BEFORE A

Andrew Shanahan

ISBN: 9781677612154

First paperback edition January 2020.

Book design by Socciones Editoria Digitale

Cover design by Yolander Yeo

"Dark Days" written and performed by PUP. Published by Rough Trade Publishing

For exclusive updates about this book and Andrew Shanahan visit www.helloshan.co.uk.

For Emma

CONTENTS

All the fat belongs to the Lord.
Leviticus 3:16

We're wasting away, bit by bit.
Everyone has gone and everything has changed.
PUP, Dark Days

CHAPTER 1

Tuesday 4th August 2020

601 lbs (273 kg)

The fireman who falls to his death is Carl, and the one who kicks him out of the window is Karl.

It seems like such a pointless thing to remember, but when the two firemen first arrive at my flat, Carl makes a big thing about him being "Carl with a C" and his colleague being "Karl with a K". It would be more accurate to say Carl with a C is the one who compulsively chips in gags and catchphrases, and Karl with a K is the one who mostly works in a tight-jawed silence. It's the sort of bobbins you say when there's very little that needs to be said and silence is awkward. Everyone who has been through the flat that morning has their own versions of this mouth noise. Mostly, it consists of a series of introductions and overly-cheerful explanations.

"Hi Ben, I'm Josie. I'm the lead bariatric nurse, and I'll be helping to move you and making sure you're comfortable until we get to the hospital."

"Hi Ben, I'm Dr Ash and I'm responsible for making sure that you're all fit and healthy for the big move."

"Hi Ben, I'm Lloyd and I'm one of the diabetes nurses that will be getting you safely out of your flat and into the ambulance."

There are more. I tune them out after a bit.

The first name stuff is supposed to be reassuring and make me feel empowered. They all call me Ben, once they've established that I am happy to be referred to that way. Ultimately, it makes it all seem like we are a bunch of mates who get together occasionally to lift a 601 pound man out of the front wall of his home with a crane. All standard stuff. Very normal.

Another of the inanities is that they all individually ask me to repeat and confirm what it is that's being done. So I tell them all repeatedly that I am having my leg amputated and once that is established, then we confirm which leg it is. They all ask me to go through this process even though Dr Ash has already drawn on my right leg and signed his initials. It's surreal to watch him do it and barely feel a thing, thanks to the nerve damage from the diabetes. Even without the messy "F.A." scrawled on my leg, I hope it would be apparent to anyone even vaguely medically trained which one is the poorly leg. If the nasty sunburn hue, drifts of peeling white skin and mottled purple and black patches don't give it away, then the four-inch scab on the top of my foot should clinch it.

"So, you're having your right lower leg amputated, is that correct?"

"That is correct."

"And you've had the process of what's happening to you today explained?"

"Yes." At least a thousand times.

"And do you have any questions?"

Yes. How did I get to this position? What went wrong? Who will care for Brown? Why can't I stop thinking about eating? Am I worth saving?

"No. It's all clear, thank you."

The council workmen arrive punctually slightly before 7 a.m. There are four men, dressed in black and grey multi-pocketed trousers, paint-spattered work boots and polo shirts with the Housing Association logo printed on them. They work purposefully with a minimum of equipment to remove the front wall of my flat and the sidings to the balcony, revealing an extended view over the surrounding buildings, the hills and the distant city that I can see from my bed if I sit up straight. One of the first things they do when they arrive is to fix a large plastic sheet diagonally across the living room, cocooning me in a bright, blank space that sucks and billows in the gentle breeze like a diaphragm. In theory, this is to protect me from the brick and plaster dust as they take down the wall, but aside from a dry taste to the air and an early fit of sneezing, there isn't much disturbance. I ask if they want a brew from behind my curtain, but a voice beyond the veil says they've brought flasks with them. I do wonder whether the sheet just makes the whole thing less awkward for them.

There is a gap in the sheeting next to the wall where I can see the men as they carry large yellow builders' buckets of bricks and the patio doors out of the lounge, down the hall and out of the front door of the flat. I watch them as they trudge back through the flat, sweat seeping through their shirts as they work in the early heat. The workers don't meet my eye and seem to feel it is easier to focus on their buckets, or the seams of their gloves as they walk past. The entire project only takes them about an hour, including removing the screen, and throughout that time they barely speak a word. The oldest of the four men sidles over to my bed and asks for a signature on a battered clipboard as the rest of his team get their tools together. I thank them for the new view and sign whatever it is he passes to me - maybe he wants an autograph.

There is a glorious half hour of quiet before the medics and the firemen arrive. I check my packing again and eat breakfast; hot sweet tea with oat milk and four sugars and six rounds of toast, margarine and jam. After breakfast, I reflexively open my last pack of bourbons and slowly feed them into my mouth until they are all gone. I assure myself that this isn't compulsive eating, the deadline of when I have to stop eating and drinking before the surgery is looming and I want to make sure I'm not going to go hungry. Plus, I've done well on my diet recently, so I've earned a bit of a treat to calm my nerves. I watch the steam curl from the top of my mug and wonder what mum would have made of it all. I know. She would have thought it was exciting, she loved having people over to the flat.

When the team arrive, there are four from the hospital - three nurses and one doctor - plus two members of the fire brigade. On Middleton Road outside and on the roof of my building, there are another five members of the fire brigade. They are liaising with the crane operator and a further two workmen who are using a cherry picker - a heavy duty elevated working platform that has a cage at the top for someone to drive and move the boom arm. I nearly have a heart attack when I first see a fireman apparently floating past the window outside my flat. I calm myself down. Too much effort and money has been spent for me to kark it now.

The "multi-agency movement strategy" was painstakingly explained to me when it became apparent that I needed the amputation. For years, the Housing Association has been aware of my living situation and tried to coax me out of the flat and into another property. They carefully explained the health and safety risks of having a super-obese man in a top floor flat. They said that after a risk assessment, they no longer felt it was safe for me to use the building's ancient lift, which would need upgrading if it was ever to carry me safely. They dropped hints about legal action, but they never quite got around to evicting me. Then Type 2 Diabetes succeeded where the persuasive powers of housing officers had failed.

Essentially, there are three steps to the movement plan – get me out of bed, get me out of the flat and get me to hospital. The first challenge is that the medical staff and firemen have to get me onto something called a bariatric med sled. This mostly involves rolling me from side-to-side on my bed and gradually sliding a plastic board with handholds underneath me. As the heat is stifling, I've been advised to wear just underwear and so the first mortification of the day, but by no means the last, is lying mostly naked in bed, being pushed back and forth by the team like they are working dough. It doesn't help that as they jostle me, I can't stop a small fart from creeping out which has just enough of a rasp that it was very obviously from me.

"I'm so sorry, it's the moving and the nerves," I explain, trying not to make eye contact with anyone.

"Don't worry Ben, it's perfectly natural, nurses get it all the time," says Lloyd.

"That's why they pay them so much," says Karl, causing Carl to snigger.

When you're my size you get used to everything having the prefix "bariatric". It's not a toilet, it's a bariatric commode. It's not a bed, it's a bariatric sleeping platform. I've even got bariatric shoes, although I don't think I've ever worn them – say all the bad things you like about being a shut-in, but it does save you money on shoes. Bariatric is one of those words that only medics and insurance companies use, and as far as I can tell, it means fat in a costly and complicated way.

Once I am finally on the bariatric sled, I am secured in place to prevent me from slipping. I experience a sting of vertigo as the foot of the bed is lowered, and the whole team carefully move me onto the floor, where another stiff plastic movement board is waiting. I suddenly have a vivid memory of seeing an adult at a seventh birthday party holding a plate with an untouched jelly vertically over the bin. I remember watching the jelly grip at first, then slowly slip and fall into the bin. I remember the adult had caught me watching and smiled at me and I recoiled with embarrassment.

I try to roll my body to find a comfortable position on the hard floor, but I can only move an inch and I am essentially immobilised. The movement board is again strapped up to prevent the med sled itself from moving about on top of it. The final act is to hook the entire sausage roll to the crane outside, which will very carefully perform the act of taking my weight and lifting me into the air. The movement board has a steadying line attached to the cherry picker, but this won't be taking any of the weight – it will just steady my horizontal movement and ensure that I don't swing out of the flat like a wrecking ball and demolish a nearby building. No one says that is a concern, but I get the distinct impression that it has been risk assessed.

The plan is then to manoeuvre me out of the flat and lower me extremely slowly over the 44 feet to the ground and onto a bariatric paramedic trolley. I will be winched into the specialist bariatric ambulance and taken to hospital. I have been told they are expecting a crowd and have erected barriers to keep people at a safe distance and to protect my dignity. In this part of North Manchester, a crowd would gather just to marvel at a crane, so the idea of seeing some fat, shut-in weirdo suspended from a crane will probably close schools and factories for miles around. I'm bracing for a commemorative issue of the local paper.

And then, for the first time since I was 16, I will be outside the flat. A lot must have changed in nine years. I can look around and see what lies beyond the corner of the road. I'll be able to see the other third of the advertising billboard just before the roundabout that is currently obscured by flats. I can turn and look back at Ellis Tower and see where I have been for nearly a decade. The thought of seeing my flat from the outside makes me feel like I am falling into a deep crevice in the earth, plunging into the core. I feel dizzy and my breathing gets shallow. One of the nurses monitoring my heart rate and blood pressure asks if I am OK. I lie and nod.

Once I am out, the council workers will come back in and fix a tarpaulin across the missing wall to ensure that my flat isn't open to the elements. Not that rain is a concern currently. It hasn't rained in 74 days now and across the country there are widespread drought warnings in place. The tabloids have stopped declaring it "Britain's Record-Breaking Summer!" and started questioning whether "The Endless Heatwave" might be indicative of a wider problem. The heat has even been blamed for the sporadic rioting we had in June and July. I'll probably be begging them to leave the wall off rather than boxing me in again. This is of course dependent on whether they'll even let me return to my flat. My surgeon has said that a creeping amputation is a distinct possibility, so I might need to have further operations before they can even discuss whether I could go home. Recently, I've also found out there are additional complications, which I have been trying hard not to think about. Weirdly, the thought of dying worries me far less than the gnawing tension of being away from the flat.

The biggest challenge of the first stage has been the missing wall and working at height, which means that the team have had to wear safety harnesses tethered to the cherry picker and secure spots in the flat. There are a lot of "excuse mes", jingling of harnesses and ducking under straps – Carl says it feels like they are doing a Maypole dance. By now everyone has realised that you don't have to react to what Carl is saying, so no one laughs and Carl seems fine. As they click the final straps across my chest shut, I feel panic mounting like a dark wave and consider asking for the sedative which I had been offered earlier. But as tempting as oblivion seems, my anxiety insists that I have to be in a state of pin-drop alertness or an unspecified calamity will occur. It isn't just being pinned down that makes me nervous; it is the sheer enormity of the moment. The air from outside the window smells vivid and different. I feel supernaturally attuned to each second and the new sensations that it brings. Even familiar feelings like the burning friction from the four deep boils that sit on the underside of my belly seem more real in that moment.

I hear one of the team call on a radio for the crane to start lowering the chains into position. I gulp and look at the crucifix on the wall. Was I worth all of this effort? Two phones ring simultaneously, and there is a burst of static from a radio and a garbled message that I can't hear. After a few seconds more phones ring and phone notifications ping. There is a buzz of strangely intense activity, the sounds of people packing equipment and leaving and then a mumbled explanation: "Um, Ben, we need to get to, um, we won't be long…".

Then nothing happens for two hours.

***

"Would it be possible to loosen the straps until we know what's going on?" I ask Karl for the tenth time. He is pacing along the length of the room, clinking gently as his safety harness adjusts to his changing position.

"Hold your horses, Fatty," he says and a cloud of sweet-smelling vape billows from his mouth.

"Please, I need to use the toilet."

"Tough."

After the medical staff had abruptly left, the mood had soured. Karl stopped pretending that he wasn't openly hostile towards me and Carl, although he'd initially been the one trying to maintain some professionalism, had transformed into a surly, tutting presence, sitting on my bed, thumbing his phone screen and biting the corner of his lip. The two firemen now meet periodically on the balcony to conduct muttered conversations and then return to their positions – pacing and tutting.

I am still lying on the floor. My arms have been placed by my sides and I am wrapped in a bedsheet. Around that are two bariatric moving sheets, made of a slippery polyester material that reduces the friction and help the medics to shift me around. The firemen have also fastened five seatbelt-style straps from my feet up to my shoulders, with each strap clicking into a fat black plastic buckle which they pull tight. I can only move my fingers and my head, which is supported by a pillow. I can feel the sweat pouring off me, which has drenched both the pillow and the bedsheet next to my skin. Earlier I'd asked for a glass of water, or for them to loosen the sheets, but Karl had ignored me and Carl had said they'd need to clear it with the medical staff. I am now left sitting in the waves of pain that radiate from my back and hips. After asking again, Karl explains in angry tones that they would need a winch to pull me back onto the bed and he can't undo me from the med sled unless I have a harness, because it would be a health and safety risk. So I am left on the floor, feeling the pressure in my bladder grow.

The radio on Karl's coat beeps loudly like an alarm and he grabs it from the bed. He moves onto the balcony so I can only hear his responses, which aren't encouraging.

"Well, how much pissing longer?" Karl asks. "He's literally here waiting to go! We had a small army of people waiting to move the fat twat! Where are they now? Well, I'm fucked off!" Another rattle of static, during which I can only hear the word "emergency". Karl steps back into the room and I see him again, he has shrugged the coat on so he can use the radio. He pushes back the hair from his forehead and in annoyance, he flings the sweat he's gathered on his hand out into the void.

"So who's coming back to unwrap the diabetic fajita then? There's no way we can do it on our own. None of this is in the movement plan, so we need to know what you want us to do."

Karl loses patience with whatever is being said to him on the radio, he mutes it and turns to address Carl instead.

"Can you believe this? Central say we've got to stay here with this turd."

He swings around and plants his boot into the wall above the fireplace so hard that the crucifix swings on its nail.

"Alright mate, what do they want us to do?" Carl asks when Karl's moment of rage passes.

"We've got to wait until they find out what's happening. There's no back up because all the crews are out. I'm telling you now, it's going to be hours. We're going to be sat smelling this lardarse for the rest of the day."

"What's happening at the hospital?" Carl asks.

"They just said there's been some big emergency. I don't think they knew. Something is off about all of this."

Karl walks back into my field of view and squats by my head. He is dripping with sweat, and a bead falls from his forehead onto mine. I try to edge away.

"Do you know how much this cost today?" he asks.

"I know it's a lot," I reply, feeling ashamed. Of course, I know today is extravagant. Of course, I know it is my fault. I just can't understand what is happening. Where are the medical staff? Why can't I just go to hospital and wait for whatever this emergency is to end? Why can't they just leave me alone and get out of my home?

"You *should* know. Not only should you know, if it was up to me you'd have to fucking pay for it, you heffalump. Why should decent taxpayers like me foot the bill for this? There's a whole bloody team of people whose entire day is going to be spent waiting around to move your fat, sweating carcass to hospital, just so that you can get your leg lopped off because you can't stop shoving KFC in your face."

His face is red and he is leaning so close that I have to turn my head away to avoid the harsh acid of his breath. Something is wrong. His voice is pitched high and his body beats with an unnerving energy. I see his fingers twitching and he blinks rapidly.

"I'm…a vegan," I say, stuck for anything logical to diffuse the situation.

"What?"

"I'm a vegan. I don't eat chicken."

"Do you think that makes a blind bit of difference? Do you think it matters one hairy fuck whether you've gorged yourself to this point on Zinger Burgers or on…or on…lentils?"

Karl steps over me and smashes his boot into the wall again. The flat seems to shake, and the crucifix falls and bounces off the fireplace. Jesus lays spread-eagled, face down on the carpet next to me. Karl coughs loudly and takes a deep, painful breath. He groans and his hand comes up to his side. Has he hurt himself kicking the wall? Carl is watching, speechless. Karl moves quickly to the opposite corner of the room, near the open wall where I can't see him and he retches. I hear a thick gush of fluid spattering.

"Are you ok? What's the matter? What's happened?" I shout.

"Mate! What's going on? Do you need me to get someone?" Carl asks moving over to his colleague.

I look at the ceiling and a rich bile smell fills the flat, which makes me gag. I realise that if I am sick I might not be able to turn my head enough to avoid choking on it. I force myself to take calm, measured breaths through my mouth and to focus on the drab, beige paint on the woodchip ceiling. Mum hated the woodchip. Beyond the flat, I hear a sound like someone dropping a large metal item in a skip and then wailing screams and the different pitches of three or four car alarms. There is a sound of grinding metal and the "Whoomp!" of an explosion.

"Please! Take my straps off! What's happening?" I scream.

"Shut up!" Carl shouts. "What's the matter mate? Karl? Mate, you're worrying me! Should I tell central?" The sound of more retching, an inhuman hurl that sounds like someone turning themselves inside out.

"Please let me up!" I scream, unable to keep the terror out of my voice now. "Please, you're firemen, you have to help me!"

"Shut up!" Karl screams, his voice sounds scratchy and hoarse. "Everything you've taken out of this system. I know people like you. You take and you take and you take. What's the point of you? What have you offered?"

Karl suddenly looms over me and raises his boot above my head. I stare at him and my only thought is who will look after Brown when I am dead. As the boot begins to travel towards my head, Carl launches himself and barges into Karl from behind, sending him sprawling onto my bed. His boot scrapes the top of my head rather than crushing my face.

"Get off! I'm going to stamp this scum out of existence."

"You can't! You'll get done for murder!" Carl stands by Karl with his arms raised at chest height, fingers outstretched, placating his colleague.

They move out of sight and I hear sounds of a scuffle and Carl utters a pained cry. They push past me again and I see Karl wrestling with his partner and inching his fingers towards the clips to his safety harness. Then they are out by the balcony and there is a winded "Unnnnnnhh!" and seconds later a distant thump. There may be a scream, but there are so many more shouts now - voices closer to Ellis Tower. The world seems to be dissolving into screams and heat. The air is unbearable. My scalp burns.

Karl walks back into my eyeline. I notice his chin and chest are covered with a bib of bloody yellow bile and his eyes are watery and red. He looks demonic.

"What have you done?" he asks me through tears.

"What do you mean, what have I done? Where's your friend? Please, you have to help. You're a fireman! Help! I'm being murdered!" I scream.

I roll my head around to track Karl's location. His harness is impairing his movements, but he paces back and forth pulling at his hair. With vacant eyes, he returns to his position above my head. He lifts his boot up high over my face and starts to bring it down. The only defensive manoeuvre I have at my disposal is to flinch.

The tether line leading to Karl from outside the window whips tight and the harness jerks around his chest, as an awful sound of shearing metal cuts through the air. Karl is pulled straight out of my line of vision with a shout that follows him as he is jerked out of the gap in the flat wall.

Frantically, I crane my neck and try to hop my body around to see what is happening, but I can't move. Everywhere, the sounds of furious, insensible shouting grow louder. Car alarms and sirens compete for supremacy among the noises of carnage that rage just beyond my line of sight. I can only listen and watch the sun gazing down from a bright blue sky onto the sounds of chaos. In the distance, I see the contrail of a plane turn abruptly from its course and trace a path straight down.

***

It is going dark. The skyline is red. The screaming hasn't stopped, but at some point it comes closer, inside the building. Earlier I could hear a roaring sound in the flat down the corridor – the only other one that is occupied on my floor. My neighbour Mr Ethiss was screaming "Joan!", his wife's name, over and over but after about an hour that stopped too. A smell of burning hung in the air and I became convinced that the whole building was on fire.

Gradually, my ears become attuned to the new raft of sounds and I can listen past them to pick out a small, scratching noise from Brown. She is locked in the bedroom down the corridor, waiting for a veterinary nurse who never arrived to take her into the kennels. I call to her, tell her it is going to be OK. I sing out nonsense songs to her until my mouth dries into silence and I pass out.

CHAPTER 2

3rd December 2017

2 years, 8 months, 1 day before

542 lbs (246 kg)

There were 17 shopping bags in total.

Graham, the delivery driver had tried to group them into categories when he took them out of the storage crates and arranged them by the front door. He wasn't quite sure why he'd unloaded the bags from the crates – after all, if there was no one in he'd have to pack them back into the crates again. He asked himself why he'd done that, and the only answer he had for himself was that it was just for something to do.

He'd put all the non-food items on the right-hand side of the door. There were four bags of these, mostly washing detergent, toothpaste and several multi-packs of Flash anti-bacterial wipes, but there was also a pack of the supermarket's own-brand four-blade razors. Graham thought this showed eminent good sense, because what was the point of paying for a brand name razor when it was just going to be scraped around your face once and then dropped in the bin? Toilet roll, bin bags and tomato ketchup were the only brands he maintained were worth spending the extra for. Ketchup because no other brand could come close to Heinz, and bin bags and loo roll because it wasn't pretty when either of them split. He'd made that very observation when he dropped shopping off to an elderly lady customer a year ago and had been surprised when he'd received a verbal warning the next week about being careful what he was saying to customers. Since then, he'd tried to keep his thoughts to himself, but he didn't always succeed.

Next to the non-food items were bags of pet foods and sundries. There were four bags of these. This was curious on an initial appraisal because there was a mix of foods – all from the premium end of the spectrum - but some of it was formulated for young dogs and others were for more adult dogs, or dogs with medical conditions. What was odd is that dogs, and by extension, dog owners were very brand loyal; very brand loyal indeed. It was unusual, once an animal had settled on a brand, to see much in the way of variation. Of course, other companies would throw in coupons to tempt customers to try a new brand, but in Graham's experience these rarely worked. Pets knew what they liked and their owners respected that. It always got to Graham when he knew a customer was on the bones of their arse and their food shopping was reduced to loaves of cheap bread, potatoes, tins of tomatoes and cheap cuts of meat, but the pet food stayed the same, even when it was a luxury brand.

Knocking on the door, he hadn't heard any barking coming from within the flat, but when he listened intently with his ear to the door, he'd heard a scuffling noise, which he thought could have been claws on a floor but then equally around here, it could also be a rat. Also in the non-food bags were a range of pet toys such as tuggers, hoops and balls – again, all premium brands. Graham concluded that this was a new dog and that the owner – Mr Ben Stone, the occupant of Flat 4, Ellis Tower – was attempting to establish what the puppy would take to, both in terms of foods and in terms of playthings.

The food bags made for an easier deduction. Three entire bags were made up of Bourbon biscuits, the large 12 biscuit packs – a quick calculation had put that at approximately 500 Bourbon biscuits –which was quite some order. There were also ten packets of Party Ring biscuits and bags of standard ready meals. Interestingly, Graham recognised these as belonging to a leading vegan brand. As something of a surprise contrast, there were also three bags which held two-litre bottles of Diet Coca-Cola and one bottle of decent malt whisky. This surprised Graham because there seemed to be some significant mismatching going on among the products. Perhaps this was an indication that this was a couple's abode and that she was a recent vegan convert. Of course, it could be that he was the vegan, but Graham didn't think so. Women tended to lead on issues of food and diet. Hadn't it been his own wife who had started to get in those low-salt crisps and whatnot when the doctor had said about his blood pressure? Potentially, the lady here was trying to promote the vegan lifestyle to her partner – Mr Stone. Graham mentally pencilled a question mark over the vegan items on his clipboard as he tapped purposefully at the door again.

"Just Morrisons with your shopping, Mr Stone – are you there?"

Another bag contained six large multipacks of Skittles, which he was particularly partial to himself and he'd entertained the possibility of mentioning this to the customer. Not because he was trying to get any of the sweets gifted to him – this would have violated several of the store's policies around accepting gifts and remunerations – but just as a means of building a rapport with the customer. They'd covered the importance of this in his training and the main conclusion that Graham had reached was that rapport could be built mostly by enthusing about some of the items that a customer had bought. Following a role-play exercise to showcase this technique, it had been clearly outlined that there were categories of products where this wouldn't be an appropriate strategy, especially those in the hygiene or medical product lines. Graham felt that Skittles would be safer ground.

Finally, there were savoury and bakery bags – large white paper bags of six sugared jam doughnuts and tubes of Pringles, mostly the red Original flavour, which Graham had always felt got undue attention in place of the stronger Sour Cream and Onion Pringles, but then there was no accounting for taste. As a veteran of more than three years delivering food to customers across the homes of the North West, Graham felt confident in his diagnosis that this customer was preparing for a children's party and that the central present for the little one was going to be a puppy. They said you shouldn't give puppies as a gift but then it happened all the time and Graham didn't suppose that was such a bad thing – better than some gaming system that would cost a fortune and just keep the child locked inside, away from the fresh air.

The only counter-indication to Graham's conclusion was that there were no banners or balloons among the shopping. Perhaps the customer had received a deal on party supplies elsewhere? If the customer had a loyalty card, then they'd probably find a year from now they'd be getting suggestions and coupons for balloons and candles. They'd covered this in his training and it was all down to something called an algorithm, which struck Graham as somewhat magical and he thought on it often. People could knock technology all they liked, but if you had an algorithm suggesting helpful things at appropriate times, was that really so bad? He felt bad about the supplies not reaching the customer, especially with the party, but it was already past the 15-minute window that Morrisons gave him for unloading a customer's shopping. He checked his watch and knocked again, this time with greater purpose, which held just the right side of being rude. No response.

This had been Graham's concern when the Cuddington Estate buildings had been approved for home deliveries. Because you had to pay in advance when you bought your shopping online, it wasn't usual to get prank orders – it would have been an expensive and easily traced prank after all – but the discussion among the drivers was that the estate would mean more thefts, more damage to vehicles and more no shows, all of which cost time and often ended up with ruined stock. Somehow, management always managed to imply the fact that a bag was stolen, or that a customer didn't show up was the driver's fault. Graham was growing increasingly keen on the idea that had been suggested at a recent drivers' meeting where they'd all wear cameras like the police, so they could prove what they did all day.

A sneeze sounded through the door, followed by a conspicuous silence.

"Hello? Is someone there? It's Graham, your delivery driver from Morrisons. I've got your order."

"I can't open the door right now. I'm…poorly I'm afraid. I wouldn't want you to catch it."

"Is that Mr Stone?" Graham replied. "It's quite all right, we come into contact with all sorts of germs and ailments while we're on the road."

He thought about how that sounded and moved to ward off any misapprehension it might have raised. "But I'm in good health myself. Clean bill of health entirely."

"I don't want you to catch anything. Can you just leave the shopping out there?"

"Well, we usually offer to take the shopping into your house. We can even unpack it straight into your cupboards if you'd prefer?" Seeing inside customer's houses was one of Graham's favourite parts of the job.

"I wouldn't want that. You don't have to do that."

"It's no bother, all part of the service."

"Can you just leave it out there?"

"Well, I can, but I'm going to have to ask for a signature to say that you received the shopping."

The door opened a crack and revealed a darkened interior. Graham picked up some of the nearest bags, preparing to pass them over the threshold, but was taken aback when the door stopped after a few inches as a short security chain prevented it from opening further.

"Oh. Ok. So are you happy with me leaving the shopping on the floor out here? I wouldn't want it to get stolen, that's the only thing."

"There's only one other person left on this corridor and he's nearly seventy. It'll be fine."

"Ok then," said Graham and smiled as a small, black muzzle pushed its way through the crack in the door. The dog was black and brown and stood approximately eight inches in height. It peered at Graham with brown eyes that spoke of both wariness and warmth.

"Oh, hello there! Who are you? You must be who all the puppy food and toys are for, eh?! Who's a lucky boy?" The dog's eyes narrowed and one of its two triangular ears raised, causing the tip to fold over like the flap of an envelope. Graham chuckled – it would be a while before there was enough dog to put those ears into proportion.

"She's a girl."

"Awww, she's lovely. What is she, a Doberman?"

"No, she's a Manchester Terrier."

"Ahhhh, you don't see many of them these days, what's she

called?"

"Brown - come back in, Brown."

"Is she all right?" Graham asked, alerted by the fact that the puppy seemed to be moving its mouth but emitted no sounds.

"She can't bark."

"How come?"

"She's been debarked."

"What's that?"

"They cut the vocal cords. Apparently, the bloke selling them used to be a vet and he did the whole litter."

"Is that legal?" asked Graham.

"No. He was just a pisshead that thought dogs that can't bark would make more money."

Graham stared at the dog, unnerved. As she soundlessly shouted at him he noticed the fading tinge of a surgical wound under her chin. It gave an odd impression, like watching the telly on mute.

"What do you need me to sign?"

Graham kept watch on Brown as he handed the palm computer to Mr Stone. Because the door was only partially opened, it wouldn't go through no matter how Graham manoeuvred it. At last the door shut and re-opened without the security chain on it. It opened just enough for Graham to pass the unit through.

"If you could just give me a scribble on that. There are no substitutions so hopefully, you'll be able to have a lovely party."

With the door opened slightly wider, Brown had taken the opportunity to force her way through and was vigorously sniffing at Graham's boot. She decided that this was something she needed to attack and fell onto her side to allow her to express her silent ferocity with full force. Graham laughed and picked her up and scratched her on the head. Up close he could see an ugly, slightly uneven scar that cut nearly an inch across her chin and neck.

Brown was barking, but she seemed unaware that she was emitting nothing more than the sound of breathy kisses.

"She's really sweet." Graham looked up to hand Brown back to Mr Stone, who partially opened the door.

Involuntarily, Graham let out an "Oh!" as he saw the customer for the first time. He was tall, six foot and then some and young - mid-twenties Graham reckoned - and he wore his dark hair long, to the neck. It was pushed back on his head and hung down to the collar of his black T-shirt. He was quite simply the fattest man that Graham had ever seen, in real life, on television, or on the internet. At every point, more of him seemed to billow into being. Graham was put in mind of the sort of rolling hills that children draw, where behind every semi-circular hillock lies yet another hillock, and behind that another.

Mr Stone's clean-shaven face was encircled by two large, round collars of fat. Perhaps most awful though was the drooping gut which hung fully to the man's shins! Even though his black shirt was comically long, the belly somehow managed to hang *below it* so that Graham could glimpse the pale, dimpled nature of the skin. It gave an impression that this giant unit of a man was melting, gut first into the floor – it defied thought, and put Graham in mind of the crudest CGI effects from the horror films. As he took all this in, he fancied he could smell a ripe undertone of urine and sweat. He breathed lightly through his mouth.

Graham visibly shuddered, again without thought or intention. The improbability of the man's size had bypassed Graham's senses and allowed his subconscious reactions to bubble freely to the surface. The handheld unit, tiny in this giant's hand, was pressed firmly into Graham's hand along with a five pound note and Brown, still mutely barking at the delivery driver, was plucked from him. The door was shut firmly and the click ended Graham's stupor.

"Oh right. Yes. So, I'll leave your shopping here Mr Stone. Um, I hope you're feeling better soon." Graham suddenly thought that this last comment might be taken as a reference to the man's weight, so he added, "With the cough and cold that you mentioned before."

He shook his head and turned to his hand-truck, loaded with the empty crates. He grasped the handles, tipped it towards himself and pushed them down the corridor towards the lift. He became aware of the fiver for the first time and smiled. He tucked it into the front pocket of his shirt – maybe the Cuddington Estate wouldn't be so bad. After all, you never got a tip from the big houses that was for sure. He shook his head again, to clear the smell and images that were clouding his mind. He turned to look down the corridor and see if the customer had come out to start claiming his shopping bags, but the door remained closed. Graham was fascinated; he'd love to get another glimpse of his bulk – he was so fat! Would he even have fitted through the door? How did he live? What sort of toilet could he use, surely he'd collapse an ordinary one? Graham's mind reeled with unanswered questions.

He wondered briefly if his comment about the party was something that the customer had registered, but Graham decided it had all been so brief that he could easily pass it off as a misunderstanding. After all, it was a reasonable expectation for someone to have if a customer was buying nearly 500 Bourbon biscuits. He'd have to write up a note on the customer file in case any other drivers delivered to him in the future – Graham was fairly certain that he had managed to retain the professional demeanour that they'd outlined in the sensitivity training modules he'd done, but he knew there were some drivers who wouldn't be able to keep their thoughts to themselves or those who might have just laughed or made a face. Thinking on it, he was proud that he'd kept his composure – this job threw all sorts at you and you had to be ready with a professional smile and an ability not to judge – at least while you were in front of the customer.

The lift doors opened, revealing a single occupant wearing a motorbike helmet with the visor up. He carried a large insulated box over his shoulder with the Just Eat logo emblazoned on the side. Graham took in the scene and determined that this was one of his people – another delivery driver. He nodded his head in professional recognition and stood back to let the guy out of the lift.

"Smells good – got any going spare?" he asked.

The Just Eat driver rolled his eyes. Graham smiled – he often laughed along with similar comments from members of the public. It was all to be expected when you were out doing your job in the public eye.

Suddenly Graham was struck with solidarity.

"Listen, pal – just between us – are you going to number 4 with that? Because if you are there's something you might want to know…"

"I know," the Just Eat driver said flatly with a foreign accent and pushed past Graham, who shrugged and pulled his hand-truck into the lift and pressed the button for the ground floor. Too late, he realised that if he'd simply pretended to press the button, he might have seen the fat man answer the door to get his take-away. Sadly, Graham watched the dimpled metal doors close on the fascinating scene in the corridor and descended back to the ground floor and his awaiting van.

CHAPTER 3

7ᵗʰ August 2020

3 days after

590 lbs (268 kg)

The clock on the DVD player goes dark several hours after I am entombed in the flat. The only way to measure time passing is by watching the movement of the sun in the sky and feeling the thirst mounting in my cracked throat. Tuesday was the day of my move, when Karl tried to kill me and the world went mad. Since then, there have been two bright and beautiful days and two nights where the walls of the flat have been alight with the flittering oranges and reds of fires. A constant pall of black smoke drifts past and sometimes into the flat, threatening to choke me where I lie. The sounds of shouting from the streets haven't stopped for nearly 24 hours. A woman has been screaming "bad baby," over and over, which has terrified me more than anything during this time of imprisonment.

Gradually, the volume decreases, and the sound of crashes and explosions returns to being the exception rather than the rule. At points I'd shout for help and plead for anyone to come and get me, but either no one hears or no one cares. The muscles in my back cramp continuously and a piercing headache blooms on the second day. My head throbs so much, I think it will crack open my skull. I can't be sure whether this is all from dehydration or when Karl had stamped on me. I sleep intermittently, woken by the chill from the night air or the pooling of sweat at my back and arms. My mouth is so dry that I can feel every bump on my tongue. I look at the prone form of Jesus on the carpet by my side and I talk angrily to God, "Are these the plans you have for me? Is this prospering me? Is this the hope and the future you promised? Well you can stick it, pal." The anger subsides and I then pray desperately for Jesus to save me and promise that I will do anything if he will just help me survive. By the middle of the third day I welcome death, but death is busy elsewhere.

The team responsible for my extraction from the flat were obviously very concerned that I could slip and fall to my death. Consequently, they spared no effort in ensuring I am wrapped tight in the bedsheet, folded in the two bariatric slip mats and encased in the outer plastic sheeting of the med sled. This was then fastened tightly with straps. When the firemen had pulled the straps tight enough to restrict my breathing they'd told me not to worry because I'd soon be on the ground and then they could loosen them. It would be two minutes maximum.

As the hours pass and the sun warms the South-facing room, it has slowly baked me. Karl said I was a fajita, in my delirium I shout that he is wrong, I am a quesadilla! Or maybe a chimichanga!

"You don't bake a fajita Karl!" I cry. There are long periods of odd and convincing waking dreams, sudden bursts of happiness and hours of frustration. Through it all there is a constant, boring pain.

From my position on the floor I can see my black overnight bag that contains my clothes and toiletries for the stay in hospital. I am aware that it also contains the Metformin I take for my diabetes. I offer up thanks for the fact that I am not yet insulin-dependent, or I'd have simply died and been pre-mummified for whoever uncovered my tomb. I have not eaten since early on Tuesday – nearly 80 hours ago. I have also been sweating heavily for the whole time, and I can feel it puddling around me. I know that I have to try one more attempt to save myself. The bedsheet that is closest to my skin is soaked to the touch. Almost immediately after Karl was dragged out of the window I started to bend my knees and "jump" within the med sled, initially it made little difference to the sheets and straps but as the hours pass, I can feel the bedsheet starting to come apart to the point where I can now open my legs as though I am doing breaststroke. This means that my belly can drop lower between my legs and it releases perhaps an inch of room around the strap on my middle.

By writhing my shoulders, I find I can move my right arm enough to push against the side of my trap. By straining against the fabric I stretch the outer material just enough to snag it on the tiny nail that protrudes from the top of the crucifix. Over and over, I stretch the material out and poke a series of tiny holes in the covers. Frequently, I stop to stretch out my legs as the pain in my displaced hips makes me whimper. My finger bleeds freely from all the times I stab myself with the nail. After hours of repeatedly stabbing the fabric, I finally push at the perforated material and feel it tear open up under my thumb. I look down and I can see my thumb protrude through the layers of restraints.

Wiggling it back and forth, I open the hole up further, so that two fingers and then three are through the gap. Finally, my entire right hand emerges from the hole and I grab the crucifix and slide the nail across the outer material, which slits satisfyingly. I reach and pinch the buckle of the strap across my gut. With a ping, it opens and I instantly feel the extra room for movement. I scrabble around and soon release the other five buckles along my body.

With a gasp, I push my arms wide open and peel back the layers of restraints, releasing a tangy smell of sweat, shit and urine into the flat. I feel the air breathe across my mostly naked body.

My arms scream as I fold them under my body and prop myself up. I look at my feet. They look grey and old, and even though they are moving, I can't feel any sensation in either of them. My right leg still has an illegible smear of ink from when Dr Ash had signed the leg that was to be removed. The scab is oozing and bloody on the top of my right foot. To save the scab from breaking any more, I wiggle the whole foot rather than flexing the toes to try and bring feeling back to my extremities. I revel in the light-headedness of taking full, deep breaths and wonder if there is any better sensation than sucking a full measure of air into the lungs.

My focus grows beyond my feet and I stare out at the town. I live on the top floor of Ellis Tower, part of a series of squat, four-storey council buildings which together makes up the Cuddington Estate. It is to the North East of the town and is built on a natural rise as the folds of the Pennines begin. Even though the fourth storey isn't enough for a panoramic view, the elevation of the estate allows me to see high rises, the industrial areas and the motorway networks that start to condense into the conurbation of Manchester beyond. I feel my hand rise to my mouth as I take in the scene – everywhere there are ruins – fires, smoke rising, some buildings are razed to the ground and there is ugly charring across the high rise blocks I can see. Closer to the flat the aftermath of crashes, vicious fights and accidents are evident. There are bodies strewn across the pavements and human shapes hanging out of smashed car windows. What has happened? Where is everyone? Most eerie of all is that despite the destruction, the outside world is a tableau - silent and still.

With a gasp, I return to myself and the immediate problems in the flat. I grasp my belly and slide it to one side, in the direction of the foot of the bed, which is still tipped downwards from when the medical team had lowered me onto the floor. I wince with pain as I roll over and push myself to my hands and knees. My belly fills the space between my spine and the floor. As it extends in front of me, the boils on the underside of my belly stretch and tear and the pain causes me to suck in my breath and swear. My legs are still numb as the blood reluctantly returns to my extremities, but they slowly propel me, so that I can lay the top half of my body onto the bed. My grabber is tucked in the corner, between the mattress and the frame, and I hold the toy arm in my hand and pull the bed's controller towards me. I press the button that raises the bed to help lift me to my feet and puzzle when nothing happens. I click again, but still nothing. I then remember that the DVD clock went off and I realise with dismay that there is no electricity.

I grit my teeth and grip the mattress with my hands, driving with my thighs to push more of my body onto the bed. I lie face down on the mattress gasping for breath and wait for the separate pulses of pain in my bad leg and the boils to abate. Slowly, I raise both hands above my head and kick my mobile leg behind my right leg. By timing a roll of my left arm, I eventually manage to build up enough momentum to flip my body over. It takes five minutes to simply turn over, but gradually, I manage to position myself so that I am lying with my back flat on the bed. Everything hurts and I'm not sure I have the strength for what has to come next, but fear drives me onwards. By pushing my gut to one side, I create enough space to reach over and grip the railing of the bed. This strains and creaks as I grip the bars and pull myself into a sitting position. When the dizziness clears, I use the grabber arm to pick up the crucifix and deposit it on the mantelpiece as carefully as possible.

My mum always told me that Jesus would save me.

My bed is in the far corner of what was once the lounge of the flat, but since I'd bought it as a present for myself on my twenty-third birthday, the bed has been the centre of my world. I take every meal in this bed. I work in this bed. I watch TV in this bed. It sits adjacent to the back wall and gives me a view of the balcony and the small kitchen next to the lounge. I put up shelves which keep all of my essentials like aqueous cream, wound dressings, biscuits, remote controls, chargers and toys for Brown all within easy reach. At the back of the room, away from the balcony, a short corridor runs off, which has three doors on the right for the bathroom and two bedrooms. One room is the box room, just big enough for the single bed that my mum had slept in until she died nearly three years ago. Beyond that is my old bedroom, which I'd had until I needed more room. I'd tried to convince mum to move into my old room because it is big enough for a double bed and has a bigger window and built-in wardrobes, but she always said that she preferred to keep it for when I needed it back.

When I had the bariatric bed installed in the lounge, we'd also had all the door-frames taken off, which meant that I could just about squeeze through to make it to the toilet. The Housing Association hadn't liked that. It is eighteen steps to the toilet from my bed and at each step, my right leg screams out in pain as I walk down the corridor. I go past the toilet and my mum's room and grimace as I throw open my old bedroom door. A joyous and urgent bounce of brown and black dog leaps through the gap and skips around my ankles and pushes into my knees. A smell of dogshit festering in roaring heat hits me and I gag, but I don't care. Again and again, Brown jumps to my waist with unrestrained glee to see me after so long. Her short whip tail flashes from side to side so fast, it generates a breeze. She is panting and making inaudible yipping motions with her mouth.

"Hello girl," I say and try to pat her head as she pogos around my feet.

I turn so that she can jump on my left side, rather than scratch at my sick leg. After a minute of showcasing her intense joy, she raises her ears and stands back, opening and closing her mouth, which I know as a bark of demand. I feel my own thirst heavy in my throat and pad as lightly as I can down the corridor, supporting myself against the walls to take some of the weight off my leg. In the bathroom, I flick on the bath taps and Brown leaps in and starts to drink greedily. I cup my hand under the cold tap and fling it at my mouth. I lap at the cold, delicious water. I drink until I feel the water swishing around inside me. With our thirst resolved, I look in the mirror and shrink in horror at the face of a bloated corpse staring back. My hair is matted and my eyes look deranged. Without daring to look at them, I drop my pants into the bin next to the sink, wet a flannel and do my best to restore my hygiene. It is wonderful to feel the shock of the cold water on my skin and to be fresher. I don't know what instinct possesses me, but when Brown has drunk her fill and hops out of the bath to sprint around the flat, I drop the plugs into the bath and sink and fill them both up to the overflow holes.

As the water runs, I try to fathom what is going on. Clearly, there has been an event which has caused mass destruction. When I was trapped I had seen crashed cars, buildings burned down and planes falling out of the sky, but my thoughts keep returning to the sound of the woman shouting at her child. Then I think of Karl and how odd he looked when he tried to stamp on me. He had been sick before then. After that, it seemed like his anger had become uncontrollable. I shudder at the memory of his colleague's scream as he fell to his death. The question that I am too scared to

31

contemplate is, what has happened to everyone else? I stand in the doorway of the bathroom while Brown skitters around my feet, her wet paws leaving little imprints on the bare floors.

I hobble over to my old bedroom and pull a fresh massive black T-shirt over my head and slip into some baggy fabric shorts. The heat is stifling, but I can't bear to be naked. I go to the front door and press my eye to the peephole. With the power gone, the only light that shines into the corridor is from the stairwell, approximately 15 metres to the right. This leaves a murk which I can only assume is empty, because there doesn't seem to be any noise or movement. I press my ear to the door and listen. After 30 seconds of silence, I put the security chain on the door and open it to listen more closely. Nothing. I peer down the corridor and look at Brown who is sniffing through the crack in the door.

"Anyone there?" I ask her. She looks at me eagerly and pants. That could mean anything.

"Good girl." She jumps up at me. At least she understands that.

"Hello?" I call gently. "Is anyone there?"

I wait for an answer, but there is nothing.

Tentatively, I push the door shut and unbolt the chain. I pull the door open again and quickly stick my head into the corridor. Again, nothing. I look out again, for longer this time, and establish that the corridor is indeed empty. I turn my body sideways and with effort edge my way out. My stomach catches on the frame and I physically force my back against the wood in order to move my belly through. Even so, the latch of the door catches on my stomach, which puts a hole in my T-shirt and leaves a red scrape across my gut. I turn in the corridor to look at my front door, pushing it back to make sure it is fully ajar. I feel like an astronaut leaving a space station, and even a metre away, a feeling of desperation takes hold of me. It has been nine years since I crossed this threshold. The thought of doing so now robs me of power, and I feel my heart starting to race but I need to know what is going on, so I take another reluctant step away from my home.

The corridor is sweltering, the air feels close and exhausting. But apart from the darkness and the oppressive silence, there seems nothing unusual about it. I stabilise myself with my right forearm against the wall and turn left out of my flat, away from the lift, and step achingly down the corridor. I haven't been able to feel my foot for months, but even so I get shooting pains across the leg like the sensation of thrusting frozen fingers into scalding hot water. Brown is oblivious to my discomfort and skips to and fro, unperturbed by the darkness. She is simply thrilled to see a view other than the bedroom she's been trapped in for three days.

Outside Mr Ethiss' door, I notice that he's put up a little plaque that says "The Ethiss' Residence" and they have a front door mat with WELCOME written across it. I am peripherally aware of my neighbours, but I never see them and I only hear them when their central heating switches on, which ignites a muffled *thump* audible through our living room wall. I don't think I've seen either of them for nearly a decade and wonder if they would recognise me. A voice in my head says maybe they'll mistake me for another 600 pound man they know. The Ethiss' put a card through the door when mum passed away, which, like all of the cards, said to let them know if there was anything they could help with - but much like the rest of them, I never actually saw the people who had written the cards. It had puzzled me why people skirted so close to opening up that human connection when they didn't actually want anything to come from it. I don't blame them but I do wonder if they would simply have endured a relationship with me if I'd insisted on them coming over and helping me grieve.

I brush my knuckles against the door and whisper, "Mr Ethiss?"

I watch Brown to see if her more sensitive ears detect anything. She looks at me and radiates happiness. "Good girl," I say.

I knock again – audibly this time, "Mr Eth-"

He starts screaming before I even finish his name.

Brown leaps back as if she's been kicked. I hear footsteps and the door rattles in its frame as something is hurled against the other side.

"Joan!" comes the unearthly voice from the other side of the door. His voice cracks as he screams the name again.

"Joan! It's kids from the estate. They're banging on the door! What do I do? Joan!" Another thump and this time I feel sure that it is Mr Ethiss who is hurling himself entirely against the door. Why? A series of thumps at head height makes me think the door is going to split open. Brown is circling around my legs, barking soundlessly at the door.

"Joan!" comes the scream again, then another crunch. There is a sound of smashing glass from inside the flat and I turn in the direction of home.

"I'll come back, Mr Ethiss," I say and start back down the corridor. Brown understands the intention and jumps in front, but her eyes never leave me.

My adrenaline is pumping, so the pain in my leg isn't as noticeable as I propel myself down the hall. I've gone about two metres when the lift light illuminates, casting a weak glow into the hall. The numbers above the arrows show that it is now on the second floor. Two floors to reach my level.

In a moment of terror, my brain ponders how the lift can be working when the lights are off in the corridors and the power is out. Perhaps the flats have a generator which powers the lift? My train of thought is disturbed when another loud crash sounds behind me as Mr Ethiss destroys something else in his flat. It sounds like a dresser being pulled over with a crash of shattering glass. I shuffle as fast as I can and am half the way to my flat by the time the lift light blinks on the fourth floor. The doors roll back, revealing a woman standing in the sharp glare of the lift's interior emergency lighting. I think I vaguely recognise her but I don't know her name. She clearly works in Greggs the bakers, as she is still wearing an apron with the company name on the breast.

We stare at each other and I know there is something wrong with her before she starts to run down the corridor, screaming. I lurch forward in response and get two metres from my open front door when she slams into me with an evil strength and she pushes me backwards.

"What's the rush, Tubby?" she bellows. "Why all the noise and banging? The Housing Association should kick your sort out! Dirty immigrant!"

"Stop!" I shout trying to grab her arms and push her back. "What are you doing? I live here! This is my house!"

"Let's pull some of that fat off your face!" she replies and kicks out at my legs.

She tries to dig her fingers into my face as she rants and I hold her off as she attempts to claw her fingers down my cheeks. I raise my hands to push her back and she stumbles. She whips her head back, accidentally thumping it against the wall and then crashes forward, attempting to head-butt me. As I am at least a foot and a half taller, the blow lands harmlessly on my chest.

Brown is holding herself low to the floor and as the woman stumbles, she launches herself and fastens her jaws around the lady's wrist. Brown may only weigh thirteen pounds, but she is a creature of muscle and fury and she sinks her teeth in and shakes her body and head from side-to-side, pulling the woman off-balance. It exposes the woman's left side as she stands back up.

Then I can see the redness of her eyes, which makes it look as though she's been crying for days. I notice that across the black apron is the drying crust of a yellow stain. She looks deranged. I've never seen someone so disconnected from her humanity. Without thinking about what I am doing, I lean into a punch that knocks her jaw at a strange angle and her ranting becomes even more unintelligible.

As I follow through, I turn my right ankle and stumble against the opposite wall. The pain shoots through my leg, all the way to my hip. I feel myself falling and grasp at the woman. As we fall she lands beneath me and there is a crunch as I fall on her legs. We sprawl on the ground, with me on top of her legs. She spits at me and I turn my face away. Brown seizes the moment to bite the woman's neck with ferocious energy. The woman screams unintelligible slurs into the corridor.

"Attk dg! Ths ack d! Ra-! A fat rapist!"

"Brown, leave!" I shout and grab at her collar. Between my pulling and her obedience training, she lets go of the lady's neck, which runs with blood and returns to my side. Another crash sounds from down the hall and Mr Ethiss finally breaches the door and comes sprawling into the corridor, his arms slick with blood and his face pulped. He absently faces down the corridor and sees us on the floor and starts to run towards us.

"Knock down ginger, is it? My wife is sick! But you don't care, do you? Too busy cavorting in the corridor! Scum! This used to be a nice place to live before scum like you ruined it!"

I physically throw Brown into the flat and pull and push my body across the floor, over the threshold and into my flat, kicking off the woman's grasping hands. Once inside, I roll onto my back and raise my legs in the air, just managing to clear enough of my body from the doorway to get behind the door. I slap my hand on the lower quarter of the door and push until I hear it click shut. The door rattles as a bloody conflict starts in the corridor between the two creatures beyond. I clutch Brown to me and sit in petrified silence waiting for them to come for us.

CHAPTER 4

20th September 2010

9 years, 10 months, 15 days before

262 lbs (119 kg)

Ben had an old YouTube channel which had one video uploaded to it. The video was titled "Parrot AR. Drone unboxing and first flight" and it had received 63 views, 2 thumbs up, 15 thumbs down and 11 comments. The time-stamp on the video showed that it was uploaded on the 20th September 2010. In the video, which ran for approximately five minutes, the camera remains focused on the drone throughout. Ben wasn't seen at all, even as a reflection in a window or a mirror, the viewer occasionally saw a pair of hands, holding scissors or picking up and manipulating an item in the video.

Ben's voice was slightly higher-pitched, but it had already broken and the hair on the backs of his hands and arms had started to darken. His voice was unsure and he coughed several times, quite close to the microphone, which caused the speaker on the camera he was using to record to redline and crackle. Despite the technical issues, Ben's obvious enthusiasm for the potential of the new technology that he was holding shined through. Throughout the video, he outlined some ideas for a new YouTube channel which would cover the development of drones and quadcopters in detail.

Several times, he exhorted viewers to keep coming back to check out his channel for everything you need to know about the world of quadcopters and drones. The channel still had two subscribers.

The video showcased Ben's new purchase – a Parrot AR.Drone 1.0. The drone had been released earlier that year and Ben was one of the earliest adopters of the technology. He'd first seen drones mentioned when the military had started to use them to deliver justice from the skies. As drones had become commercially available, Ben enjoyed the thought of sending missiles of his own onto adversaries from school. For someone who had already concluded that the outside world was a challenging place, the concept of drones shone in Ben's mind as a potential way of bringing the world to him. Why would he need to leave the safety and peace of his flat if a drone could bring him everything he wanted? Food, equipment, entertainment – all of it would be flown to the balcony of Flat 4, Ellis Tower. Best of all, it wouldn't just be him – everyone would get things delivered by drone. In that way, Ben would no longer be a weirdo - he would simply be an early adopter for a new way of living.

The video gave a rundown of the specification of the drone and a short history of Parrot that Ben read from the company's website. There was a brief interruption when Anne can be heard singing Lady Gaga's *Bad Romance,* and Ben covers the microphone on the phone to shout, "Mum! I'm recording!" The rest was a straightforward first-person view of Ben's hands and arms unboxing the drone and outlining the items that come with it. The Parrot was designed to require minimal setup, so Ben was able to quickly progress to the section of the video where he powered up the Parrot for its maiden flight. Because of the size of the drone and the relative size of Ben's bedroom, he essentially just flew the drone to the roof in a rush of motors and blades. He laughed nervously when it bumped into the ceiling and, after a wobble, steadied itself. He ends the flight by landing it on the double bed. The video showed the feed from the Parrot's two onboard cameras, which looks pixelated, but Ben was clearly impressed with the possibilities. The video ended with a repeated request to keep checking out the channel and a promise to upload more footage later that week.

The comments were brutal.

Alerted by the appearance of Ben's arms, hands and fingers nearly all of the messages focus on Ben's weight. There was one comment that said simply, "Good vid", but the others point out that Ben was a "sausage-fingered fucktard". The top comment said: "Cool drone dont eat it."

***

Ben was 14 when he started home-schooling. Anne was surprised when she discovered that all it took to remove her son from school forever was to write a single letter, confirming that she was happy to be responsible for Ben's education. There was no obligation to follow a curriculum, no commitment to provide a school day or even to sit exams; just some wishy-washy language around providing an education that "achieves what it is intended to achieve." The council were supposed to send someone round for a check-up and to see that Ben was actually learning something but no official ever knocked on the door of Flat 4, Ellis Tower to see what Ben was doing with his time. This was good because Ben's education was the very definition of eclectic.

Anne had thought long and hard and employed her own life experiences to create what she saw as the perfect curriculum. For the first six months, she was adamant that Ben would learn how to learn. Her argument was simply that if she taught him how to teach himself then this was a skill that he could employ throughout his life and he could then pursue what interested him. Learning to learn meant that Ben was schooled in the art of research; including how to perform Boolean searches, how to understand the nuance of the Dewey Decimal system and how to find experts in any conceivable field and to get them to talk to him. Ben was drilled in interview techniques and note-taking by a friend of Anne's who had been a journalist. He learned shorthand and different techniques for revision. He was taught the different ways that people learn and understood how being a visual and logical learner should inform the way he studied. He was also sent out to see another friend of Anne's who ran a second-hand car dealership. He taught Ben the art of selling while using him as free labour for a month. Anne tested each of these attributes, and once he had convinced her that he was up to standard, she widened his curriculum.

This meant that Ben was made to read daily, play chess and do crosswords, volunteer, to exercise and to watch films. Anne divided cinema into "classic" and "popcorn" and taught Ben her opinion on the difference between the two forms and the values of both. Above all, Ben was challenged to explore what interested him and to become as proficient as he possibly could in everything he studied. Consequently, Ben did enough glass blowing to have produced an attractive, if slightly lumpy, swan which sat in pride of place on his mum's windowsill. He learned Esperanto, much to Anne's disgust, as she would rather have seen him study Latin but she kept her reservations to a minimum. For several months, Ben joined in at a daytime DIY group designed for men with dementia. They loved having him around, although he always had to remind them of his name, and why he was so much younger than everyone else. They passed on their knowledge of working with wood and metals. He did an online course in drop-shipping and became a pro-seller on eBay, connecting the people of the West with the products of the East. Golf balls and face masks were his most lucrative products and made him more than £20,000 a year, for doing little more than answering emails from customers and placing orders. He shared his wealth with his mum, but she insisted that he keep studying as well as working.

Throughout all of his education, Anne kept a respectful distance and didn't push him on why most of his studies saw him confined to his room for weeks on end, but constantly engaged Ben at mealtimes about what he was learning and what he was excited about learning next. Ben would talk about the military tactics of the Romans or the odd properties of the element Argon, and Anne would listen actively and probe the depths of his understanding. Ben discovered that through his mum's job at the café and her church, she had access to an incredible network of experts. Anne believed one of the most important elements of the Bible was to follow the example of Jesus, who saw no shame in washing the feet of his disciples. She saw a noble and Godly purpose in serving people cups of tea and washing up - it wasn't just a job; it gave her fulfilment. It also allowed her to ask people about how they were and who they were and to try and understand who they wanted to be. Her loud, carefree laugh meant that people warmed to her instantly once they'd got over the volume of her guffawing, and her gift was that people quickly came to love her. Ben benefited from this repeatedly through his studies when he would find that a truck driver from the café, when asked nicely by Anne, would happily flout customs and bring stick insects back from his travels, which Ben then mated and sold. A fellow parishioner who had previously been a curator at the local museum taught Ben how to use a metal detector. Anne felt she had done her best to equip Ben with both curiosity and the means to assuage that curiosity. She believed that in this way, Ben's education achieved what she intended it to achieve.

Ben loved home-schooling. When he compared it to the relentless, daily shitshow that was going to school, it was paradise. Ever since Ben had started high school, his size had made him an instant target of verbal and physical attacks. Ben always remembered the cold shock of sitting on the uncomfortable toilet at lunchtime once and seeing his name on the wall: "Ben Stone is the first in our year to get tits." It may have been true, but he hated the infamy that his weight brought him. There was nowhere to hide when you were the fattest in the school, never mind your year. He liked talking to the girls, but none of them would commit the socially suicidal move of actually making friends with him. The boys just ignored him or hit him. Even the teachers openly resented him. His P.E. teacher advised him to fake a note from home so that he wouldn't turn sports day into a comedy event. At home he had time to pursue his interests, he had freedom from the barbarism of his classmates and in his mum, he had someone who inspired him to learn and to develop in the direction that he wanted to go in.

The one element of his mum's regime that he hated was exercise. Ben felt confident when his mum told him that he needed to be doing at least four hours of P.E. each week that in time, he could convince her to reduce this to zero. He attempted this through his usual routine of good-natured whining and outright pleading. Nothing happened. His mum held firm in her conviction that there was a sport out there for everyone and that he could either get out there and find what his sport was, or he would be returned to school at the earliest convenience. He argued that as her sport was darts, perhaps he should be allowed to try that, but for once Anne insisted and Ben was tasked with finding something that raised his heart-rate.

So it was that every week, for six whole months, Ben found himself on the bus to rugby training with the local club three miles away. Some weeks he claimed that training was cancelled and some weeks he simply sat on the bus and saw where it went, but other weeks he found he had no choice but to go. Rugby had been arrived at more by process of elimination than anything else. There just weren't that many sports where someone of his size could flourish. Naturally, he hated it. He resented the jostling of running and his self-awareness around his growing body made him feel sick every time he had to contemplate getting changed in the sight of other boys. He hated the shouting of the coaches. He hated the cold of waiting around for someone to pass you the ball. He hated the heat of when you eventually did get it and it started this complicated push and shove phase of the game, which seemed to have new rules depending on the most mindless things, such as the direction in which you ran into the pushing. None of it made sense to Ben and his confusion and unhappiness meant he ate more and his weight rose again.

One day, there was a tournament where his team played a number of other local clubs. He had to endure a two-hour bus ride just to get to the tournament at some freezing God-forsaken hillside, which was so sloped that the balls would constantly run downhill if they weren't kept in a kit bag. Ben decided enough was enough and enacted a plan that he had been pondering for some time. His argument was simply that rugby had rules. If Ben refused to follow those rules, then sooner or later someone would need to remove him from the pitch in order for the game to carry on. The whistle blew and much to his team's surprise Ben threw himself into the heart of the action. He allowed himself to rage. He threw punches. He levelled people with brutal tackles. He took the ball at every opportunity and ploughed into each tackle with such ferocity that often he found the opposing team would simply back off and allow him to go straight through. Ben felt certain that the referee's whistle and his subsequent dismissal were only seconds away. The referee blew for half time.

"Gents," said the coach as they gathered around at the break and swigged watery orange squash. "If you want an example of what rugby is supposed to look like, then take a look at what Mr Ben Stone has just achieved. He has single-handedly demolished that team. I doubt they'll want to come out for the second half at this rate. Ben, we've only played one half of a game, but you're player of the tournament for me. More of the same please, son."

Ben couldn't quite believe it. He had actively tried to get sent off, but all that had happened was praise? He took to the field for the second half. He threw everything into it again. He swatted players away like flies. He stamped. He gouged. He dropped his head and charged like a bull. He was scratched and bruised, but this was a small one-time price to pay for being banned for all time from competitive rugby. However, all that happened was that the cheering from the side-lines intensified, his team-mates gave him more pats on the back and the ball found its way to him more often. They won the first game by ten tries. Ben was dumbstruck. So this is what they were supposed to be doing after all? He decided to go with it for the rest of the tournament and see how far he could push it. His play throughout the day was a study in brutality. Apart from one quiet word from the referee when Ben gathered in a player fleeing a ruck by the throat and held him tight, there was no official admonishments. His team didn't win the tournament, but the coach's prediction came true and Ben received a small trophy for being his club's player of the tournament.

Ben's mind reeled and he didn't even experience his customary discomfort as he waited for the other boys to shower and change. Somehow, as his mum had promised, he had discovered a form of physical activity that he could do. Weirdly, he decided that he was excited about training on Wednesday. Even better, the coach realised that he was getting the bus home and said he'd give Ben a lift so he didn't have to wait around for hours in the cold. Compared to the bleak playing fields, the car was stifling and warm after the frigid pitch and Ben dumped his bags and his trophy into the back seat, which was a chaos of cones, balls and bibs. The coach joyfully relived a number of Ben's more memorable moments of sporting rage with him and Ben laughed and relaxed. He wasn't sure, but he thought that he might be happy.

They arrived home and the coach parked his car at the back of Ellis Tower. Ben reached for the handle, but his coach stopped him.

"Just wait a minute Ben. Look, this isn't easy to say, and I don't want to overstep the mark but the role of a coach isn't just about telling you when to pass and when to hold the ball with both hands. Sometimes, we have to talk about the whole player."

Ben was suspicious. He felt his fingers on the cold chrome handle of the door and wondered if he should get out.

"OK."

"I know your dad isn't around and I know you've had difficulties with school, but I wanted you to know that rugby can be a family. That might sound like bollocks, but it's true."

Despite his wariness, Ben laughed to hear his coach swear. He decided that he was happy.

"Thank you. I never liked sport before. Ever."

"But one thing that families do is that they speak the truth to each other, don't they? Now what I want to say to you is that in rugby, it's fine to have weight, it's the *wobble* you don't want. Have you ever heard of ProTeen440 shakes before? Hang on, let me get you a sample pack."

The coach turned around in the seat and rummaged amongst the sporting detritus in the back of the car. He turned back and passed Ben a crumpled sachet of ProTeen440. There was a picture of a husky young man on the front of the packet looking happy and drinking a brown shake. Ben stared at the packet.

"The great thing about ProTeen440 is that it's specially formulated for young men like you who need to lose weight, but who don't want to lose muscle. It's all down to Mucanacil, which is their trademarked protein strand. Take a look online and see if you can get Mucanacil anywhere else. Best of all, I'm a retailer for it. Give that one a try and you'll love it – then you'll want to look at getting something like the Ultimate Starter Kit – that's nice because you get your own shaker for free."

Ben knew he wasn't happy with his weight. He definitely had both weight and wobble. But there was something about the moment that was making him deeply uncomfortable. His mind was blank and it seemed his coach was waiting for him to say something.

"What's a shaker?" he asked.

"A shaker – you know, it's like a cup you put the powder in and shake it up and it makes the shake for you. You can bring it to practice as well."

"So, it's free?" Ben asked, trying to understand what was going on.

"It's so cheap it might as well be free," said his coach pulling a laminated sheet from the side pocket of the door. "So to qualify for your free shaker you'd want the ultimate pack which would be about £3 per day. That's not much, is it? The smart thing though is that you can only get these in six-month batches because they want people who have committed to the ProTeen440 system, so you'd be looking at about £600 but you'd get my coach discount so you'll be investing £550. We can speak to your mum about it. Will she be in now?"

"Um, no. She'll be at darts," Ben answered. "It looks really good though, I'll try the sample."

"Good lad."

Ben opened the door and stepped out into the crisp Autumn night and watched his breath cloud in the air. He opened the back door and got his kit bag out. He looked at the trophy on the back seat and shut the door. His boots clicked on the carpark tarmac as he headed back into the flats.

CHAPTER 5

11th August 2020

7 days after

585 lbs (265 kg)

The cold water is gone.

I am filling Brown's drinking bowl and the stream of water from the cold tap thins out, returns briefly to a full flow and then disappears with a final drop hanging from the mouth of the spout. The cold water taps in the bath and in the bathroom sink have both dried up too. I leave the taps open in case the cold water comes back, but I don't think it will. I don't think it ever will. The idea that survival now means leaving the flat, perhaps permanently, makes me shiver. I try the hot water tap and it dribbles out a meagre stream of cold, flat water that tastes of metal and possibly pigeons. Brown looks at me suspiciously when I fill her bowl with it and turns her back on the bowl in a piece of canine theatre, which she completes by melodramatically returning to her basket. I share her reluctance.

Having to rely on a tank of hot water somewhere in the building that has who knows how much left in it scares me. No water is a faster death than no food. I realise I am in shock and have been since this weird riot began, so I've not had much time to react to what's happening. But when the water disappears, I feel tears of desperation welling in my eyes. An image of Brown lying thin and desiccated on the floor springs into my head and refuses to leave until I physically shake my head like I am trying to dislodge a hat. I tip my head back and battle against the teardrops – the drinking water has gone, I am not going to just let this priceless resource fall out of my face and onto the floor. The stupidity of the thought makes me laugh and the dam breaks and I weep with disbelief until snot flows from my nose and my eyes go puffy. Brown barks silently, upset at my distress, and eventually I wipe my forearm across my face and smile at her to show that everything is OK. I throw her ball for her and her trauma is undone.

It's one thing to fake a smile for Brown, but she's a dog and it's pretty apparent that everything is not OK. It's really very evident that everything is fucked. I've been processing what's happened and discounted an array of theories that runs roughly from zombies to Godzilla. My working theory is that there is some sort of illness or virus at large. The evidence for this is that Mr Ethiss, the lady from the lift and Karl all appear to have been ill – their skin has a grey tint - and they have those red, strained eyes that look as if they've been swimming in a heavily chlorinated pool, or like they have really bad hayfever. That could point towards it being something airborne like a chemical or pollen, but then why isn't everyone affected? Why don't I have it – or is that just a temporary state of affairs? Also, if I haven't got it, surely some other people are ok too, in which case where are they? The only broad conclusion I can draw is that something has happened to a number of people from different genders and ages that makes them physically and verbally aggressive. In short, I don't have a clue and the places I usually look for answers are gone.

The power is still off and nights are pitch black. This darkness extends across everything I can see from my window. The pinprick lights of the stars swarm the sky, but it's clear that there are no more planes. That's not good. By day, the endless sunlight shines down on no human movement. I find some ancient toy binoculars which give a weak magnification among the wardrobes and I scan the streets and surrounding homes for signs of life. I see no fires for cooking or warmth and in two days I hear no more explosions or screaming. Birds sing, cats hunt among the bodies and the occasional loose dog are the only indications of life I've seen. It's so still. Here and there across the areas of the city I can see, there are the remnants of destruction, lines of smoke curling into the sky, indicating where disaster has visited.

Aside from the loss of the water, the thing that scares me most is the bodies. They're just left where they fell. It's not just normal civilians, either. Aside from Karl, I can see two of the firemen who were helping to move me and they're both just left there too. If there is any remnant of society still functioning, that wouldn't happen, would it? On TV programmes about the police or the fire brigade you always see that when it's one of their own in danger then the emergency services go into overdrive. Outside my window, the bodies of the firemen are as abandoned and uncared for as any of the bodies. That suggests that society has broken down to the extent that there is no longer any emergency services. Not in the North, anyway. Maybe London is just getting on as normal and they'll be amazed to hear that there even is a North, more so that it has ended. I have this growing feeling that I am alone. I have known many nuances of loneliness over the last nine years and this feels different - more emphatic. For my own sanity more than anything, I paint the word "ALIVE" on a bedsheet with some old olive paint from when we decorated the bathroom and hang it over the balcony.

Looking cautiously out of the letterbox, I see that Mr Ethiss and the lady from the lift are still slumped in the corridor. They don't seem to be dead. I can't see if they're breathing but there's something animated about them. The lady's mouth looks odd because it's wide open and juts forward slightly. I feel sick that I dislocated someone's jaw. She was attacking me, but it all seems so brutal. I've never hit anyone before. She works at Greggs as well, how could anyone inflict pain on someone like that? They created a sausage roll for vegans. I feel so guilty that I've had to argue with myself several times that I absolutely must not step into the corridor and see if I can push it back into place. What am I supposed to do about them? Just let them rot out there? There are so many questions.

I did find one answer at least. Karl is suspended by his tether underneath the platform of the cherry picker. The operator of the machine down on the ground was collapsed across the controls, with a large wound at the back of his head. My guess is that this is what accounted for Karl being dragged out of the flat. If that's correct, then it appears an immaculately-timed act of violence saved my life. I try not to think too much about that. From the flat, I can see at least forty bodies covered in blood. I think a lot of those were the crowd who wanted to see me lifted out of the flat. Most of them seem to be the victims of assaults or accidents – their wounds range from bloodied faces to missing limbs. I can see at least twenty who also have vomit stains similar to Karl's.

I keep thinking about mass hysteria – I vaguely remember that humans are sometimes susceptible to outrageous behaviour if they all do it together. I remember reading something on Wikipedia about everyone in an Italian town where they all started dancing and couldn't stop – is this like that? Obviously, I'd look it up but there's no power and no internet. I'm pre-digital thick.

To fill time, I am taking an inventory of my resources. Food is an easy one – there is none. There's a home delivery booked with Morrisons for a week on Wednesday when I'm due to come out of the hospital, but that's not looking likely to happen now. Since mum died, I have operated a ruthlessly inefficient Just In Time form of food shopping, combined with extensive usage of Just Eat. Consequently, the bounty of the cupboards extends to three tubes of tomato paste, a multi-pack of vegan lasagne sheets, a few tins of sweetcorn and one and a half bags of self-raising flour. I soak the lasagne sheets in water until it softens and nibble at them until they are gone. I mix flour with water and make paste disks which I leave to dry on the balcony. When they have air-dried, I squeeze tomato paste on top which serves to make them revolting rather than just inedible. Even Brown rejects them. She has perhaps another day of food left and I've already rationed it out to an absurd level where I count the pieces of kibbles into her bowl. It goes in two mouthfuls and Brown looks at me with an expression somewhere between reproach and sadness.

"Good girl," I say, but she can't eat sentiments.

I've not eaten for two days now. I tried a piece of the kibble but it made me heave – plus, what would it solve if I ate Brown's food? I may as well eat Brown. In place of food, I am drinking lots of water from the hot tap, which means I have to hobble to the toilet frequently. Well, I say toilet but really I just stand on the balcony and urinate while I survey the world around me. Because I can't reach my penis to direct the stream, it just floods forth from somewhere under my gut. I worry about the trickling noise it makes on the balcony floor because a dark animal instinct is willing me to remain as silent and as hidden as possible. I get urine burns on the underside of my stomach because I can only sluice water over myself in the bathroom, which never quite reaches all the areas that need cleaning. Fortunately, I have an industrial tub of

Vaseline which goes some way to protecting the skin but there's no escaping the fact that I smell like the laundry bin from a care home.

I find a short length of crêpe bandage, which is too short to go around my right ankle more than twice, so I'm not sure what good it's doing, but it feels better than doing nothing. Where I turned my ankle in the fight with the lady from the lift, there is a deeper shade of red than I'm used to with the leg. It's more like a purple around the ankle compared to the crimson colour which is up to my mid-shin. The scab on top of my foot is just hideous, the fall loosened it and the whole piece of the scab sits like a badly fitting lid on a pot. I can feel the pressure of infection underneath it. Moving even a single step is pure agony and I've started to use an upturned broom as a crutch. I don't like the way the broom bows slightly as I lean on it, but it will have to do. The whole leg feels too full like it's going to pop at any moment.

Thank God for the prescription boxes of Ibuprofen in the shelves over my bed. I've been taking twice the maximum dose and I swear that's the only thing that has stopped me going mad with pain. In less positive medical news, I have run out of the Metformin, which I use to control my blood sugar levels. I read through the leaflet inside the medicine box and it warns that dizzy spells and death are possible side-effects I should look for in my future. Good to know. Interestingly though, it did state that if I was on a very low calorie diet of fewer than 1,000 calories per day, then I should stop taking the Metformin anyway. I'm fairly sure that my new dietary regime of hot tap water sneaks in under 1,000 calories, so maybe it won't be the dizzy spells that kill me after all.

To add to the fun, I've had to go cold turkey from using my mains-powered, sleep apnoea machine which helps me to breathe during the night. Without it, I revert to waking up clawing at the air and gasping for breath like I've swum to the surface of the sea from a thousand fathoms below. When I was 17, I paid to have a sleep study conducted at home and the doctor who reviewed the statistics said that he was amazed I'd not had a heart attack already, because of the severity of my symptoms. Apparently, I stop breathing for anywhere up to 40 seconds and that can happen 30 times a night or more. The CPAP machine prevents that by keeping my airways from collapsing, or at least it would if there was power. I've also had two nightmares where I see the lady from the lift's distended jaw, wobble and then snap shut through Brown's hind leg. Consequently, I often don't know whether I'm waking because I'm choking or because I'm terrified. It might be easier not to sleep anymore.

In the evenings, I power up my phone to check if any messages have come through, or if the BBC or Sky app has updated. Most of the apps now freeze when I open them. It feels nice to at least open the Just Eat app, even if it only brings up a screen saying "Sorry, there has been an error." Even this gives me some hope. An "error" feels salvageable. It feels like tomorrow the army might roll in, and within a few hours, I might be able to tap a screen and have two 12" pizzas with vegan cheese left outside the door. I want that to happen so much that a few times I've tapped on the Just Eat app so longingly and forcefully that it's brought up a sub-menu to ask if I want to delete the app. No! I never want to delete this app. I never want this pinnacle of human achievement to be lost.

On the question of food, there is an uncomfortable thought that I have pondered from as many angles as I can, namely, starving to death. The essence of every diet ever created is to deprive the body of calories, whether through a restricted intake of foods or increased output of activity. The aim is to force the body to look for other sources of energy to use instead, such as your body's fat.

There's no denying that I have limited resources at my disposal, but one thing that I have in great abundance is deposits of fat. Could it be as simple as burning through the calories I've draped across my body? I suspect that it might be, but the thought that makes my blood run cold is that the same cannot be said of Brown. She carries no extra weight, which is why she spends half of her life snuggling under fleeces for warmth. This question looms over our daily life.

Most of the time, I sit on my bed and look out of the flat, over the city. Because the bed is frozen with the foot lowered, I had to build it back up with piles of books. It's now level again, but it wobbles, which is annoying. The weather has continued to be hot and my skin has a permanent sheen of sweat, which only adds to the smell in the flat. I swig water from a two-litre stein and fill the four two-litre bottles of Diet Coke that were still in the recycling bin. That saves me from having to make the painful trip to the tap more often than I need. Brown mostly sits on my bed, watching me swig water and pining for me to throw her ball. It has surprised me that she's not more scared that one of the walls of the room has gone, but Manchester Terriers are resilient. As long as I'm here, she knows that things can't be that bad. I wish I had her perspective – there is so much danger around her and yet she continues to look at me sweetly and sleep and cuddle as if things are fine. In some ways, she might even prefer life now, as she doesn't have to nudge me to open the door so she can go for a shit on the balcony, she walks out whenever the need takes her.

I was on the balcony yesterday and I noticed that after the cherry picker had been accidentally repositioned, it came to rest about three or four metres from the edge of the balcony with Karl swinging below it like a grotesque piñata. The harness was pulled so tight that his thick work trousers had ridden up nearly to the middle of shins. But he tried to stomp me to death, so I wasn't going to feel sorry for him getting an atomic wedgie. The cherry picker has been going through my mind because I had started to think about how safe my position was in the flat. The front door clearly represents a point of weakness because even though I've pushed wedges under the door itself and tried to brace it as much as possible, it remains the only feasible way that anyone could get in. However, it's also blocked off as a way for Brown and me to escape should we need to, but then I can't use the lift or stairs anyway, so where would I go?

The cherry picker has a platform which is usually where someone stands to work and drive the unit. Currently, it's sitting about a half a metre lower than the balcony. On the platform itself is a control panel about one foot across, which the firemen had explained could be used to drive the whole machine from the top of the platform. That way, someone could work at the top but still drive the machine back and forth. This saved having to go back to the ground, move the unit and then climb back up. Through the binoculars, I can see that the keys are still in the base of the unit, and it appears that there is a simple joystick on the platform control panel that I'm guessing is what's used to drive the vehicle. If I can reach it somehow, then I think I might be able to bring it over to the flat. If I do that, I've got a possible escape route - should I need it.

It takes a few hours to put together a stick long enough that I can reach towards the platform. I take down the curtain rails from my old bedroom and tape them together with enough overlap to form a semi-rigid structure. The slight bend on the stick is useful, as it allows me to hover over the control panel. To the end of my improvised boom, I tape a small loop which I make from a length of the washing line from the bathroom. The heat of the day and the throbbing in my ruined leg is enough to ensure that I am covered in a sheen of sweat the entire time, but I eventually get a set up that I think could work.

I feed the pole out of the flat, using the balcony rail to keep it steady. It's like fishing, and I hover the loop of wire over the platform, trying desperately to keep it steady and hook the loop over the joystick. I try for forty minutes with my arms aching and my head spinning with pain and frustration. The difficulty is seeing what I am doing. I think that a latch might have been left up on the control panel which keeps snagging the line and preventing me from working my loop over the joystick. Finally, the loop falls onto its target, and I lower the rod and check through the binoculars to confirm that it is now secured around the black pommel on top of the joystick. I delicately pump my fist in celebration to avoid dislodging the loop.

My heart is thumping, and there is a banging sensation in my temples as my excitement mounts. I stop to clear my head and take a long glug of water. I return to the pole and, agonisingly slowly, to avoid the loop jumping off the joystick, I pull it towards me – hand over hand. I feel the line go tight, and I exert the gentlest of pressure on the joystick. Nothing happens. I pull a little harder and feel it give, which my binoculars show has moved the joystick – but again, no movement from the cherry picker. I peer through the binoculars but the angle means I can't get a better view of the control panel.

As I pan the binoculars about looking for what else I can do, I scan over the body of Karl hanging under the platform. His face has changed – his eyes are open, and he is staring straight at me. I take the binoculars away and look at him directly. He is looking back at me, his face gripped in anger, his lips pulled back from his teeth which are clamped tightly together. His face is red from the exertion of hanging in the air, but he still manages to put serious volume into the scream that he directs at me.

"What are you doing, you big fat fuck?"

The accusation reverberates around the streets, and on the ground, I see a doorway open as one, two and then more of the bodies on the ground are awakened by Karl's shouting. Even some of the bodies that I assumed were dead on the floor, bring themselves to their feet, in a rickety fashion. More shouts join Karl's voice.

"What's that fucking racket?"

"Why won't everyone shut up?!"

"Hurry up and jump!"

I recoil in fear and step back into the flat so that I am out of Karl's eyeline. Not wanting it to be seen by others, I quickly pull the rod and line towards me, but it catches on something. The sound of a diesel engine turning over springs from the unit of the cherry picker on the ground. Even among the shouting, the noise of the engine seems phenomenal, like a grand piano being dropped into a shipping container. I sneak to the edge of the window and notice more heads looking up and ranting about noise and pollution. Someone screams something improbable about Greta Thunberg. I try to lift the pole off and tug gently at it to try and free it. With a jerk, the whole platform lurches forward several feet. I pull the pole again and with surprising speed, the platform turns and crashes into the side of Ellis Tower just to the right of my balcony. There is a creak of metal on brick and the rage in Karl's scream intensifies and then stops.

"I'm so sorry!" I say into the air beyond the balcony, as I finally manage to unloop the line from the platform's control panel and pull it back into the flat.

Approximately twenty people are moving in the street now. They scream as they see each other and clash. The scene below resembles a full-on brawl with people intent on fighting each other, and the sounds of chaos rise as the combatants vent their fury. I hobble backwards away from anyone's view and sit heavily on the edge of the bed, feeling weak and shocked. Brown runs to me from the kitchen where she is hiding and leaps onto my lap. I stare at the wall and hold Brown's head close to me as the noises of another riot float up from the street. What is going on? What sort of chemical or illness allows people to be motionless for days at a time and then wake up? I've never heard of anything like this before.

After an hour, all is silent again and I risk peeking over the side of the balcony. I'm surprised by how eerie and still it is already. Some newcomers have tumbled to the ground and lie splayed across the floor, or propped against vehicles but there is no movement. Are they all dead? I don't recognise any of them, but they all seem so vacant, or perhaps they are so filled with anger that it leaves them hard to identify as human. I can clearly see the control panel on the platform now, and I use my reaching pole to press all the buttons until the sound of the engine below stops abruptly. Despite the disastrous way I'd achieved it I could at least celebrate the small victory of now having an escape route.

Until I see a small notice on the control panel, which even upside down I can read: "Maximum operator weight 150kg" That would mean that about half of me could escape. I want to scream with the frustration of it all. No water! No medicine! No escape! I feel an urgent longing for a biscuit. Not just one biscuit, a thousand biscuits, enough to eat away all this failure and just briefly block out the world. I simmer with frustration as I watch another perfect, deep pink sunset predicting another sunny day tomorrow. I look again at Karl and see close-up where he has been smashed into the side of the building when the cherry picker moved. His face looks ruined. There is a smear of blood about a metre long, across the side of the building where it seems he's been dragged face-first against the wall. That's when I see that he is still wearing his coat and that clipped to the breast pocket is the thick, robust-looking emergency radio.

I limp back into the bedroom and switch out the end of the reaching stick and attach the toy grasping arm I use for extending my range when sitting in bed. I force it open to give me a hook shape for the end of the pole. I feed the pole carefully down the side of the building and manage to gently tease the radio from Karl's uniform and pull it into my flat. Karl doesn't move at all and I resign myself to the fact that I have now assaulted and possibly killed two people. I feel a surge of panic, a desperate need to explain to someone that this isn't who I am! My head feels light and I think I am going to fall over. I'd been having fewer hunger pangs since about the fourth day, but when they hit, I feel like they might actually kill me. I try to breathe as feelings of guilt and pain and hunger war within me. After a minute I feel strong enough to carry on.

The radio unit is heavier and squatter than a mobile phone. It has two dials on the top of the unit and a digital display on the front. I hobble down the corridor, away from the lounge and into my old bedroom to try and contain the noise. I shut the door and sit on my old bed which makes the springs squeak. I catch my breath and flex my toes, wincing as the scab pinches and starts to bleed. I give a long push on the power button and watch the unit flash into life. The battery indicator is tinged red, and only a single sliver of power remains, I have to work quickly. I turn both the dials and start pressing buttons.

"Hello? Can anyone hear me? Hello!" I pant into the receiver.

I look again at the unit and press and hold the power button to try and reboot it. After a couple of seconds, it illuminates and goes through a brief display cycle. Another button says "Seek" and I keep pressing that and listening. There is a pause and then a dry burst of static each time I press it. Every few seconds I repeat, "Hello?". I jab at another button on the top of the unit and a shrill alarm sounds, scaring me so much that I immediately hit the power off button just to get it to shut up. In the corridor outside the flat, I hear footsteps and voices raise and Mr Ethiss and the lady start another screaming battle. I lie back on my bed and hope it stops.

Eventually, the noises die off and I pull the duvet over my head to contain the noises while I reboot the unit again and wait as the LED display lights up again.

"-await further instructions…"

"Hello!" I whisper urgently into the unit. "Can anyone hear me? Is someone there?"

There is no response, but a voice is broadcasting, so I shut up and listen. It is a woman's computerised voice reading in a calm but officious tone.

"Attention. This is a crisis broadcast, recorded and distributed on…Wednesday the 5th August 2020…the message follows: There has been a global incident resulting in massive loss of life and the destruction of property. This has resulted in the disruption of travel links, power networks and communications systems. At this time emergency, military and governmental responses are compromised. The cause of this incident is unknown, but if you witness someone demonstrating significantly altered behaviour and symptoms including severe vomiting, then you are advised to avoid contact with them…This broadcast will be updated every 24 hours with the latest information. The advice is to stay calm and to stay in your homes."

There is a pause and a clicking sound before the message continues.

"Attention. This is a crisis broadcast, recorded and distributed on…Thursday the 6th August 2020…the message follows: Where is everyone? Is anyone left? I think the wraths have killed everyone. They said we weren't supposed to use the broadcast system, but I can't get hold of anyone on the radio and all the COs are dead. Is anyone out there? I'm on my own now, please send help…This broadcast will be updated every 24 hours with the latest information. The advice is to stay calm and to stay in your homes. This message will now repeat."

I listen through one more time and power the radio off.

CHAPTER 6

16th November 2010

9 years, 8 months, 19 days before

289 lbs (131 kg)

"Ok, we start the session with sharing. Remember – this is a space where honesty creates healing and that creates hope. Remember the triangle we looked at last week? So let's share whenever you're ready. Does anyone want to share? Anyone? At our Tuesday group, you can't get everyone to stop sharing! Sometimes it's a bit much and you're like, "Ahhhh! I didn't need to know that!" But it *is* good. It is good to share and often, the hope that you create can be seen on the scales next week. So, who wants to start us off this week?"

The silence that followed Karen's introduction was thick and immediate. The chance of anyone voluntarily sharing anything was slimmer than Karen herself, who in comparison to the group members seemed transparent. Ben sat forward in his chair and looked at his feet. The pressure of squashing his belly into the top of his thighs, restricted his lung capacity and made him feel light-headed. He watched the sparkles of light dance in the periphery of his vision. He rocked back in his seat and counted to see how long before the sparkles went. It felt like blood was pooling in his ears, so it was a shock when Karen's shrill voice pierced his awareness.

"Ben? Are you with us?! Ben – how about you share how your week has been? Did you manage to stick to the green face foods we looked at?"

"I don't know."

"Come on Ben," Karen implored - clearly she had decided that this was the moment that she would unlock Ben Stone's heart and lead him to honesty, healing and hope. "Did you find the green faces this week? How was it?"

"I had some salad -"

"Ok, great! That's great! Remember what we say – salad on half of the plate is a green face and that's great!"

"-on Monday."

"Oh. OK. Well, that's a start – that's a good start. Did you see any other green faces through the week? How about your oats and your lean meats and fish?"

"Well, I can't do meat and fish, remember I told you I was a vegan?"

Karen looked confused briefly and consulted her notes.

"Was that you? I didn't have that down on the Friday group. For some reason, I thought the vegan was Tuesday. Beth – do we have a vegan on Tuesday?"

Beth was Karen's second-in-command who made notes when Karen talked and noted the members' weights down on a spreadsheet in an ancient laptop emblazoned with Eat Great, Talk Great, Feel Great stickers. Ben had been to two meetings now and he didn't yet feel great; although to be fair he hadn't been eating great or talking great.

"No, that's me," Ben admitted.

"So what do you eat? Nuts? Because what I need you to do is look at the nutritional labels on the nuts because yes they're high in fibre and some minerals, but they are also high in, someone?

Don't leave me hanging!"

"Fat," Lucy By The Door said. The seats by the door always filled up the fastest, but Lucy always got the prime spot.

"That's right – fats and high fats are, someone?"

"Red faces." That answer was a combined mumbled effort from Bingo Wing Beryl and Relapse Rachel.

"Yes, red faces. So let's keep off the nuts this week, Ben, and aim for more green – check your booklet if you need more green face foods. But don't forget eating great is one element of the triangle – the other is to talk great – so Ben, why don't you share how your week has been?"

Ben had never felt more visible. Sitting in a Scout hut alongside eight middle-aged women, he felt every centimetre and each pound of his size. He felt as though he was inflated with helium and tethered to his chair by a luminous orange guide rope. The unspoken agreement of the members was that they didn't make eye contact. They had made a silent pact to treat this group in the spirit that it was intended - as a "screw you, fatties" from the local authority.

Ben knew he had to offer up a sacrificial virgin to the dragon. He thought he'd try being honest.

"My week has been horrible. I don't have any friends. I sometimes wonder if there's something in me that's broken. I feel like I don't know how to behave or live. Food is the only thing I look forward to or understand."

Karen had heard enough. "Don't have any friends! It's the best time of your life, school! You ask any of these ladies, who I'm sure they won't mind me saying are past school age, and they'd tell you that they'd give anything to be back at school. Look at Beth! Me and Beth were in school together and she was the popular one! All the boys! Getting her exams! Ask her if she'd like to have a chance for all of that again!"

Beth raised herself up slightly so that she could peer over the top of the laptop. "It was -"

"This week, how about you think about all of the good things about school, OK, Ben? Don't focus on the negatives."

"But, I don't go to school, I'm home-schooled."

"You're what?"

"Home-schooled. I don't go to school."

"Well, that's your problem then isn't it – if you were at school, you'd have plenty of friends."

"But I left school because everyone hated me."

"Listen, we've had enough of this downer talk. Remember what we said: "Life isn't about waiting for a sunny day, it's about learning to dance in the rain.""

"Dance…in…the…rain, got it," said Ben pretending to take a note in his booklet.

"That's right," Karen said, measuring Ben's sincerity with a look. "OK – Lucy, how has your week been?"

Ben leaned forward again and watched the sparkly lights in his vision return. He knew it probably wasn't healthy, but it was something to pass the time. Ben had spent a lot of time just passing the time. Waiting in corridors for teachers. Shuffling to find comfort in the plastic chairs they bolt to the walls of hospital corridors. Even at home, he often felt like he was just waiting for someone to explain something fundamental to him – what he was supposed to do, so he could just get on and do it. Until that happened, he passed the time.

Karen's scales were wider than his ones at home. The platform was nearly half a metre across, and it was topped with some special material that allowed a better grip. Ben knew that he was the biggest of all the members and he had wondered to himself with a surge of panic whether these scales would be able to register his full weight. After all, he was here because he had maxed out the ones at his doctors, who had then referred him to this group, and he had been unable to resist his mum's gentle pleadings that he give it a go. He dreaded to think what circle of hell lay in wait for those who maxed out Karen's mighty scales.

"OK then – before you jump on, let's have a quick look at your food diary for the week shall we? Don't forget if you've got more than nine green faces, then you'll be eligible for this week's prize draw – although I will warn you that one of our Tuesday group got 30 green faces! Couldn't believe it, could we Beth?"

Beth peered over the lid of the laptop again. "Um, no."

Ben handed Karen a thin sheet of paper with some hurried scribbles in two of the boxes.

"Ok – first red face here, Ben, is that you've only tracked on two days. Monday and yesterday. Monday you've got two green faces which are for the salad you mentioned earlier. Although two tomatoes is the bare minimum that you can get a green face for, so just be aware that you're right on the edge there. Then yesterday you've got one, two, three, four, five, six…forty six…this is a bad day, Ben – you've got nearly 100 red faces. Do you remember a pizza is one of the worst things you can have? Why would you eat two?"

"I don't know," Ben replied. "I just thought that maybe I should be honest and just say what I actually ate so you could see…"

"So did you actually eat all these Bourbons? Over 60?"

"Yes."

"Did it not make you feel sick?"

"I didn't really notice eating them. I just know that I had two packs by my bed and then by the time I got up for lunch, there wasn't any left. I had another pack in the evening when I was watching TV. I figured it out by counting the wrappers."

"That's really worrying Ben. That's never right. Combine that with the pizzas and the Pringles, and you've got a lot of red faces. What are you doing to yourself?"

"I don't know."

"Do you get any enjoyment out of eating all of that rubbish?"

"Not really."

"Well, this week, as well as having a think about all the good things about school, or home-school or whatever, why don't you see if you can just happen to snack on healthy foods. Chop up some celery and dip it in a teaspoonful of marmite. Or try buying a big punnet of mushrooms, dry fry them and wait for them to crisp up and then you can have those like crisps."

"Sounds good, I'll do that."

"Let's see what it's done on the scales shall we?"

Ben reluctantly stepped up onto the platform and stared ahead at the grey curtains across the rear of the stage, wondering what it would feel like to be wrapped up in them. He imagined it would be warm and quiet.

"Eight pounds on, Ben," said Karen with barely contained spite.

"On? So am I still in the obese BMI range?"

"Well, you've not gone under it, have you?"

"No, I mean am I still obese, or am I in the one above?"

Karen checked a chart in the back of her notes. "No, you are *just* still obese, but another couple of pounds and you're in Obese Two."

"Well, it's good to have a goal," Ben replied. Karen's face looked thunderous.

"Ben, you need to take this seriously – if not for you then for me – we have targets for you, you know? At this rate I'm worried that we're not going to even get paid for the work we've done with you.

You need to start filling out your food diary and getting those green faces. I'll put in your book that you shared in the group, so that's one green face for this week – the rest is up to you. Lucy, do you want to come up? Everyone give Ben a clap, he put eight pounds on."

Ben took his food diary back from Karen and crushed it down into his jacket pocket. He walked down the aisle of feeble plastic chairs and out into the car park. He would skip the cooking demonstration. He wasn't sure he could stomach the idea of enduring another 45 minutes of Karen demonstrating how to make a baked potato – after all, the name of the dish also contained the recipe.

He emerged from the building into an unseasonably warm winter day. He zipped his black coat up anyway and felt his neck prickle with sweat. Ben aimed himself at the ginnel, which would take him out onto the high street. It wasn't yet 2pm so it would be relatively quiet and he could get a large portion of chips to eat as he waited for the bus that would take him home.

A horn sounded out close to him, and he jumped and looked around. He saw that he had walked right past his mum's Nissan Micra, which over time had seen the paintwork fade from its original red to dark pink. It always reminded Ben of strawberry ice-cream. His mum was waving from the driver's seat, he swallowed his disappointment at seeing her and opened the passenger door.

"What are you doing here?"

"I wanted to see how you did, so I thought I'd wait outside for you. Thought it would save you getting the bus home as well."

Ben lowered himself into the car by holding onto the grab handle, which creaked in alarm. He noticed how uncomfortable it felt in the passenger seat like there wasn't enough room, and he pushed the seat back as far as it would go and unzipped his coat a few inches.

"I thought you had loads to do today?"

"I got my bit of shopping done and thought I'd come and see how you did – well? Don't leave me in suspense!"

"Eight pounds."

"Brilliant! Brilliant! Brilliant! I'm so proud!"

"On."

"Oooh. It was definitely on? You've done so well this week, there was all that salad."

"Definitely on."

"Well, eight pounds is nothing, you'll lose that in a fortnight."

"I put it on in a week mum!"

Anne reached between the seats and with a struggle, brought a large Toys R Us bag through the gap and passed it to Ben. It barely fitted between his stomach and the glove box.

"What's this?"

"I just wanted you to know how proud I am. It's not been easy of late, and I know you've been worrying about something. I wanted to get you something to say I love you."

Ben instantly felt tears well up in his eyes. He didn't dare look at his mum, so he pushed back a corner of the bag and uncovered the corner of a Lego box. He peered inside and saw that it was a huge set – Eiffel Tower: 1 in 300 read the words in the top corner.

"You are my son, you always were I think, even before you were born. You'll be my son even after I've gone, and as your mum I know you better than anyone. You're special. You're going to do something amazing in your life and even if you don't take the same path as everyone else to get there, maybe God has a reason for that. Perhaps that's part of the reason why you'll be able to do these special things. But in the meantime, you'll get people saying you're doing things wrong. They'll sit in their Eiffel Towers and assume they're right and you're wrong. I want you to know that as long as you're following your own choices, I will always be on your side."

Ben couldn't look at her. He lay the Lego set flat on his knee and turned to pull the seatbelt out. As he clicked the belt into the buckle, his mum did the same and he brushed his fingers against hers. He held the contact and nudged his fingers gently into hers.

"Can we get chips?"

"Of course we can get chips."

CHAPTER 7

4th September 2020

31 days after

543 lbs (246 kg)

The Just Eat app has crashed. Every night at 9pm, I have been powering up my phone to check for messages. That's usually the time that I'm at my hungriest and need distracting. Although weirdly, the pain of the hunger has gone now and it's mostly just like this ache of regret that there's nothing to eat. In lieu of eating, I open the Just Eat app. Until last night, the main screen displayed a message about an error and then allowed me to browse some of the restaurants I'd looked at when the internet was still a thing. Yesterday it just froze, so that tapping the little red circle icon did nothing, like there was a force field that repelled the touch. I just thumbed it and wondered where it had gone. God, it's depressing.

The radio broadcast is still the same since and there are no new additions. It's just stuck on the Thursday 6th August message with the desperate request for help rendered in that calm, automatic voice. I wonder what happened to the person who wrote the message? The message suggests that maybe someone else survived, at least initially. In hindsight, the broadcast does provide a few useful pieces of information. Firstly, it suggests that this is a global incident. It doesn't say whether other countries fared better or worse than Britain, but if our power, travel, communication and emergency services have gone, it's hard to see how a country could be doing worse.

A slightly riskier assumption is that if this is happening on a global level then it probably isn't an act of terrorism. It's just too insane to think of a co-ordinated worldwide attack. Surely, that wouldn't be possible? The final message from the next day had referred to "wraths". I listened a few times before I properly understood it, as the computerised voice had mangled the pronunciation. Initially, I thought it was wraiths, but actually a wrath is a pretty good description of what I'd seen in Karl, Mr Ethiss and the lady from the lift. The thing that I keep returning to is the advice from the broadcast to stay in your home.

In many respects, the flat is an ideal safe place. After all, it is on the fourth floor and the building as a whole is accessible with a key fob that only residents have. The council built the doors to withstand scallies trying to break in, so I am reasonably sure that the building is safe, but I appreciate that 'safe' is a relative term in this new world. Equally, I feel that as long as I keep my front door protected, then even if someone did get into the building, they would struggle to get at Brown and me – if they even knew to look for me here. If I am safe from physical attack, then the real danger that presents itself is from the questions around the water supply. I know that the cold water is gone and that the hot water is probably being pulled from a tank in the building somewhere. I'm pretty sure drinking hot water gives you Legionnaires' disease, but that is a shitshow for another day. What I don't know is if there is anyone else drawing from the same supply. I haven't seen any trace of other people in nearly a month, so I feel that it is a safe bet that I am the last human in the building. Maybe the last in the town.

That leaves food.

There have been two main surprises about not eating for nearly a month. The first is how little I miss doing it. Don't get me wrong, if I could get online, I would have a line of Deliveroos bringing a steady chain of pizzas to the flat. They could have forgotten the bikes and just formed a human chain direct from the kitchen I would have ordered so much food. I spend the evenings planning out the menu – vegan Puttanesca, portions of doughballs and squares of carrot cake. I'd get Morrisons to pick up some Bourbon biscuits and Skittles and I'd crumble those on top of the cake. I'd get a load of Diet Coke and Original Pringles as well. I can feel myself salivating just thinking about that knock on the door. Just a simple "Thanks" and a tip and they'd leave all that food on the floor outside. I could wait until the lift doors close and then scoop it all up and lay it out on the bed and feast. There was no doubt that modern technology had truly improved the quality of life for a shut-in.

That said, I've not been thinking about food as much as I thought I would. The aching of hunger is just a background noise against the pain in my leg and the soreness around my groin from the urine burns. I'm nearly as desperate for a packet of Flash anti-bacterial wipes to wash myself as I am for food. Before the wraths, I spent nearly all day thinking about food. If I was eating, then I was thinking about how it felt, I was feeling the relief as the food was in my mouth. I was enjoying the fullness in my stomach, which was always accompanied by the question of what was next. I'd start thinking to myself just as I swallowed my last mouthful, "That was nice, I should do a bowl of some pasta and bacon bits in a few minutes." The days were divided between eating and thinking about eating. Food meant that nothing else could intrude. But now I have nothing but the intrusions.

The other big surprise about not eating is that you don't stop pooing. I assumed that if you don't eat then you don't poo. The only thing that's going in is water and surely that's eventually converted and expelled as urine? Apparently not. Around every tenth day, I still feel my colon tightening and having to roll off the bed, which pulls at the boils under my belly and makes my leg throb. The walk to the toilet became too painful so I dragged the large commode straight into the lounge. It's facing the balcony and now I use it as a time to scan the skyline with the binoculars and look for signs of life. Often all that's produced is a thumb-sized stool, which has a slightly greener shade than normal. There's no real smell to them but maybe they're just too small. I push myself to stand and fling the turdlets into the air outside the flat. No one has complained yet. The loo roll is long gone, and so I use an old sock which I rinse and leave to hang on the balcony.

I can tell I'm losing weight. I can't bring myself to walk all the way to the bathroom just to weigh myself, but there is more room in my body than before. Normally, when I lie flat on my bed the weight of my belly pushes my legs open and splays them wide as if I was strapped in a gynaecologist's stirrups. Before, my belly reached down to just below my knees. When I was washing, I'd have a red heat rash from my kneecaps upwards, where the skin prickled with sweat. Now I've noticed that the hang of my belly is above my knee. When I noticed, I thought of Karen and wondered if she'd be proud of me. I could have filled in my food diary with great accuracy as well, so that would have been another green face.

I assume that there are minerals and vitamins that the body needs to survive, so I am taking one of the extra-strength daily vitamins that mum bought in bulk from Holland and Barratt when she got cancer. They are speckled orange tablets the length of your thumb. They taste like shit, and they're practically bigger than she was, I don't know how she managed to swallow them. I've been washing them down with my favourite beverage – stale water from the hot water tap. I'm working on the hypothesis that for the foreseeable future I have stored about me enough calories to stop me from dying. I'm now in no doubt that I'm starving to death, I just think that process is going to take a while. The irony of my morbid obesity keeping me alive is not lost on me.

My main concern is Brown. She drinks water and trots out to the balcony to wee, but other than that she has changed considerably. As a breed, Manchester Terriers tend to be thin and wiry – everyone always mistakes them for Dobermans and I think the comparison makes them seem smaller still. Brown is definitely a small Manchester though, she's only about a foot high and she normally weighs around 6 kilogrammes. I haven't dared to put her on the scales in the last week. Her ribs are showing though and she's listless when I stroke her flanks. Even her tail, which is usually alert and whipping around like a conductor's baton seems to have drooped. She's also lost some of the power that her small body used to generate. Most of the time she rests on the bed and looks beseechingly at me as if to try and understand why I would put her through this hell. I wish I knew how to explain it to her.

Although I might have longer to go before I starve to death, I don't know how long my leg will survive. The toes are such a dark purple now that they're close to black. The skin feels brittle and stiff when I dare to brush my fingers across them. It's the strangest feeling to look at your body and know that part of you is already dead. It's like a localised form of time travel – where my leg already knows what lies beyond the grave. The foot and up to the knee is swollen now and the scab on top of the foot is bordered with virulent green pus. Any movement forces the scab to crack and shortly after a rank smell wafts up, which gives a good indication of what lies beneath. I feel sorry for Brown with her superior sense of smell. The pain is massively restricting what I can do. The two journeys I have to make are to the toilet and to the tap. Both of these now leave me short of breath and weeping with pain. I hobble with the upturned brush under my right armpit to avoid putting any weight on my entire right side. When I return to the bed I'm covered with droplets of sweat and looking in the mirror I see a pale froth that has gathered at the corner of my mouth. To make matters worse, I used up the last of my Ibuprofen yesterday. Overnight, the pain has magnified to near unbearable levels.

I keep fantasising about rescue. I dream about seeing black military helicopters looming overhead, broadcasting appeals for survivors to make themselves known. Usually, I wave and they magically transport Brown and me aboard and we're off to get food and find what remains of civilisation. In the more pessimistic dreams, they see who I am and open fire on me when I start to wave. I feel so unready for this new world. What could I offer to this imaginary new civilisation when they'd need to get a crane to even take me out of the flat? I was a liability before the wraths, and I'm still a liability – the only thing I have to offer the world is my dog. When I've been sitting on the commode, I've sometimes thought that it would all be over if I just stood up and took ten steps forward. The pain would go – I'd be free from this horrible shell I've built around myself. But I can't even do that because I know Brown would follow me. She watches me every time I drag myself to the kitchen. I know that if I chose to jump out of the window, then she would jump down from the bed and follow me unquestioningly. The thought of her loyal body lying broken next to mine on the street is enough. I won't do that. So, we go onward.

The only sliver of advantage that I have is my drone.

When mum bought me my first drone, I think she was trying to pierce the cocoon I was building for myself. A lot of her gifts were about that. She didn't address me being shut-in directly, as she respected that it was my right to make bad choices, but she never stopped trying to tempt me with glimpses of the world outside. The drone was one of her more inspired attempts at building a bridge between the world and me. But I managed to push past even that. I hung on and did everything I could to push myself further into the shell. The food helped. It pushed things further away and broke the world itself so that it had to reform in the way that I wanted it to appear. Things had to come to me. Dentists. Shopping. Work. They all had to make a pilgrimage to the cocoon. It was the power I had.

I always found flying drones intoxicating. For many pilots it is the power of flight itself that absorbs them, but for me, it was the world the drone's cameras recorded that drew my attention. I loved to fly my drone somewhere I could land it secretly, and just watch. One of my favourite places to land was on the roof of the local supermarket. I would land the drone on the big sign at the front of the building and angle the camera towards the entrance. That way, I could watch a constant stream of people coming in and out of the shop. A young mum with too many bags and children. Someone tying up a dog and petting his ears before he left. An old person with a shopping trolley dropping the wrapper of a Toffee Crisp on the floor. It was all so normal and it just went on.

My current drone is a DJI S1500, which has been heavily adapted so that rather than using conventional power sources, it runs off hydrogen power cells. This is still a relatively new approach for drones and it means sitting a cylinder of hydrogen on top of the drone, which isn't aesthetically great, but it has the great advantage of extending the drone's flight time by 35 minutes and gives me an extra range of four or five miles. Since her death, mum's room has become the storage centre for the drone and along one wall is a row of six-litre hydrogen tanks that create the on-board electricity source. I had held off on taking the drone out since the wraths arrived because the blades and motors make noise and I didn't want to attract their attention. In the end though, I'd simply run out of options.

Dragging the drone out of mum's room and setting up the eight individual rotors takes nearly an entire day of sweating and pain. I work as quietly as I can and, finally, I have the drone set up on its usual launch pad at the end of the balcony. The drone is around a metre wide and half a metre tall. Taking off and landing on a balcony requires a fine touch, but I am an experienced pilot, and it means that I don't have to leave the flat to fly. Brown is desperate to get involved, but I keep her tucked tight by my side as I slip on the VR goggles and power up the rotors. The transmitter remote control unit that allows me to control the drone is fully powered, so I have more than 10 hours of flight time. The headset which allows me to see what the onboard cameras are recording only has 45% battery, which means I am going to have to run it at slightly less than full HD to conserve power, but I can worry about that later.

I lift the drone quickly and quietly into the air and set the cameras to track my head movements. Essentially, the on-board cameras look where my head is pointing. This is disorientating for many pilots because the natural assumption is that you go in the direction you're looking in, but I found that it makes more sense when I am flying. I take the drone straight up to 250 feet as quickly as possible and set a wide circle around the immediate area. The first obvious thing is how little movement there is.

I see some of the wraths looking around for the source of the noise, but I keep moving and they simply stand and fight with each other. At this altitude, silence reigns over the various scenes of destruction in the local area. I fly around Ellis Tower and establish that there doesn't seem to be any signs of life in any of the other flats. I pull back and conduct a sweep across the area. When the drone gets too close, the wraths wake up and rage at the source of the disturbance. To keep things simple I fly high and fast.

I take the drone to the nearest high rise to look for signs of life inside the building. I am hoping to see others holed up in their flats like me, and despite the silence and lack of movement I feel a nervous excitement building. The building has been badly damaged by fire, and the brickwork is charred for the first six storeys. I hover close to the windows and inside the rooms, the walls and furniture are black and broken. Every item has soot marks and here and there, blackened skeletons are visible. I lift the drone up the side of the building and try to peer into the windows higher up. I notice a swish of movement and an elderly woman in a dressing gown and nightdress presses up against her window. Her face is contorted with rage and down her front is the now-familiar stains of the yellow bile. She bangs first her clenched fists and then her face against the window, all the while bellowing something at the drone. Some of the other neighbouring properties show the same bemused and furious faces at the window. I think again of the computerised voice asking if anyone is left alive.

A blur of movement streaks past the camera and at first I think it's a bird – sometimes buzzards and bigger birds of prey will try and attack drones – so I throw the control sticks backwards in an evasive move. Another streak flies past the cameras and I think I see a human hand among the blur, the fingers outstretched. I pull further away again, just as another body falls past trying to reach for the drone. I try not to think of the wraths landing far below as

I pull it away from the high rise to try and stop other wraths being tempted into making the leap. I circle around, gazing at the dry landscape and finally drop down to the ground near to the high street. I don't feel safe landing, but I descend close enough to see that as the noise approaches, faces that I think are dead look at the cameras. When they spot the drone, they shout and jump on cars and benches to try and get closer. Often they fall, and then they stand again, bleeding and dazed but still focusing on the drone. I can't hear what they are saying, but I can see their mouths moving and even through a camera I can sense the raw anger coming from them.

Hovering over the high street for less than a minute draws out close to two hundred wraths who scream and gesture at the drone. As they come closer to each other, they forget about the drone and attack each other, pulling themselves onto the floor where they kick and headbutt until one of them goes still, and the other looks for something else to fight. It occurs to me that none of them thinks to throw anything at the drone – they chose to fling themselves from the high rise rather than using objects. I scan the crowd, I can see that where they are fighting each other, it is all hand-to-hand combat rather than availing themselves of any of the debris on the ground that they could easily use as weapons. Does their hatred make them stupid? I pull the drone up high and circle back slowly in a wide loop to ensure that as few wraths as possible notice the drone dropping onto my balcony. It lands without a bump. I feel weak with the realisation that this is the world that I am going to have to send Brown into.

CHAPTER 8

9th December 2017

2 years, 7 months, 26 days before

543 lbs (246 kg)

Father Donnell brought the tea into the lounge and placed the mugs onto the adjustable table that Ben kept next to the bed. He returned to the kitchen and brought in a pack of Bourbons as well.

"Have you thought of a name yet?" the priest asked, indicating the small black and brown blob in the fleece basket, placed between Ben and the wall.

"I'm no good with names Father, I think I'll stick with Brown."

"Right. But one could make the argument that she's very much black?"

"Yeah. I think it sort of sums up the mess of it all."

The priest looked around for something to sit on and not seeing any chairs, he indicated the foot of the bed.

"Help yourself Father, as long as you don't jiggle," said Ben.

The priest sat gently and reached to take his tea and a Bourbon.

"The king of biscuits, the Bourbon. You know it's often pronounced *borbon* but actually, it's the softer *burban* that is correct. And did you also know that they are so-called because you're supposed to dip them in whisky?"

"Is that true?" asked Ben, shocked. He didn't consider himself a connoisseur of much, but he'd probably eaten more Bourbon biscuits than anyone alive and this was news to him.

"No, I don't think so, but if you've got some whisky maybe we could try?"

"You'd have to look in the cupboard down there." Ben indicated the cupboard next to the TV and Father Donnell sprang up from the bed causing Ben to wince. He knelt next to the cupboard and removed some of the bottles at the front. He took one from the back and held it up.

"This is the good stuff! How about a drop of this in your tea?"

"I'm all right thanks, it always makes me think of my dad. I think that was his, so it might have gone off."

"Malts don't really go off. I'll take the risk though." He leapt nimbly to his feet with a flexibility that surprised Ben. The priest uncorked the bottle and dropped a solid glug into his tea. He dipped his biscuit in.

"Oh Mary Mother of Jesus that's awful, don't try it."

Ben laughed and gradually they settled into a warm silence punctuated only by Brown's snuffles. Ben drank his tea and the priest looked around the room. He smiled at the crucifix on the wall.

"She had a powerful faith, your mum. We miss her dreadfully at church."

"Yeah, would it be too cynical to say that her faith didn't help her much?"

"Not at all – it's a good question. Did the almighty zoom down on a bolt of lightning and blast the cancer out of her? He did not. But in her walk with him, is that what she expected? I prayed with your mother many times and I can't recall her ever asking for healing. Sure enough we prayed for the cancer anyway and it didn't save her – I believe it helped her though. It was healing and protection for you that she prayed for. Always."

Ben put his tea on the table and looked at the ceiling as tears fell from his eyes and a choke caught in his throat.

"I can't stop crying. I've never been a crier and now I'm weeping at crinkly old tissues of hers that I find around the flat. I can't face sorting her room out, it's all exactly the same in there."

"Be fair to yourself Ben – it's only been a month since she died. Tears are better for you than bourbon or bourbons. You'll do well to let the tears come. And there will be time enough for you to sort things out. For now, just focus on you and this thing." He tapped Brown lightly on the back, and she stood and repositioned herself in her fleece crib.

"I wanted to come to the service, Father. I asked the council about how we could do it, but they said they couldn't cover the cost of getting me out of the flat unless I left altogether," Ben sobbed and the priest smiled and nodded. "I don't know what I'm doing, Father. I'm scared. What will I do without mum?"

The priest sighed and put another solid drop of whisky in his tea. "I know you've not got religion in the same way as your mum, Ben, but I remember your confirmation well enough, so there's a story you might know from the Bible. This is from just after Jesus gets baptised and your man's on fire! He's just walking around doing miracle after miracle. Raise the dead – sure! Blasting demons into pigs and driving them off cliffs – done! It's mad, you should read it. Anyway, Jesus is walking along this road and because he's doing all these incredible things there's this powerful crowd following him and then there's this woman. This woman is well known in the area because she's had this illness forever and once. It's not nice, but basically, it sounds like the arse is dropping out of her. She's seen every doctor going and they've all looked at her like it's a miracle she's not dead already. She sees Jesus walking past and despite this massive crowd she says – I don't need to chat with him, I don't need him to do anything, if I just do something tiny like touching his coat then I know I'll be healed. So she steels herself and pushes through the crowd. You'd imagine that they'd probably maybe back off, as you might if you saw some lass known for having a bleeding arse coming towards you. And this woman, she doesn't even make eye contact with our Lord, she just reaches out and the merest bit of her fingernail grazes Jesus' robe. Because she knows, you see? She *knows*. Well, he feels this, even though he's being jostled every which way – he feels his power going out of him and he turns around and says, "Daughter, your faith has made you well, go in peace." And this woman is completely cured. Completely – she's made whole."

The priest drained his tea and put the cup back on the table. He picked up another biscuit and jammed half of it into his mouth. Ben looked at the priest.

"But Jesus is dead – how does that help me?"

"No, Jesus is very much alive, but I concede that until he returns permanently, he's temporarily without earthly form."

"I'm sorry Father but how does that help me? What can *you* do to help me?"

"I can pray for you Ben. I can keep you in my heart and I can tell you this simple truth: you have to find that belief in you. Listen, I can tell you for free that the right way is reaching out for Jesus knowing that if you touch him then you'll be healed, but at this stage, I think you need to just find a belief in *something*. Because if you can't reach out and touch something knowing that it will fill you up and complete you, then all of the prayers of the world and its Saints won't bring you back." He smiled at Ben with such warmth that Ben felt himself starting to cry again.

"I really miss her. She was so nice. She was so kind. She loved me so much and it kept the world away."

"Ben, why do you think she got you that mutt?"

"I don't know. She was always buying me presents. She heard about someone who was selling dogs and she bought one."

"Now, if you had a young man such as yourself who had decided to hole himself up in his house and eat himself to death – said with the respect that only a man who has dipped you in a font can give – why would you buy him a dog? It's a disaster! Your mum knew she was dying, so she went to the pub and asked around and was offered one of these dogs. She brings it home and now she's yours. Pass her over here."

The priest threw the rest of the biscuit into his mouth, clapped the crumbs from his hands and held his arms out expectantly. Ben reached into the basket and lifted Brown to his face and smelled her. She smelled of quiet things and happy things. He ran his cheek across hers and she blinked at him. He looked at the dog with her little mole face and the scar on her neck still raw and shocking. Brown briefly yawned. The priest held out his hands. He too looked at the dog and then cradled her in his arms.

"She's a beautiful dog, Ben. She has a great heart, I can feel that. She's not going to be taking any messing though, I can feel that too." He closed his eyes and his voice assumed an authority. Ben caught on and closed his eyes too as the priest prayed. "Father God – what have we here? Would you look at this dog, her name is Brown. God, me and Ben have a difference of opinion. I believe you created all living things and that you walk with us on this earth whether we accept that or not. Ben believes in biscuits and fear. Please Lord, can you show us which one is right, because if it's the biscuits then I need to get some in. Bless this dog, Lord. Make her a mighty dog. Make her a powerful dog. Make her a dog that when Ben looks at her, he sees your face and your love. We thank you for the woman who brought Brown into Ben's life and we ask that you make her plan come to fruition with your wonderful blessing Lord. Amen." Ben muttered an Amen.

"Mum wasn't much of a planner."

The priest squished Brown's ear and passed her back over. Then he stood up and pulled on his black overcoat.

"Oh, she had a plan all right. This isn't a dog, it's a portal. You might not want to go out into the world, but this dog is going to bring the world to you. We'll keep you in our prayers, Benjamin, and I'll pop in when I can if you want me to? God bless you, my son."

Father Donnell hadn't waited for an answer to his question, but he was true to his word and once a month, he'd come in to see Ben. He was the one person who Ben could tolerate being in the flat and that was mostly because he'd been so close to his mum. In him there was a connection to her, no matter how tenuous. He could ask questions and he loved to listen to the priest talk about her – even if it was just trivial nonsense about how she washed up after a Beetle Drive or how she helped serve communion. Ben even started buying decent whisky to keep in the cupboard for when Father Donnell came round.

For his part, the priest talked to Ben about the Bible, he shared his own thoughts about faith and he helped Ben to find books of the Bible that weren't just long lists of dead kings. The one thing Father Donnell resolutely refused to do was help with Brown. The notion that Brown was a portal had stayed in Ben's head and even made him slightly wary of the dog; was she really part of some plan of mum's as the priest suggested? On his more paranoid days, Ben could feel the outer edges of a concerted effort to get to him, which made him feel like eating more and embedding himself further into the flat.

The arrival of a dog certainly threw up some practical considerations. Chief among these was that Brown was a perfect size for a pet to accompany someone in a flat, but she still needed exercise. Ben often wondered what would have happened if the dogs that were for sale in the pub were German Shepherds or Mastiffs. He knew he would have coped somehow. The thing about Manchester Terriers was that they love to be around their owner, who they adore with such a fervour that it can sometimes be overwhelming. They didn't bark unnecessarily, although that option had been brutally taken from Brown anyway. Getting food and drink for her was easy, especially when the local supermarkets started to do home delivery. The real problem was exercise.

Ben hadn't been outside the flat since he was sixteen, but Brown needed walking at least once a day unless it was raining, in which case a stick of dynamite couldn't have persuaded her to leave the warmth and comfort of home. A health and safety assessment had decreed that the building's lift was no longer suitable for carrying Ben. There were also several doorways and stairs that he would have to negotiate if he were to go out through his front door. Some of the doors were fire doors that couldn't be expanded or have the frames removed and that meant Ben had only one option of egress: through the wall of the flat. The council had clearly stated that the only reasons they would be prepared to fund such an expensive extraction would be if he was in a life-threatening medical situation, or if he was leaving the flat to give it up permanently. They even refused Ben's many requests to help to get him out for his mum's funeral, which he had ultimately ended up listening to via a mobile phone, on speakerphone in the church.

The Housing Association offered him a number of ground floor flats in special units which they would be able to move him to. They even said that in some of the flats, there would be an enclosed area for Brown to run around in. Ben just couldn't do it though. He'd lived in this flat for his entire life. He'd been brought home as a baby to this flat. His mum had made their meagre home into a place of security and happiness. They'd been proud of their home. Yes, it was small, and the area around it was rough, but then there were moments of pure magic in this place – staying up late on New Year's Eve with hot chocolate and watching the fireworks around them explode in colourful lights and shrieks. Pancake races down the corridor outside the flat, both of them tossing cold pancakes in the pan. A lifetime of Sunday dinners and the smells of the perfect roast potatoes hanging in the air with them in the flat. His mum had helped him build the world in here, and Ben had too much invested in it. And now he physically couldn't leave the flat. If he tried, his heart hammered through his chest and his breathing dried up. It was only inside the flat that he could exist.

All of this left the problem of walking Brown. There were dog walkers who could have taken her out, but to his shame, Ben couldn't accept them. He didn't want to have someone coming into the flat every day. It would daily show him how he was failing the one thing that he had allowed himself to love. He also didn't trust anyone else to protect his dog. So, he'd decided to use the drone. In Ben's mind, warped with fear, it was an elegant and modern solution to a problem. It was unusual certainly, but not absurd when you really thought it through. After all, they put a dog in space, why was this so very different? Manchester Terriers take patience and time to train, but they are strongly motivated by food and so if you have a ready supply of wafer-thin roast chicken (another concession that Ben could never believe he'd made for the sake of a dog) then you could access their ready intelligence and train them to do pretty much anything – even fly.

The first barrier had been getting Brown used to the noise, smells and sight of the drone so that she wouldn't panic when she saw it and would, over time, learn to associate it with good things. This was relatively easy. Ben set the drone up on its launch pad at the end of the balcony and put it through a simple pre-launch programme that set the drone's eight rotors in motion without actually moving it. This caused some downdraft and a noise like a particularly determined kitchen blender. As this went on in the background, Ben liberally fed Brown chicken so that she gradually came to accept the noise as being connected to food and, therefore, happiness. It was no more than a week before she barely even noticed when the drone was activated. If anything, she seemed excited to see Ben taking it out of his mum's room.

The next problem was how to safely transport his dog using the drone. This required some thought. In the end, he scoured the net and found a number of products that could create an automatic opening arm. He secured this onto a lightweight pet carrier about the size of a large picnic hamper, which had been bought to provide maximum comfort for Brown during her flights but not allow her to move around too much and cause balance problems for the drone in flight. The carrier was secured using 15 feet of paracord and some industrial strength karabiner clips. The idea was simple, Brown would fly in the carrier as a contented passenger and Ben would land the drone. After a set time the carrier would automatically pop open. Ben went through the same familiarisation process with Brown and the carrier. They turned it into a game and went through endless packs of roast chicken and ham, until the point that Brown was reluctant to play anything else. Inside the pet carrier case, there was another time-activated box which was set to open after 30 minutes which played an MP3 of Ben's voice calling to Brown. Once this box opened, it also revealed a piece of salami, which Ben had discovered was the key to Brown's heart. Usefully it not only had a strong smell, it was also reserved as a very special treat, so Ben and Brown practised in the flat until she had a 100% recall rate for when the box opened and the MP3 played. Most of the time Brown was waiting by the box minutes before it opened. The automated arm would then click shut and Brown would be safely on board for the return journey.

Ben tried several unmanned test flights around the area to uncover any potential problems – including once nearly catching the trailing carry case on tall trees, which meant he upgraded the drone's cameras to full night vision, allowing him to spot obstacles even on the darkest nights and which handily also gave him thermal imaging. Ben also adapted the drone to take hydrogen power cells. This increased his flight time and maximum payload to around 15 kilogrammes which meant that destinations further afield were possible. Because the final piece of the puzzle was where Ben would fly Brown to. After all, he couldn't fly Brown to a public place. Not only would the arrival of a dog via drone cause significant discussion and probably lead to a visit from the police; equally Ben wanted the place where he took Brown to be isolated and entirely under his control.

In the end, Ben was inspired by the trend for commercial dog walking grounds. These were large, enclosed fields where a dog could safely be allowed off the leash. Ben couldn't use any of the commercial fields, so he bought some land and created his own. After extensive research and repeated flyovers to test the approach to the land, Ben made an offer of £10,000 to a surprised farmer for a three-acre patch of scrap land eight minutes flying time directly North East of the flat. The farmer held out for £12,000, and the deal was done, even though Ben would have paid twice as much for the location. The land had long ago held wooden industrial sheds, which had since been demolished. It bordered a country park which was closed at night, so Ben rarely ever saw anyone as he flew Brown to her walking grounds. On their land, she had access to a section of grass and concrete slightly larger than the size of a football field. Ben ensured that the entire area was fenced securely so that Brown couldn't escape and she could enjoy a massive space to run, chase and urinate. After experimentation, they discovered the time with fewest people on the streets was at 3am. That way, by 4am Brown could be home, where she would leap contentedly from the transporter, her breath smelling of salami, and instantly run to Ben to sniff and check he was still there, which of course he always was.

CHAPTER 9

23rd September 2020

1 month, 19 days after

494 lbs (224 kg)

Parts of me are escaping. As I sprawl on the bed, I am aware of that. My belly now extends to my mid-thigh, and when I look in the mirror, I see a smaller, younger face looking back, somewhat surprised. I've succumbed to a dark, shaggy beard which is growing quickly. The strangeness of it further serves to reinforce the impression that Ben is fading away, and I think I know where he's going. Karen said once that when we lose weight, the actual fat that we get rid of is metabolised by our body and exits through our breath. With each day that passes where I don't eat, my body burns through the still ample store of fat deposits about my stomach, arms, chest, legs and face – I breathe out a part of me. A hated part, but a part of me all the same. The breath rises in the heat of the flat and skirts the top of the ceiling like the drone rising on an air current, and slowly it finds its way to the edge of the room and it escapes – off into the air, away into the atmosphere, rising above the carnage that the world has become.

The pain in my leg wakes me from a shallow, sweaty sleep at about 3am. Brown raises her head from the bed and quizzes me with a single ear lifted. She is so thin. I pat her bony flank but even that minute movement shoots a rivet of pain through my entire right side. I lean to the left and eject a thin spray of vomit over the side of the bed. It's all water, but it has mixed with enough of my internal fluids to smell rank. I suddenly panic and examine it closely to see if it is the yellow vomit of the wraths. It is not. I cough and pull a pillow across my face to remove the sweat and bile from my face. I fall asleep and wake to see dawn creeping across the horizon. My leg has felt entirely numb for a few days, but now it burns like it is plugged directly into the mains. I can't bring myself to touch the skin, but it seems black all the way up to mid-shin, and the scab on the roof of the foot is barely even visible now, among the rot it is just another ruined element.

I push onto my elbows and drag myself to a sitting position, I cock my right leg behind me on the bed so it doesn't hang off the edge, as I have a weird premonition that it will simply fall off and I don't want it to happen like that. There is so much loss. Not just outside the wall of the flat, but with every breath that pulls me inside out - and now I know the limb must go too. I sit and look at this room that has been home for so long. I consider the day and realise that there is nothing left for it – if I don't amputate my leg, then it is going to kill me today. The truth of that understanding lands heavily on me and shudders run through me, a flash of fear and then, slowly, acceptance. This is the way of things and I can't simply hope for that not to be true; it is time to make a change. A failure to act now will kill me.

I knew that this moment was coming and I'd started to assemble something resembling a plan. Ideally, I would put Brown in the bathroom to keep her out of the way but there is no way that I could move that far any more. Also, I couldn't abide the thought that I might die and she would be simply stuck in the bathroom until she starved. In the kitchen in previous days, I had started to assemble the tools of this dark business without ever really admitting what I was doing. I had selected the chef's knife and honed it with the whetstone until it whispered its sharpness. I'd also found and piled up the last remaining tea towels.

One of them showed the massive radio telescope at Jodrell Bank, picked out in a fading pattern. It reminded me of when mum took me there as our one and only home-schooling educational trip out. We'd gone on the train and tried to walk from the station up to the dish, only it was much further than I could manage. We'd stopped at the nearest pub and called a taxi. It had taken an hour and a half to arrive and when we got in and mum said that we wanted to go to Jodrell Bank the driver had rolled his eyes and said it was only a mile away and he looked me over with a disdain that provoked my mum into an unusual retaliation.

"Do you want the job or not?" she'd asked.

He'd lapsed into a surly silence and driven us around the lanes. Jodrell Bank was marvellous. So daunting and futuristic, real science rising out of the agricultural Cheshire landscape - one of those unusual pairings that somehow just fit together. Plus, the vegan cakes in the café were incredible. We'd got a lift back in the same taxi. We didn't speak to the driver.

I put the Jodrell Bank tea towel on the pile on the floor and clear a space to work in. I have seven tea towels in total and a bath sheet. I also put down the bariatric sheets from the med sled across the operating area so that there is something resembling a medical setting for what is going to happen. I lay the knife and a pair of kitchen shears to one side. Next to that I place a staple gun which is loaded with new staples. I have a roll of duct tape which I take different lengths from and stick them onto the TV stand within easy reach. On the balcony, I build a small fire in a wire waste paper bin and use the cutlery pot from the draining board as a grate. On top, I lay paper, small threads of sticks and then next to that some bigger pieces of wood from the chairs. Checking that everything is within reach, I lower myself onto the bariatric slide sheets and scream low into my chest so as not to upset Brown as my ruined leg folds under me.

With much panting effort, I use my hands to move my belly to my left side, which feels unnatural as I usually hang it to the right, but this gives me better access to my leg. I then gingerly lean over the top of my stomach and pull my leg inwards so that I can reach. The sheer effort of doing this leaves my body drenched in sweat and I feel sick again. I breathe deeply to try and control my stomach – I can't be sick in this area – it's my operating table! The lunacy of the moment dawns on me and I laugh. I reach for the whisky which is full to just under the neck of the bottle. I shudder as I take a mouthful and the brown heat and spice of the liquid rolls down my spine. A hot breath of indigestion returns in response and I swallow a drooling mouthful of saliva. The whisky hits my stomach, and I swear I can visualise precisely where it is inside me. The alcohol swiftly hits my brain and I breathe more calmly. I take another big drain – two sizeable swallows - of the whisky and wait for it to mute the rational part of my brain that is imploring me not to go through with this.

By now, the sun is low in the sky, illuminating the fields and brushing the houses and flats with a soft light. It is a warming light and I feel the kinship between the light and the warmth of the whisky. I understand momentarily why people drink – to spark that sunshine inside themselves – creating internal sunsets as they willed. I blink to try and clear my head and realise that I need to save the rest of the alcohol to disinfect my leg. I don't know if that works, but I am willing to give it a try. I reach over and light the fire. It catches, despite the slight wind that pulls at the balcony and soon it is blazing nicely, providing an unnecessary source of heat. The smell intrigues Brown and she jumps off the bed to see what is happening. She sniffs at the knife and her pathetic figure with her ribs to the fore and the shape of her skull nearly visible make my resolve harden. I have a path of doing nothing that leads to death. I have a very narrow path that might lead to life. I must at least try this route for her. I reach out and touch her collar and whisper a long prayer.

At the Amen, I take up the knife and place the point just below the left side of my right knee, the wide, white expanse of my inner thigh pointing at the ceiling. I decide to start the incision at the original point where the consultant had intended to amputate. I suspect it might have progressed to the point where a further amputation higher up the leg will be necessary, but for now, I fix in my head the procedure that he outlined for me when we met to discuss the operation. I close my eyes and take a calm, even breath. I release it, open my eyes and push the knife's point in where the rolls of fat from my thigh join the upper calf. The pain is intense but not debilitating – it requires a mental strength rather than a physical strength. Rather than screaming, I utter a sustained "Ohh-oh-oh-ohhh-uhhhhhhh". I push aside the years of conditioning that suggests that you don't cut off your own limbs and simply allow the weight and sharpness of the blade to do its work. As soon as the knife pierces the skin, a slick of blood begins to run out and wet the back of my leg. In some ways, this makes cutting easier. I release a high pitch moan as the point of the knife digs into a hard point, which I assume is a bone. Brown appears by my side, her expression questioning my actions. Her mouth is full of a tennis ball, which I tremblingly take from her and throw into the corridor.

"Good girl," I say as she gives chase.

Moaning to myself I let the knife guide my hand towards the softer tissues – a light yellow substance spills out and I have a sense of recognition that this is my fat, agent of so many of my problems. The knife snags on the white stringy elastic tendons and I resist the urge to cry out as I snip through them with the tip of the shears.

I continue to cut away at the back of my leg and more tissue and gore piles up. This has gone past the point of being able to back away now. I am committed. I dig on with the knife and tea towels blotting away the blood so I can try and see what I am doing. My leg shakes with tremors as I lift it from the floor so that I can pass the knife around the back, negotiating another hardened piece, which I assume is the other bone. After about 10 minutes have passed I have encircled the leg with my knife, and I am sat in a puddle of blood. I reach for one of the bottles of water and drink nearly the whole thing down. The whisky is still inside me, but the pain is managed more by my brain's refusal to believe that this is truly happening. I put the knife down next to me and push Brown back who is sniffing around – intrigued and concerned in equal measures. As she retreats, her feet dance out bloody pawprints across the floor. The Housing Association are not going to like that. Tentatively, I extend myself over the top of my gut and reach my hands around my leg. I stare in horror as I pull downwards – there is a liquid sucking noise, and I realise that I can now see more of the inside of the leg.

I quickly pick up the kitchen shears and snip at the darker looking tissues. The outer ones are whiter and more fibrous, and I assume that these are the tendons, they ping as they are cut, recoiling off to who knows where inside the leg. The bundle next to this gives way at a snip, and suddenly the slick of blood that I am sitting in rapidly starts to increase with each pump as the artery blasts a constant throb of dark red blood onto the floor. My eyes roll back and I realise that I have to be quick, or I will simply faint and bleed to death. Picking up the knife again, I chop quicker at the remaining tendons and muscle until there is a clear gap between my upper leg and lower. Again, I reach around my leg with my hands and tug downwards. I stop and wrap another dry tea towel around my leg to increase the grip. I find that with a slight agonising twist I can move the leg downwards by a fraction of a centimetre. The wet suction noise increases and with a comical *slurp,* I lift my hands and hold my leg aloft in front of my face. I place it carefully to my side and look horrified at the raw stump of my leg. Blood is oozing from the muscle and the yellow fat is stained red, isolating and outlining each clumped cell of fat. In the centre, the artery rhythmically gushes.

Hanging down at the front of my leg is a thin plate of off-white bone which I belatedly realise is my kneecap. Tentatively, I touch the kneecap and find that it is hinged. I push it with my fingers and see that it folds over the knee and neatly covers the artery. I plunge the knife into the side of the wire basket and wait for it to heat. In seconds the red embers touch the cheap, thin blade and the moulded handle begins to heat up. I wait until it is barely possible to touch and then pull the blade out. With a gasp, I force the blade against the red stump and listen to the sizzle of the heat as it singes the wet flesh. I have no real idea what it is that I'm doing but I repeat the process three times until all across the stump, the knife has at least tried to seal the bleeding. At points, I hold the knife too long and it sticks to the cooked flesh underneath, and I have to yank it off and seal it again. Finally, I drop the knife and push the patella down across the stump, trapping the artery underneath. I reach over to the TV stand and pull a length of duct tape from the side and stick the patella into place. I pull the other end of the tape up the back of my thigh and repeat the process until there are four pieces of bloody duct tape holding the patella in place.

With my awareness starting to fade, I pack tea towels around the wound in a parody of a bandage and dump the remaining whisky onto the tea towels. I fall back into blackness.

***

Flies are buzzing around my leg stump, so I try to move it, but congealed blood has pooled underneath and sealed me to the sheet. In the end, it's easier to shake the sheet with my hands to get rid of them than it is to peel myself from the sheet. Brown has settled on my left arm, and I turn to look at her. She's gaunt and although she's still black and brown she seems to have taken on a ghostly white pallor in my mind. It's for her that I sit up. The world recoils and tilts to the right. There's a battlefield from my waist down. Everything is covered with blood and it's hard to pick out the tea towels from the leg. Some of the duct tape has come loose and I look around for the roll and reseal the patella in place. I consider if I dare to attempt to seal it further with the staples, but my nerve fails. Everything on my right side throbs. Weirdly, my neck on that side is where I feel the most pain, and I run my hand over my beard and feel a lump in my neck. Maybe I hit it when I fell back. The wooden embers are still just visible in the fire, so I screw up some paper and throw it on top and wait for it to spark. Slowly it catches and I feed on some of the leftover pieces of the chair. I hold my hands to the warmth and puzzle at the dark stains that cover me to the elbows. It's dried blood, I think woozily. Of course it is.

I stroke Brown's ears and plant a kiss on my hand and push it onto her nose. She sniffs at my hands. I reach down and scoot my bottom closer to the fire. The late evening is still warm but I'm chilled and shivery. I lean into the heat of the fire and upend the final dregs of the whisky into my mouth. I put the bottle down and notice my foot for the first time. I laugh because the foot, my foot, is naked. I touch it and it feels cold and pointless. I lift my foot to my face and smell it deeply. It smells metallic and ripe. It's heavier than I expected. The darker areas of skin have resolved themselves into crusty blackened remnants. They look like the toes of a mummy we saw in a museum once on a trip at primary school. My foot is as dead as a mummy. The upper parts of the leg still look relatively healthy. I tug at one of the toes and it snaps relatively easily into my hands. I feed it into the fire. It burns brightly until it's subsumed in the embers.

I'm left with the calf muscle down to the front of the shin which looks ok, despite the edges being nibbled with a rising blackness. I try and channel what my doctor would say and imagine him declaring the operation a complete success. Despite the throbbing in my throat and the aching in my back from lying on the floor for the better part of a day, I'm amazed at the current state of affairs. I audit my blessings: I'm not dead. I have done what I can to resolve the issue of my leg, which has kept me all but bed-bound for the better part of 50 days.

I move in closer to the warmth of the fire and Brown comes and puts her head on my lap. She silently barks at me once and I think I hear a declaration of love. I lean my amputated leg against the wastebasket and after the singeing smell of hair is burnt away a fragrance of charring meat rises to my nose, which causes me instinctively to salivate. I turn my leg on the brazier and risk burned fingers to pull off a strip of skin and fat. It runs with juice down my fingers and hisses into the fire. I hold it out to Brown. She looks at the meat as if she's forgotten what food is and then reaches out with gentle teeth and plucks it from my hand. At first taste her face eagerly looks up at me, even as she's eating the long strip I gave her.

"Hold on, there's plenty more," I say as she leaps onto my lap and noses at my chest. I ignore the throbbing pain in my stump and neck. I pull another piece from my leg and smile as I hold it out for her, "Just don't get a taste for it."

CHAPTER 10

25th January 2015

5 years, 6 months, 10 days before

402 lbs (182 kg)

Ben lifted the tab on the box and pulled the scales out of the box. He put them on the floor next to the old pair and compared them – they were precisely the same. Same colours, same dimensions. The only difference was that on his old set the platform was slightly worn where he had assumed the position over the years. Ben tried to calculate the hours of disappointment those scales represented. Since the age of twelve, he had weighed himself every morning, it was his daily act of self-sabotage. A little fuck-you, that daily renewed his decision to turn his back on the world. He knew that the numbers never revealed anything that he wanted to know about himself, but every morning after he went to the toilet, he would shrug himself out of his shorts and T-shirt, pull the scales out from behind the sink's pedestal where they were stored and lay them on the floor. The lino had an implausible pattern of flowers and dolphins and there was one dolphin that Ben always lined the scales up with. This way, everything was perfectly the same and he could be certain that any fluctuations on the dial were purely down to his weight.

Ben had scoured eBay to find a set of scales that were exactly the same make. He positioned the new set just to the right of the old ones and decided that he would separate them by the width of his little finger. That way, there wouldn't be any friction between the two units and again he would know that the weight it registered would be all him. Of course, Ben knew that it would be better if he could have bought a single set of scales that could register his entire weight, but he'd been using these scales for so long he felt that it would invalidate any previous comparisons. Even if there was a tiny margin of error in his technique of weighing himself across two scales, he'd rather that than start a new journey on an entirely different set. The other obvious point was that he could have lost weight and used only one set of scales. Ben had considered this option and then bought the second set.

Ben stepped his left foot onto the original scales and his right foot onto the new set. For the previous two months, the scales had simply leapt around the dial and settled at the maximum 329 pounds. For more than a few weeks, Ben had allowed himself the thought that maybe this was his actual weight, but he had now accepted that this was extremely unlikely. There was something about the way the needle surged around the dial and hammered against the plastic stopper, which suggested that if given free rein, the numbers would be much higher.

Ben examined the dual dials of his scales and squinted to make sure he had both numbers correct. The left dial read 261 pounds, and the right scale read 141 pounds. The numbers would adjust depending on his balance between the two units, but even leaning heavily to one side the two numbers always added up to over 400 pounds. Ben put both sets of the scales behind the sink, put his shorts and T-shirt back on and flushed the chain. 402 pounds – a new high. Ben imagined time stretching ahead of him, and a sudden thought of a third set of scales arose in his head. An image flashed into his mind of his legs straddling two scales and leaning over to push his hands onto a third set. That would give him a weighing capacity of 1001 pounds. That number seemed so unlikely though. Didn't it? Humans couldn't get to over a thousand pounds, could they? Wasn't that half a ton? Ben ambled to his bedroom and took down the exercise book he used for his weight diary.

There was any number of moments that could have shocked Ben into action around his weight. There had been the time that he was unable to go on the dodgems at the fair with his mum. He remembered focusing on the seams of the black vinyl seat of the dodgem as the attendant told him that he would break the cart if he even managed to get in it. There was the arrival of the first shapeless, characterless clothes that had to be ordered from a specialist website. Drab tent T-shirts and utilitarian trousers, even wide-cuffed socks. All the clothes were black, naturally, because everyone knows that black is slimming. The relentless, cruel internal commentary generated from some hateful part of his sub-conscious once told Ben that his wardrobe choices made him resemble nightfall, and he'd never been able to shake the thought from his mind. Then there was the last time he walked up the steps to the flat, and his heart had hammered so hard and so fast in his chest that he felt death was inevitable. Ben didn't say outright that he wasn't leaving the flat again – at first, a day had gone by, then a week. Things had fallen into place that had enabled him to plant roots into this spot and then it was three months since he'd left the house and it took on the status of a conscious decision which Ben never allowed anyone to challenge.

After the decision had been made to shut himself away in the flat, it was surprising how few people had disagreed with it. Ben's mum had always been the only one that ever had a chance of convincing him that this was not a sound path, so Ben made sure to terminate all conversations about it with extreme prejudice. He was never violent, but he was loud and aggressive and the simple fact that he dwarfed his mother in size made even his vocal disagreements tantamount to an act of violence. This shamed Ben to his core, but it did at least mean that his mum's attempts were reduced to tentatively laying breadcrumbs that led to the outside world. Ben was wise to these tactics and he mostly just ate the breadcrumbs and kept his door shut. School had put up a token resistance, but the decision to home school had allowed them to tick the box that said they'd cared just enough to raise the issue, but not enough to do anything about it. Doctors had given a series of dire warnings and referred Ben to a range of patchy council resources that always tried hard and meant well, but were altogether too comfortable with accepting failure.

As he grew, life became a stream of occupational therapists, bariatric specialists and the gradual invasion of the sort of equipment that had supported Ben to carry on eating as he chose. There were beds that turned him automatically to try and reduce the number of bedsores that he got. There were a series of additions that armoured the toilet so Ben could continue to use it, until eventually a specialist unit had to be installed and a commode brought in to give him further options. There was a chair that mechanically lifted Ben from a seated position to standing, that had to go back when he exceeded the weight capacity for it. There was talk of an even bigger model they could access from America, but Ben preferred his bed.

Then there were the various medicalia which had slowly infiltrated his world until the flat looked like a pharmacist's storeroom. The plasters tipped with silver to draw out the pus from the searing boils that inevitably formed where his belly rubbed against his thighs. These were horrid deep pouches of pus that Ben would sicken himself by bursting and then wince as the rancid smell rose to his nostrils. He had to though – if he didn't they would build into focused points of exquisite agony that made moving an impossibility. There were industrial vats of aqueous cream which Ben slathered across his growing form. There were the stinging lemon Flash wipes which he mostly used instead of showers, having grown too big to use the bathroom regularly. The harsh chemicals of the wipes dried his skin, but he felt it at least did something to ward off the bacteria that he feared lurked in his body's crevices. But, oh, when he did make the effort to shower and that hot water hit his face and hair! The pure, normal joy of towelling off clean, shampooed hair and the swallowed disappointment of knowing that it would be weeks before he felt this clean again. The choking, reluctant acceptance of dry shampoo. The CPAP machine that opened his airways at night.

As the flat and his person was further reinforced to support his weight gain, Ben did everything he could to reverse the trend – at least on the surface. He faithfully signed up for blogs, social media accounts, products, magazines and YouTube channels about losing weight and exercise. He understood the biology of weight gain and weight loss at a molecular level. He knew the numbers that lipid profiles should show and the numbers that it revealed in his blood. He monitored his HBAC1 long before the diabetes actually appeared. He consumed back issues of Men's Health while eating Party Rings and fantasised about the magazine's promises to give him a six-pack in just six weeks. He knew it was a lie, but for a time, it was a relief to believe it. He digested long screeds about the philosophy and morality of weight loss. He resisted the impulse to align himself with any of the movements and politics around weight loss – he was neither healthy at every size, or a thin man trapped inside a fat man. He was fat-shamed by people and the environment they designed, but he found it hard to engage with the polemics. His physical health screwed his mental health which crippled his spiritual health. But throughout it all he was simply Ben - a person who became overweight as a child, then obese and obese class II as a teenager and when he moved into his twenties, obese class III and then super-obese – denoting he had hit the jackpot and his BMI was now over 50.

These were the markers and metrics of the medical and insurance community, but they didn't hold much significance for Ben. Even the numbers that he wrote down in his weight logbook didn't hold much meaning for him. His own metric was simpler. There was the stage of being fat where you could still see your penis and there was the stage of being fat when you couldn't. Ben was 19 when he had lost his penis to his belly. His weight charts state that he was just over 350 pounds. Ben reasoned that this was the tipping point because accepting that your penis had been consumed by your fatness was the ultimate symbolic defeat. If you could accept the loss of your manhood, then fat had won. Fight it, and you could lose weight and recover your member. Ben had found that if you could accept the indignity of losing your penis then the stretch marks, the urine burns, the jiggly tits, the pendulous underarms and the grunts he made when he moved would always be a distant second.

That's not to say that Ben didn't try to lose weight. There wasn't a method that Ben didn't investigate for at least three or four days and then dismiss. He did keto, low carb high fat, the cabbage diet, raspberry ketones, caffeine pills, sauna suits, fasting, intermittent fasting, very low calorie diets, 80:20, 5:2, 16:8. He had counted fats, calories, macros, he had imbibed pills of every sort, he had sent away his blood, his urine, his hair, his poo, he had received back pamphlets, booklets, powders, injections. He had consulted dietitians, experts, quacks, champions and a mystic. The 100% failure rate of all of the above had been down to the underlying truth that Ben had opted for none of them to work. The psychologists, the counsellors and the trolls had analysed his choices and made their statements about why Ben was choosing this path, but ultimately none of that mattered – the only thing that mattered was the moment when Ben lifted the biscuit to his mouth and reached for another until the lightness of the packet meant he reached for another packet. Ben decreed that was the only thing that mattered.

Ben's only connection to the process was to record the data. So every morning he weighed himself and logged the weight in his red, dog-eared exercise book which bore the words Ben Stone, English, Class 2B. This was crossed out and underneath, in a serious block lettering, were the words Weight Diary. Ben never recorded anything other than the date and the weight. He never plotted graphs, explained his inner-feelings or recorded the milestones of weight gain. Just the date and the weight. It had begun as a suggestion from his mum when he was starting to bloom from being a chubby child into a heavy-set young man. He had maintained the diary for over a decade now and sometimes when he recorded a weight, he looked over the scrawl of the preceding pages and was aware that these data told a story that would one day be his only legacy. There was something stark and brutal about the look of the biro on the book that somehow suited the story that it told. Occasionally, Ben would run his fingertips over the indentations of the pen on the pages and think of all the days that they represented. Other days, he would wonder why he never worried about the story these numbers told.

Ben had considered showing the diary to the diabetes nurse who had been assigned to him and wondered if it might be useful information for her to have. In the end, he'd kept his mouth shut and simply agreed with her assessment of his situation, that Ben would be lucky not to lose a leg to diabetes if he didn't change his eating. In truth, she hadn't been overly emotional about the situation – Ben had found that the response of healthcare professionals was proportional to the emotion shown by the patient. If the patient screamed and shouted, then this ignited something in the carer – they wanted to give them the healing that the patient so clearly wanted. If you were like Ben however and just went grey and watched the scene unfold, then they would pick up on that and simply be professional. They would give you the medicine or the advice that they were there to impart and then they'd move on to the next patient. It made sense – no one had enough emotional energy going spare to care 100 per cent about all the people they saw on a daily basis.

Ben thought again and rued the fact that the two scales approach would lose him accuracy when he recorded his weight. There was nothing that could be done, though. He noted the weight in his diary, closed the book and put it back on the shelf.

CHAPTER 11

20th October 2020

2 months, 16 days after

408 lbs (185 kg)

I had fabricated a pointlessly complex story to tell the company who fenced off the land I bought for walking Brown. It involved a barely-believable fantasy where I had been bequeathed the land, but a family squabble had arisen about the rightful ownership and, although it was only for the principle of the issue, I wanted to protect my inheritance. I needn't have bothered. The first fencing company I spoke to in the area were happy to undertake the work without any need to meet me and be paid by bank transfer, no questions asked. We never met and, as requested, the company submitted a series of photos and videos documenting the work they'd done fencing the land off and installing CCTV cameras. The work took a little over a week and cost me around £5,000, putting the total cost of the walking field project at around £18,000, once you added the legal work needed to register the land. That put a sizeable dent in my savings, mostly accrued from the drop-shipping work I did on eBay, but it was worth it.

The result was three acres of scrubland mixed between grass and concrete, surrounded by palisade fencing with W section posts, meaning that the individual posts were split into three prongs on the top like a fleur de lis. These posts were set narrowly, approximately the width of a hand apart – too narrow to allow Brown through, but there were also two runs of chicken wire next to the fence, dug into the ground with fox-proof prickle strips, which dissuaded dogs from tunnelling their way out of the compound, or foxes and badgers from tunnelling their way in. In the middle, I'd instructed the fencing company to dig and concrete a shallow indentation which rainfall would fill up and provide a gently sloping pool up to about three feet deep for Brown to splash about in. I also thought it would attract birds that she might like to chase. Aside from solitude and security, the real natural resource that the scrubland had was rats. The combination of easy access to water and low shrub cover meant that there was a ready supply of rodents.

As I bring Brown into land, I scan the ground with the thermal imaging camera, and when I'm sure that we ditched the last wrath miles before, I set the pet carrier down in the middle of the property near to the pool. A couple of small, dashing creatures flash past the camera's lens which suggests that this will be a good hunting-ground. The 30-second delay on the opening of the pet carrier means that the drone is safely idling and its blades are still as the lid springs open and Brown raises her head and senses the air with excitement.

I installed a basic CCTV camera set up on the fences of the walking ground for extra security, but it relies on mains power, so like everything else that requires electricity, it is as redundant as my right shoe. The power on the drone is another question. The radio control transmitter is battery powered and currently has an 80% charge. It never really draws much charge from the battery though as there isn't a great deal that it has to do – it is more likely that the hydrogen will run out before the transmitter batteries do. The only other thing that I worry about is the display – the part of the drone set-up that means that I can see what the drone's onboard cameras are transmitting. Without a display, I will be forced to fly the drone blind, which means a good chance that I'll get lost and fly in the wrong direction, or crash into a pylon. I have three options for the display – my virtual reality goggles are at 24% charge, my laptop is on 41% and my phone is down to 17%. I decided to use up the goggles first as they give the most detailed visuals, and that could be the difference between life and death for Brown.

The truth I have been forced to confront is that this trip is a binary choice for Brown – I either find her a source of food that she can access safely, or she will die. It has been nearly four weeks since I amputated my leg and inadvertently created a temporary food source for my dog. For two weeks I rationed out the leg meat, which I stored in the warm freezer, wrapped in clingfilm, to try and preserve it for as long as possible. During that time, she regained some of her vitality. Her eyes reclaimed their warmth, and as the edible sections of my leg were depleted, I let her gnaw on the bones. Intuitively, she sensed that the necrotic areas of flesh weren't going to provide her with nutrition, and I ended up throwing some of the flesh over the side of the balcony. I filleted my foot to remove the smaller bones and prevent her from choking, but rather than waste them I put them in a pan with water and boiled them into a toe soup. She devoured it with glee when I poured it into her bowl. I even held it to my own nose and thought of taking a sip, but my stomach rebelled, and Brown got the full serving.

Brown's favourite was my tibia, or the fibula, whichever is the thicker of the two bones in the leg. She carried it round in her mouth proudly, banging into the furniture and refusing to cede it for even a second – even as she slept she had her teeth wrapped around it. It was surreal to see this part of me being gradually gnawed by my dog. As the caloric content was consumed, I started to feel sorry that I only had that one leg to give her. I suppose I could have lopped off a finger, but it didn't seem to create much of a solution – it was a miracle that I survived the amputation. I had spent three weeks recovering, feeling shaky and weak. I got a fever about a week after the amputation which consigned me to bed for 48 hours to endure some truly psychedelic dreams and led to a few days of watery diarrhoea. I felt stretched and at one point I felt my breathing becoming painful, and I worried that this might be the end. Instead, I slept lightly for hours unable even to get up to use the toilet. Eventually, I managed to rouse myself from bed and drink lustily from the tap again. Slowly, the strength had returned to the limbs I had left. While I recuperated, I watched the wound on the stump go from a gnarled purple gash, to a yellowish skin covering the wounds, with sticky patches sat alongside islands of drying scab. By the third week the wetness had dried up and the new skin was starting to reclaim the end of the stump.

During this time, I realised that the unavoidable reality was that I had to take Brown back to the walking grounds and hope that she could find something to eat there. It was a neat solution – I could almost guarantee that there wouldn't be anyone else on the land because of the fence. The rats would also provide a near-endless source of food. I'd never actually seen Brown eat a rat before, but I'd seen her catch plenty. When you watched a Manchester Terrier go after a rat you understood the purpose of breeding. I'd read that originally, Manchesters worked alongside a ratter in a ship's hold when it returned from sea. The very close relationship between the ratter and the dog was imprinted on the breed and it was singular in its devotion to hunting and killing rats.

It had been verified that a single Manchester could kill upwards of 100 rats in an hour. I didn't know what the exact nutritional value of a rat might be, but I was relatively certain it had to contain protein and fibre. Eyes must have calories, right?

I have left the flight until the very last minute for two reasons. The practical issue is that even though Brown is experienced at flying with the drone and catching and disposing of rats; I am sending her into a vastly different world. I have no idea what caused the wraths to start behaving like they do, but I know that if one somehow manages to catch Brown then it will kill her. It isn't until my inactivity will achieve the same thing that the risk feels worth taking. The other issue is that I am scared. Brown is the reason I am not alone. I haven't seen another living human being for months – the fear of losing her isn't just terrifying, it is paralysing. How could I even force my hands to fly her away from me and into hell?

At the field, Brown sniffs the air long enough to convince herself that she knows where she is, and then hops out of the pet carrier. Looking at her through the thermal cameras on the drone, it is all too apparent how thin she has become. She seems to have lost stature and height as well as muscle, she is a different creature from her when she is in her prime. I think again about the possibility of amputating another limb for her, but accept that my choice is made. Brown shakes her body and sniffs at the ground. She looks like a purple spirit in infrared, with a small yellow mask around her muzzle and eyes. She pees a long stream of urine which glows white in the thermal vision and creates a pool of light at her feet. Then she gives a soundless bark and runs into the undergrowth and the carnage begins.

I count at least three rats that are caught and despatched within sight of the drone's cameras, so who knows how many others there are off-camera. The destruction is operatic. She sights another victim, drops her nose to the ground and launches herself at the target. Once it is seized in her jaws, her head flicks from side-to-side and the rat nearly snaps in half. She then drops it on the ground and focuses on the next quarry. After a ten-minute killing frenzy, she returns to the bodies she has despatched and eats. She settles the body of the rat between her front paws and takes the head off, looking around her as she chomps through it. She then works the rat's body to the back of her jaws, turns her face to the side and chews it between her molars.

While Brown feasts, I sit on the edge of the bed. My nervous energy demands that I pace up and down the flat until she is safely wrapped up in her carrier and delivered back into my arms again. Unfortunately, I still haven't worked out the finer intricacies of pacing with just one leg. I was now up to hobbling about with the broom crutch under my arm. Recently, I'd started to think about making a prosthetic and had tried to make a cast of my left leg using strips of some of mum's old magazines that I couldn't bear to read for the hundredth time. I sometimes think the end of the world may have been a small price to pay for the fact that there will never again be another edition of Hello! magazine. Unfortunately, I had used all the self-raising flour with my failed balcony biscuits, so I had nothing that would make the mush set. Consequently, all that I managed to achieve was pasting a ghostly image of Prince Harry at a polo match onto my left shin that took two days to fade.

As I watch Brown eat her fifth rat, I shuffle off the edge of the bed and slowly lower myself to the floor, while still wearing the VR headset. I lie face down with my belly pooling underneath me and stretch my one and a half legs out and press them against the floor. Still unsure of what I am doing other than releasing some tension, I place my hands square to my shoulders and push down through the palms of my hands. Nothing happens. I push harder until the top of my chest moves up approximately an inch. By this point, my arms are shaking and I am breathing so loudly that I shock myself. Agonisingly slowly, my arms straighten until they are almost locked out. My belly is still on the floor and my knees are supporting me too, but I pause for a second and slowly lower myself to the ground.

What was that about?

Apparently, I am not finished. With much jostling and rearranging of flesh, I roll on my back. I hook my left foot underneath the rung at the bottom of my bed and move around until I am flat on my back at right angles to the bed itself. I link both hands tightly behind my head and try not to dislodge the VR goggles. I guess where my stomach muscles might be and focus my attention on this area. At the same time, I heave with my arms and neck and feel a strain pulling down the back of my neck. I keep the pressure up and breathe hard with the effort. Slowly, the top half of my body curls from the floor and I feel my head lifting off the ground and rolling over the top of my chest. I take the weight of my head in my hands and lower myself to the ground. I feel the pulling generate a warm sensation in my stomach. I lie on the ground breathing fast. My nerves are still jangling for Brown, but in my mind, a shocked whisper passes from neurone to neurone: Ben exercised.

The timer on the pet carrier pings and the recording of me shouting her sounds. I see Brown give a reluctant look at the delicious carcasses she is leaving behind, but her training is too strong and she stands obediently and hops back inside the pet carrier. I saved the one good toe from my right foot to go into the reward box. I figure it is the most obvious salami alternative I can offer under the circumstances. The lid of the carrier shuts and I awkwardly roll over on the floor and scoot myself to my knee and stump which rubs painfully on the ground. I grab the controller and power up the rotors of the drone. She is coming home to me.

I try to stay alert but my mind drifts. One of the attractions of piloting drones has always been that it takes me out of myself and away from the flat like a form of meditation. I skim the drone slightly lower and look over the landscape. A lorry is turned on its side and on a billboard a faded image of a smiling woman with perfect white teeth catches my eye. My mind drifts to my mum. I remember the wrinkled plastic of her purple cagoule the last time I saw her. It was such an ugly coat. If I'd known that it was the last time I'd see her, I would have hugged her and told her that I recognised everything she did for me. I would have acknowledged the sacrifices she had made for me from the moment of my conception to the time she wandered out and returned with Brown – pushing the puppy into my hands with a smile that still warms me when I think of it.

She only went out to get a Lemsip. She was fine, just a bit of a cold. The second round of radiotherapy was done and it had been a success. She was nipping to the chemist before it shut, did I want anything? She had some Lemsip blackcurrant in, but she preferred the lemon flavour. She tripped on the step outside the shop and skinned her knee. She went back in and asked for a plaster from the pharmacist, who maybe sensed a claim on the horizon, so he insisted on getting an ambulance to check her over. Ludicrous. She had a graze! When the ambulance came, they gave the pharmacist hell for wasting their time and then to protect themselves, they took her blood oxygen levels, which were low. They did her blood pressure, which was low too and so this seemingly healthy woman with a skinned knee ended up in the hospital, where they slowly concluded that the radiotherapy hadn't been as effective as they first hoped. She never came home. We spoke on the phone, but the last time I saw her she was wearing a shit purple cagoule and I was asking her to get me biscuits.

My thoughts return to Brown and I pan the camera around. In the streets below the drone I see the red and orange shapes of wraths - even in infrared, something sets these things apart from humans. They move like they're rusty. They collide into each other and fight. They sprint haphazardly, following the sound of the drone. Arms are outstretched, willing the drone and my dog to fall to earth with them. By the time I bring the drone overhead, over a hundred wraths are baying in the street below. The sounds of fighting and shouting rise to the fourth floor and I focus on the precision sounds of the rotors and the thump as the pet carrier lands heavily on the balcony.

"Bang! Bang! Let me up there and I'll make some noise by banging your skull against a wall!"

I lean over the balcony and in shock I see Karl is clawing at his tether, fruitlessly trying to climb up. I don't know why but I'm almost glad to hear him threatening to murder me again. Maybe it's because it takes my bodycount down and lessens the guilt I feel. I ignore his screaming and focus on Brown. The lid of the pet carrier pops open and my beautiful dog noses her way through, she is spooked by the noises from below and Karl's threats. I sit on the bed and she launches herself into my arms and turns around in my lap, her ears raised and alert for dangers. As I pet her, she relaxes slightly and drops to the floor to drink heavily from her bowl. Exhausted from her activities, she jumps back onto the bed and gives me a measured look.

"You probably don't recognise me because I've been working out, thanks for noticing."

By way of reply, she farts quietly, and the scent of digesting rat fills the flat and makes my eyes water. Within minutes she is asleep and dreaming happily, thinking of an eventful day. I watch her sleep and try not to listen to the sounds of rioting from outside the window. Everything is changing. It's not just that the world is now full of wraths - I realise that I had convinced myself to believe that this flat was a place of safety, somewhere away from the eyes of the world and away from time itself. I convinced myself that as long as I was in this flat, then nothing would hurt me. The food gave me a purpose and allowed me to ignore life, which simply went on without me. I can now see that this was an illusion. I have not been safe here for nine years, I've been trapped here.

CHAPTER 12

11th September 2018

1 year, 10 months, 24 days before

570 lbs (259 kg)

Ben had one profile photo which had been taken by his mum. He was 19 years old and he was already well into his adventures in obesity. In the photo he was stood on the balcony wearing a black ruffled shirt, which clung tightly to his chest and contrasted against the light grey sky behind him. Looking at it, Ben was amazed by how much weight he'd gained in the following years. He felt like he was twice the width now. Yet he found he could flashback to that point in his memory and he knew that he'd felt fat then. But here he was now much, much heavier and it was impossible to avoid the thought of whether he would look back at this time in the future and think about how thin he looked right now. And yet right now he felt incontrovertibly fat. He *was* fat.

Fat doesn't play well on dating websites. Ben had learned this after nearly three months of swiping right without a match. He logged onto Tinder twice a day as part of his digital routine and gamely approved the majority of women whose pictures appeared in front of him. This in itself was an interesting experiment as he realised he had a type. Age, race or height didn't bother him, but he noted, somewhat ashamed, that he tended not to choose plus-size women or very thin women. This wasn't an aesthetic choice, but he was conscious that he *might just* have a few eating issues himself and more than anything he didn't want someone like him. He felt that comfortably healthy-sized women who looked like they could eat a cake without a crisis, but who didn't put icing on their toothbrush, might be an appealing middle ground.

Primarily, he liked women with interesting faces. The ones who he rejected tended to be heavily made up, to the extent that their faces didn't seem to register any expression at all. He wondered if there was an app that airbrushed profile photos to this extent because it was a popular look. The women who used these images seemed artificially young, but also because there was no emotion of their own on display, it invited you to superimpose your own feelings and for Ben that was never a good thing. He found himself worrying for these women. If they were prepared to offer potential partners a blank space that they could fill however they liked, then what did it say about their self-esteem within the relationship – would they ensure that they were equal partners? Would they protect themselves emotionally, physically and sexually? Ben would have loved to discuss this concept with a woman and to get their views, but no one ever swiped right on him because he was incredibly fat.

He knew his profile was an important piece of text - if you don't have the looks then you have to give them the old razzle-dazzle with the words. Ben's read:

Let's address the elephant in the room: me. A BMI shouldn't be three digits. But there are positives about dating a fat guy: there's always leftover takeaway. I will *never* suggest we go jogging. Anything I sit on is instantly ironed. Even linens.

HMU and let's talk Pringles.

I have a really cute dog.

I realise that this last USP sounds like I'm trying to entice you into a van. I'm not, it just happens to be true, I have a cute dog. You're free to leave at any time.

It had taken a simply staggering amount of time to write and hone that description. He hated himself for the fact that he'd gone "fat but funny" but really, what other option was available to him? Could he have tried being scholarly? He didn't have a cycling proficiency certificate, let alone a degree. Rich? He had a good job working as a home-based travel agent and he had savings from his eBay selling, but he lived in a Housing Association flat and didn't have a car. He'd watched a YouTube video where an impeccably coiffured man had discussed the pros and cons of using a shirtless photo on your profile. On the good side, it apparently showed off your physical attributes and got women hot. On the bad side it made you seem excessively shallow and only interested in sex. Ben had given serious thought to using a shirtless photo, he'd even taken one of him side-on in the bathroom, but the sheer enormity of his gut had made him cringe so badly that he swore he could taste the embarrassment. "But that's why it's funny!" he told himself, but he locked that voice in the further reaches of his brain and went with the one where he was approximately half the width he was today.

Ben was self-aware enough to appreciate that who he actually wanted to find was someone like his mum. He knew how creepy that sounded and if anyone ever chose to speak to him on a dating site, then he wouldn't lead with that particular piece of information. What he meant was that he wanted someone who shared her characteristics. Namely, a strong and independent woman with her own thoughts and beliefs. People had been conditioned by the media to see a single mum in a council flat and think nothing more than "benefit fraud", but Ben's mum was a fiercely intelligent woman. She was passionate about her religion, although she often criticised the church and held the Pope in particular disdain. Above all, the things that she had committed to, she held fast to her heart and never abandoned. Ben was so grateful that one of those things was him. It struck him that this was probably why those women who airbrushed themselves horrified him. He wanted warts and all – he felt that all he had to offer was warts.

And so the daily humiliation of finding no matches on Tinder continued until Helen matched with him. Ben was so confused by the new notification sound that he initially thought the app must have accidentally matched them. Helen was a nurse ("that could come in handy" Ben had joked during their incessant back and forth messaging), she was five years younger than him and she was weirdly normal looking. In certain profile pictures, she was actually rather beautiful, in a particular, Northern way. She had short blonde hair that hung in a neat bob and her deep green eyes always seemed to convey the impression that she was waiting for an answer to a question. The fact that someone this incredible had matched with him instantly put Ben on alert and he spent a depressing evening researching catfishing scams. Helen was frank about Ben's weight. Her dad and his brothers were all very overweight and as she had grown up around fat men they were just the norm. Ben noticed but didn't comment, on the fact that this aligned them, in the sense that in some way she measured suitors against her dad.

They talked about work. Ben explained the thrilling world of online travel agency and booked Helen's cousin into Disneyland for next year. That was just what happened with Ben and work – nearly all his sales were from word-of-mouth recommendations. Helen's cousin would tell her mates about how helpful he'd been and how he'd got them a better deal than they could get on the web and in the next month he'd have another three calls and probably one or two bookings as a result. Helen talked about nursing and often wondered about whether she should move to Australia, where there was a desperate need for nurses. Plus, the pay was better and the weather wasn't drab and miserable. Ben responded to this threat with a not-so-subtle campaign whereby he sent a stream of images showing the aftermath of spider bites, shark attacks and drop bear attacks. The latter he was particularly proud of because the Australian drop bear looked essentially like a koala, which Helen thought was cute - but then he revealed that the drop bear was so-called because it dropped out of trees onto the heads of passers-by and could inflict horrific bites on their scalps. Helen won in the end when she found that the drop bear was a hoax. She didn't move to Australia though.

They chatted for four months, every day, sending anything up to 100 messages a day. Ben's sales figures for those two months were the lowest he'd ever recorded. His manager sent him a couple of jokey emails, the sub-text of which was very clearly: "Please keep selling lots of Disneyland trips." Ben ignored the emails and they stopped coming and his sales figures recovered. He and Helen progressed from messaging and soon spent evenings on the phone talking about their days, discussing television programmes and laughing about their veganism. Following his mum's example, Ben had always felt passionate about animal welfare and hated the thought that his actions could result in the death of any creature. It had never seemed a particularly arduous thing to Ben, especially when he discovered a range of foods that were vegan but also delivered high fat and sugar content. By contrast, Helen had nearly choked to death on a sausage when she was nine and had developed a fear that meat was out to get her that she could never quite shake.

When they were talking, Ben would put Helen on speakerphone so that Brown could hear her voice too. He wanted to know that Brown would be comfortable around her and he wanted Brown's approval. For Christmas, Ben flew the drone to Helen's house with Brown's pet carrier laden with a bouquet of fancy ciders and gifts. She got him a giant Bourbon biscuit made by a local bakers', which said BourBen on the top. Ben found that somehow Helen didn't threaten him in the way that the world usually did. Throughout their conversations, Helen would frequently request that they could meet up, but Ben couldn't bear the thought of smashing the precious relationship that they had developed. He also wasn't sure he could even get outside anymore. Anyway, in his heart he knew that if she saw him, she would find him abhorrent – who wouldn't? And that would be the end of that. For all her promises that she didn't care about size, he knew in his heart that he would horrify her. So he did everything he could to keep her at arm's length.

In the end, Helen tricked him. They had a tendency to keep messages word-based rather than visual, but Helen started sending him photos of the view from her window and they began to send sunsets to each other, which they then rated and critiqued God's handiwork. Ben joined in and started to send views of the sunsets from his window to her as well. Even though he was careful not to include any notable landmarks in the pictures, Helen somehow used the various views to triangulate a location, figure out where he lived and then one evening she simply knocked on his door.

Ben opened the door and saw the real-world version of Helen, who for so long had simply been an avatar on his phone. Such was the association in his mind that he felt as though he heard a notification ping when he saw her face.

"Hello Ben, I'm Helen," she said and she held out her hand. Ben shook it.

"It's very nice to meet you, Helen. My name is Ben."

He froze, aware that now was the moment where she would see that he was twice the man he'd been pretending to be. She smiled at him. She was shorter than he imagined, but she was so pretty that Ben felt giddy. Her hair was so shiny, there was a band of light all along it. How did that happen? Was it a shampoo thing? He recognised that his intellectual faculties had stalled, so he covered by not saying anything and staring dumbly at her.

"I have a present for your beautiful dog, Brown, may I come in?"

"I don't feel like I can stop you, short of physically barring the way." Ben stood back and let her in. "I can't believe you've just turned up like this. I've not hoovered or dissolved the body of my last victim in the bathtub yet."

"Ordinarily, I'd say that it doesn't matter Ben, but your flat looks and smells horrible and I think you've earned my honesty."

"Thank you Helen, I'll show my gratitude in making sure I kill you thoroughly first before I dissolve you."

They were now in the kitchen. Ben saw the flat through her eyes and was aware of how odd it all was. He had an insane thought run through his head that he should lean in and kiss her on the lips. He panicked as he was leaning across and aborted the action and touched her warmly on the shoulder, which awkwardly evolved into giving her an arm's-length cuddle. Brown looked confused as Helen spotted her and went into paroxysms of delight. She figured that this stranger was ok when she received several slices of ham from Helen's coat pocket.

"This is Brown then? She's so beautiful." She pulled a new tennis ball out of her other pocket, which Brown instantly tore from her fingers and sprinted gleefully around the flat. "And you're Ben?"

"Surprise!" said Ben weakly. "Marginally less beautiful than Brown, but what I lack in beauty I make up for in buoyancy."

"You're buoyant, are you?"

"Wildly."

"Ben, I'm leaving and I wanted to see you before I went."

"What?" Ben felt unstable like the world had suddenly picked up the pace of its revolutions. "Are you going to Australia? What about the drop bears?"

"No, not Australia. I'm going to America. I've researched it thoroughly and the only dangers are guns and ignorance."

"Some of their rodents are huge too. High pitched voices. Respond to Mickey. Why…why are you going?"

"Because I want to try leaving. I always have. But I needed to see you before I went. I honestly don't know what we have. It's weird. I love speaking to you. You make me happy. You make me furious. But most of all, you make me sad."

"OK."

"This isn't right, what you're doing. I don't want you to always be in here. If that's what you want then I can accept that, but I wanted to at least ask you to come with me."

Emotions coursed through him and with a certainty he'd never experienced before he recognised that this woman was everything. Ben thought again about kissing her. He wished he could keep up with the conversation, he felt out of breath and his heart rate felt fluttery.

"I don't think I can."

"I think you can."

"It's so far away."

"Life is often far away Ben. If you come with me, we can go towards it together. I'd really like to go with someone as buoyant as you, that could be a very useful attribute to have on an adventure."

"What about Brown?"

"She's allowed, I checked."

"I'm scared of the drop bears," Ben said and he knew it was feeble but he needed to think and process what she was asking him to do.

"I have a month to get my VISA sorted and I want to be there in time for Christmas. I want to go and have turkey dinner with Mickey and Donald and the whole gang. I want to pull a cracker with Cinderella. You might even qualify for a special VISA because you're self-employed. You could potentially get a green card if you wanted."

"I don't know. It's a lot to think about."

"I know. You've got plenty of time to make a decision Ben, just promise me that you'll think about all the things you can go towards, rather than think of all the things that are holding you back?"

She stepped forward and placing her hands on his shoulders she reached up and kissed him. Her lips held his with intent and Ben thought of gooseberries and a memory of speeding downhill on a bike when he was a child. He was acutely aware of his arms dangling by his sides like big awkward ropes. Where should hands go? Then it was over.

They left it there. Ben replayed the moment of the kiss and the question she asked him as he paced the flat. He threw the new ball for Brown and wondered if he dared to go. He sized up the front door and imagined himself walking through it, with a suitcase and a pet carrier. He imagined booking three seats on the plane journey to ensure that he wouldn't find himself spilling over the armrests and ruining other people's flights. He crafted the image in his mind's eye of having *that* picture taken with Helen in Disneyland, them side-by-side and smiling, with Cinderella's Castle on Main Street USA in the background. He even wondered what it would take to join the tens of thousands of people who propose at Walt Disney World every year.

And while he was wondering, he ate. He decimated packet after packet after packet of Bourbons. He doubled his order at Morrisons and doubled his eating. He ate until he felt tired and irritable. He stuffed his face until his lung capacity reduced. His joints ached and he creaked as he moved. He added new items to his standard takeaway orders, and he switched Diet Coke for Coke. He ate spoonfuls of sugar until his teeth ached and his breathing was shallow in his chest. He had pains shooting down his arms, and he had to change the settings on his sleep apnoea machine to account for the sudden and alarming increase in his weight.

Helen had offered him a glimpse of something startling and new in Ben's life, and Ben was desperate to take the opportunity, but Ben was also determined to dash it away from himself and ruin it. He didn't respond to Helen for a day. Then it was two days. Then after a week of not being able to reply to her messages because he simply didn't know what to say, Ben deleted Tinder.

CHAPTER 13

9th November 2020

3 months, 5 days after

373 lbs (169 kg)

It must be about two in the morning and I am engaged in my nightly internal argument about whether I can be arsed to go through the rigmarole of getting up to have a wee and suddenly the room starts to get brighter. It's as if someone is shining a torch, then a headlight, then a spotlight straight into the room from the balcony. It burns with a raw, white light, like the magnesium strips we held over the Bunsen burners in Chemistry. I initially lift my head to see what it is, but the light just keeps getting brighter and something about it makes me scared. I grab Brown's collar and pull her under the covers and try to cover her with my body. She's understandably confused and struggles to get free, so I pin her down. She bites my hand hard, but I pull the sheet over my head and push my face into the mattress with my eyes squeezed shut. Even so, the brightness seeps into my awareness. After a few seconds, I risk a glimpse, but the room is still too bright. Another few seconds and I look again – the light is still there but the intensity has diminished slightly. I think about the shepherds on the Bethlehem hillside being told by Gabriel, "Be not afraid!" Easy for you to say.

The light outside diminishes enough that I let go of Brown and rub the side of my palm. She hasn't broken the skin but there was real intent there. I scoot my leg out of bed and grab my crutch. Somewhat warily, I limp to the balcony, shielding my eyes from the light which is coming from somewhere slightly over the horizon to the North West. The light finally fades and then disappears entirely. As it recedes, I find that the brightness has left me with an after-image which I can see when I blink my eyes. The retreat of the light allows the darkness to return. Above, the massed glories of the constellations go about their celestial business, entirely unaware and uncaring of what is happening on earth.

I rack my brain trying to work out what direction the light is coming from and with a jolt I wonder if Heysham power station would be over that way. The idea of it exploding doesn't seem unlikely, but would it really be visible? It must be about forty miles away. Have I just witnessed a nuclear meltdown? That would be a first to put in my baby book. I think of mum and one of her favourite sayings, "If you can do something about a problem then you should do it; if you can't, you should should pray about it and go to sleep." For once, I take her advice and I say a prayer and go back to bed and sleep soundly. In the morning, there is nothing on the skyline, Not even a column of smoke. I wonder if I dreamed the whole thing, but a series of little teeth-shaped bruises along the side of my hand show it was real.

After the amputation life settles into a rhythm. The days remain resolutely sunny and hot, with night times stifling and close, but bitterly cold shortly before dawn. I make the most of the relative cool of the early mornings and get my flat-keeping done. First, I monitor the essentials – water and drones. I have four two-litre bottles and a series of pans, which I store water in. I have discovered that if the water from the hot tap is left to sit for a while it takes away some of the brackish taste. I like to have as much water in reserve as possible for the inevitable day when the water from the hot tap runs dry. With a full bath, eight litres in bottles and another ten litres in the pots and pans, I anticipate it will give me roughly seven days in which to plan my next move. Fortunately, the water is still running this morning.

Breakfast is a bowl of water for Brown and a litre of water and one multivitamin for me. I chop the vitamin in two and crunch it slowly to make it last. It tastes strongly of metal and dried herbs and just as I find every day, it is utterly horrible. At no point do they get any better, but just the process of crunching something in my mouth makes me feel like I am ticking something essential off a to-do list. I have lived so long with hunger now that it feels like my body has adapted. The early days of hunger pangs and long rumbling sessions where my stomach seemed to vocally protest the deprivation are long gone. I think I remember reading that survival is about a rule of twos. It's painful how much I miss the internet for checking things like this. I've come to the realisation that I'm pretty thick, but me plus the internet could just about pass as a functioning human being. My recollection is that you can survive two minutes without oxygen, two days without water and I'm debating with myself whether it was two weeks or two months without food. Two months seems like a ridiculously long time – if that is the case, surely there wouldn't be any need for food banks, you'd just opt not to eat. "Huh, we're too poor to buy food at the moment, never mind, I'll just get a sandwich in June." On the other hand, I have survived for nearly three months without food, and I'm almost certain I'm not dead.

In a back issue of Closer which I've now read five times (The feature on 20 Sexy Halloween Costumes Celebs Have Rocked keeps pulling me back in), I found a factoid which says that a gram of fat is nine calories. When they were planning to take me into hospital for the operation, they brought a set of bariatric scales into the flat so they could ensure I got the right dose of anaesthetic during the operation. People really did work so hard for me. I hope they're not all dead. Those scales said that I was 601 pounds, which is 42 stone and 13 pounds or 273 kilogrammes. I gave those numbers in so many conversations with nurses and doctors, I remember them better than Helen's phone number. If you work on the estimate that I was around 70% body fat then that means I contained about 191,100 grams of fat or 1,719,900 calories. If my body burns 2,500 calories a day then that means that it would be 687.9 days until I am whittled down to the pips. Shit, a family of four could make it until next Christmas on me. It puts into context the fact that I now haven't eaten in nearly 100 days.

The thing I miss most about food is that eating filled so much of my day and consumed so many of my thoughts. Bypassing food means that I have so much time to get things done and then time to think and to remember. The question is, what do I want to do? I sweep the flat, which means having to hop around the flat using my broom crutch for its original purpose. This always makes me sweat, but I no longer find myself breathing so hard that I have to double over to catch my breath. I take my sheet and pillow onto the balcony and survey the street. Nothing seems to have changed. The nighttime fireworks haven't reanimated anyone or caused the corpses to glow green. Good to know. Just the same bodies arranged in various broken positions, it's easy to tell the wraths from the dead now because the dead have mostly decomposed.

I risk a look at Karl who is still flush to the wall – he seems fine – there's no decay, just a sort of heavy weathering which gives him a windblown and chapped appearance. One side of his face is scabbed from where he was pulled against the side of the building. I flap the bedsheets and pillow to give them some air and return inside and make the bed. Housework complete, I sit on the bed and look around. Brown is nosing unenthusiastically around her water bowl and considering which tennis ball to chew on for the day. I don't know why, but sitting there in the warmth of the early sun, I feel a sudden wash of positivity come over me. I audit my recent experiences and feelings for why I might feel that way. Most of the world's population has suffered a catastrophic change which renders them as beings of pure, murderous anger. Nothing cheery there. I am trapped in a flat where I have already been entombed for nine years, wasting approximately a third of my life within the same four walls. Nope, still pretty dour. Last night there was a potential nuclear explosion on the horizon. Not good either.

Then it hits me – when I was sweeping the flat, I passed through the doorway into the hall, and I hadn't caught my hips on the archway. I get up and shuffle over to the doorway and pass through it. I try it sideways and straight on. There is no denying that there is clear air between the door frame and my sides. Previously, my hips were constantly scraped as I passed through like the flat was physically holding onto me. I'd had to prise myself into rooms, back scraping against the door frame and mauling the flesh of my stomach like beating down a rising loaf of bread. But now I can sail through without harm. I call Brown over and make her watch.

"See? I can go straight through." I crutch through the doorway to demonstrate. She drops her tennis ball at my feet, which I think shows her appreciation at this turn of events.

I feel the bagginess in my T-shirt, and with the broom under my arm, I swing into the bathroom and sit on the side of the bath, which groans under my weight. I take this as a warning that I shouldn't get too far ahead of myself. I pull out both sets of scales and position them on the lino. Brown watches from the threshold. She remembers my weighing ritual well enough that she is aware I hate to deviate from my set procedure, which means not getting under my feet while I am setting the scales up. Once they are in position, I put my crutch on one of the scales and note that it weighs four pounds.

I push myself to my foot and grab my crutch and hop around to the scales. I put the crutch in the centre of one of the scales and jump my left foot into the centre of the other scale. The dials are more erratic than usual, probably due to the addition of the broom, but even so, I have to get back off and on three times before I accept that they are giving approximately the same reading each time – 377 pounds. I lean over the sink and take a long drink of water to celebrate, I splash Brown and she barks silently to express her surprise. She skitters down the hall and then returns and looks around the side of the doorframe. I splash her again. The number keeps reeling through my mind – 377 pounds!

With a jolt, I remember that the crutch weighs 4 pounds, which means I am 373 pounds. I whoop and pinch my thumb under the running tap causing a triangular spray of water to blast across the bathroom, soaking the walls, the scales and causing Brown to run away altogether. I can't help myself – for a second I don't care about Mr Ethiss or the lady from the lift, I scream a long "Yesssss!" and soak my face and hair and laugh. Brown comes into the room and insists that I stroke her ears to prove that everything is ok, which I do. Touching her fur, it feels brittle and like it is hung too loosely over her skeleton. I know I am going to have to fly her to the walking grounds again tomorrow. I hate doing it, but she is starting to show signs of malnutrition, and I don't want to leave it so long that she is too weak to hunt the rats by the time I get her out there.

The evaporation from the day's heat means that by the time I get a towel from the airing cupboard in the hall, everything is almost dry. I reflexively find my red exercise book and mark the date, which takes a long time to figure out and means I have to check the neat rows of tally marks I have been keeping on the wall next to my bed. I proudly write the numbers 373 next to today's date. It looks odd next to the previous entry of 601 and in my mind I imagine the sudden plunge that a graph would show. I think of Karen giving me several sheets of green smiling face stickers. Somebody from the Tuesday night group would probably still have pipped me to that week's rubbish fruit bowl prize though. Karen is probably dead, but I hope that wherever she has ended up, she can somehow claim the credit for my remarkable weight loss. I feel something stirring inside me. It is such a lost emotion that I have to try hard to place it. It is that positive feeling again. I feel hope. I smile.

I return to the lounge and lie on my bed. It feels as though I am suddenly starting to spot reasons to be cheerful everywhere. I think about the figure of 601 pounds. It already seems such a long way away, but the thing that really makes me feel joyful is that 601 pounds is undeniably the high-water mark. Whether I like it or not, I now live in a world where the delivery of calories to the front door is over. The global obesity crisis is solved and all it took was the total destruction of civilisation. I know that I will never go beyond 601 pounds. Something about that fact rings like a gong in my head. At 601 pounds I reached the zenith of my weight gain and it wreaked a terrible toll on my life – but my weight is now on the downward trajectory and it makes me giddy to think of where I might go. I dare to imagine a time when I am not fat. At all. I can't conceive it – if I'm not obese who will I be? While I am pondering this I notice that I can see my thighs.

Of course, even at my biggest, I could have seen my thighs by moving my gut out of the way, but normally my stomach spills over them like a giant bib of skin. But now when I sit up in my bed, I can see my thighs. The left thigh even seems to have some definition to it. I prod it and push this tougher swelling under the surface of my skin. I can't believe I have a muscle! I suddenly want to show someone. I imagine calling Helen and asking if she wants to see my muscle and I think I hear her laugh indulgently. Where is Helen? Did she get to America? Is she in Disneyland right now, somehow sheltered from all this horror? Is Disneyland even still there? Of course it is. It has to be. Disney is a universal constant, like time or gravity.

I lie in bed for an hour just flexing my thigh muscle and watching the changing tone of the skin and feeling the emergence of this form underneath. In those moments I make a decision: I am going to get fit. I create a promise to myself and burn it into the deepest part of my heart. I get up and go to the bedroom and retrieve my weight diary. I turn to the back and find a fresh page and draw a chart as neatly as I can. On a column on the left, I write out the names of a series of exercises, which I feel will account for all of the different parts of my body. I work muscle by muscle and write out a list of squats, curls and squeezes that I remember from issues of Men's Health. When I don't know the name of an exercise, I do my best to imagine one and put it into words – "Side push with shake", "Tennis ball squeeze (until forearm burns)" "Dip to elbows". In the end I have a list of over 30 rows of exercises and a series of columns for dates over the next 30 days. I add in a row at the bottom of the chart for 10,000 steps every day as well, although I'm not sure if that should be halved now that I am no longer a biped.

It strikes me that mum used to have some hand weights and I think that if they are anywhere, they will be in the back of her wardrobe. I crutch myself through to her room and start sorting through the endless shoes at the bottom of her cupboard, pleased for once that I never tackled the issue of getting rid of her old things. Among the shoeboxes and a black lacquered box with the Ann Summers logo embossed on it, which I vow to instantly forget I've seen, I find one of the weights – a 5-kilogram dumbbell. Just beneath this, I find a carrier bag from Tesco, which holds a very large sealed white plastic packet with a familiar logo on the side. I pull back the bag and read, "Limited edition lavender bourbons." A moment from life before the wraths flashes to my mind. I was helping mum to bring the shopping into the flat, and she stole a bag away to take into her bedroom claiming I'd ruin a surprise if I looked. It was about a month before she died. I rip open the packet of biscuits and start to eat.

CHAPTER 14

9th May 2018

2 years, 2 months, 26 days before

531 lbs (241 kg)

The silver foil material of the sauna suit rustled as Ben shuffled in the chair to try and release the dull ache in his back and hips. He muted the triangular speakerphone on the desk and pulled at the collar of the suit. Despite buying the biggest size they had, the suit was still pulled as tight as a drumskin across his stomach, which just enhanced the discomfort. His face was bright red and sweat fell freely from his head. He reached for a small hand towel from the radiator in his room and dabbed at his head and neck. He stood, exhaling long and loudly and pulled his bedroom window closed. He retook his seat and made sure the suit was settled before unmuting the call.

"Can you hear me ok, Marcy? Steve? I'm still getting quite a lot of crackling?"

"I don't think it's our end Ben, it could be a bad line I suppose. Do you want to call us back?"

"No, it's fine. I think it's settled. Maybe it was just a patch of interference. Ok, let's just recap on the package so far," Ben scrolled up on a tablet being careful not to crinkle the arms of the suit too much and read from the screen. "We have flights for four to Walt Disney World, we've chosen the Atlantic Clubhouse upgrade on the flights – which gives you access to the VIP lounge at Manchester, Heathrow and Florida. This is also available for the entire year in case you decide to take any other flights. You are going to get the two-room suite at the Garden View Beach Club with added access to the sands and games section of the resort there, which I really think is going to be a blessing for Olivia, especially. You have your seven-day park hopper ticket and your deluxe dining plan. Don't forget that if you or Steve wants to have a particularly big night, then you can transfer drinks across people within the same party, but you can't hold me to account if you lose your lunch on Space Mountain! I'm going to check with park services about whether I can transfer some of your Disney bucks into a Princess makeover experience for Sophie – and I will let you know on that. I think the only other thing we had to decide on was the upgrades for the ride tickets, but I know you had questions on that."

"Wow – it sounds like such a lot when you put it all together!" came Marcy's voice from the speaker.

"I'm not going to lie, it's Disney, it's stupidly expensive. I've had people in tears when they're giving me the long card number, but ask yourself this – have you ever heard of Loopy?"

"Loopy?" Steve's voice from the speaker this time.

"Yep, Loopy – have Olivia or Sophie ever mentioned Loopy to you?"

"I don't think so, not to me – Marcy?"

"No, is it a ride?"

"Nope," Ben answered and he started tapping into the tablet computer he had resting on his gut as he leaned back in the chair and crinkled again. "Loopy is an eight-foot grey rat, with a little tuft of white hair like a cloud. I'm not going to lie, the look in his eyes tell you that he's killed before and he might again. He's the mascot for the holiday village at Cleethorpes and for the week that you'll be in Disney I can get you a triple berth static home for…£749. I don't know if that includes access to the Fun Range, which I think is their pool complex. The trade-off is that when you're sat in the bar in the evening, Loopy the Rat is going to come over and you're going to have this conversation with Sophie: "Who's that dad and what will make him go away?" "That's Loopy the Rat Sophie! He wants to be your friend!" By the end of the holiday the nightmares will be getting a lot better."

"Do you remember the carnival?" Marcy asked.

"Oh no," said Steve. "That poor man."

"Loopy?" Ben asked.

"Close enough, it was this weird beaver mascot they had. It…didn't go well," said Marcy. "We know what you're saying Ben, it's just the reality of the money!"

"I'm not going to tell you that paying this bill is not going to hurt. If you do Disney right, it should make you wince so hard you pull a muscle, but when Mickey comes over – and he will – Sophie is going to cry. Olivia is going to cry. I strongly suspect that Steve will cry. But no one is going to cry because they're terrified that they're going to be abducted. The girls will hold out their hands and Mickey will give them a hug and you're going to get that photo of the whole family with the most famous mouse in the world. And in two years when you finish paying this bill off – that photo won't have even started to fade."

"Do it for Loopy," said Steve with a note of finality.

"For Loopy," agreed Marcy.

Ben wiped his face from the fresh sheen of sweat that had taken hold and took them through the final upgrade options. They took the seven-day express ride ticket that Ben recommended. They also got the platinum souvenir package, the Cinderella's Royal Table experience and Ben fiddled the order details, so they got the Bedtime Story with Mickey add-on for free. The sale would put him another twelve thousand pounds past Dougie Collins to make him the top Disney salesman for the month. Again. The truth was that he could have moved two or three sales from next month into this month's figures if he really wanted to crush Dougie, but he quite liked keeping his closest competitor engaged. On a conference call with the whole Northern sales team, Dougie had accidentally muted the room rather than his own phone and described Ben to someone as "the fatted fucking calf."

It was undoubtedly true. Ben was fat but he resented it being pointed out. It just felt like lazy thinking. Ben knew there were far more glaring flaws in his character that Dougie could have highlighted. What about the fact that he let fear rule his life? How about his relatively lax standards of hygiene? Don't go obvious with your insults, Dougie. After discussions with HR, Dougie had been forced to write a letter of apology which Ben had magnanimously waved off and, genuinely, he didn't hold any real rancour towards Dougie; it just amused Ben that this latest win would bring the total to 19 months of victories.

Other salesmen often asked what Ben's secret was when it came to selling Disney packages. Ben had resisted polite requests from management to record his calls and as he was technically self-employed, they couldn't really force him to comply – besides they knew their competitors would love to swoop in if Ben was ever actually forced out of the company. Also – top business tip – you don't annoy your best salespeople, you give them whatever they want. They want to skip the mandatory training events at HQ? No problem. They refuse to have their picture on the company website when even the CEO has had to submit a fun picture of themselves on holiday somewhere? I'm sure we can sort that. Dougie had his mythical creatures mixed up. Ben wasn't a fatted calf, he was a golden goose.

So, what was his secret? Why could Ben sell Disney better than anyone else in the entire Home Travel Advisor network? Ben had a few tricks and tips. He never pushed a sale, he tried to listen to what customers wanted and find ways to deliver exactly that, with as many bonuses as he could get them. He always gave people the option of changing course or backing out altogether, but if they were going to skip away, then he gave them a clear view of precisely what they were doing. They were choosing Loopy. They were choosing a second-rate rat. On a simple level, it was also because Ben enjoyed the experience of talking to people. He liked learning about them and helping them. He didn't speak to anyone in the normal course of his life and so getting a peek into other people's dreams was fascinating.

It never ceased to amaze Ben just how insane parents could be. There were certain experiences that they were seemingly biologically compelled to provide for their children. He had spoken to single mums who worked during the day and did waitress shifts at nights just to put down five grand on a basic holiday to Disney. It was a validation he supposed. If you did what you had to do and got them to Disney, then that was a marker. It said to the parents that they were good at their job. They had provided a good childhood. It was nonsense of course – Ben's mum had never taken him to Disneyland and he felt like he'd had a good childhood on the whole.

He stood at his desk and thought about taking a sip of water, but the instructions were very clear. The sauna suit worked best when you didn't take on board any extra water while you were wearing it. He felt woozy but he supposed that meant it was working. He shook his head and checked the time on the tablet and saw that he still had 14 minutes until the month's sales deadline. He decided to challenge himself and pecked a finger at the tablet screen, he reached across to the handset on his desk and tapped in a number. The speaker gave a few rings and a voice sounded out.

"Hello? Peter Crow speaking."

Ben swallowed hard, trying to marshal the saliva in his rapidly dehydrating body.

"Hi Peter, it's Ben Stone from Home Travel Advisors, I had 15 minutes spare, so I thought I'd get the final booking details in the system so you could get the discount benefits that we talked about – unfortunately, Disney work to the end of the month, so if we don't do it today we'd have to wait until the end of next month. Entirely up to you though, I'm happy to call back in a month?"

"No, if you can sort it that would be great – I've got 15 minutes spare," said Mr Crow.

"That's great, just to warn you I've had some problems with my phone today so if you hear a crackling, don't worry we shouldn't get disconnected," said Ben and he tapped his tablet screen and smiled. Poor old Dougie.

CHAPTER 15

"What power do you have over me? You're so small! You're nothing!"

I pull my arm back and fling the bourbon off the balcony. It flies far and true and bounces off the bonnet of a car on the opposite side of the road. Brown looks at the biscuits imploringly.

"They'd kill you Brown. Remember the chocolate buttons?" Brown continues to look at me. "I'm not going to let them kill either of us."

I pull another of the overly-fragrant bourbons from the massive pack and let it fly out over the balcony. I wish I had a shotgun to blast it into crumbs. Instead, I watch it fall and glance off the side of a woman's head. She's long dead, but I apologise anyway.

Finding the bourbons right when I was experiencing a surge of hope has been hard. When I uncovered them at the back of mum's wardrobe, it made me feel emotional. It was yet more tangible evidence that mum was the greatest – in the middle of fighting cancer, she'd found a pack of biscuits that she thought I'd like and hidden them away as a present. I say a quick prayer asking God to give mum a hug from me.

And then I started to eat.

113 days since I've last had food and suddenly I have a glut of my favourite biscuits. OK, they are a weird limited-edition flavoured with lavender, but the muscle memory of bingeing is still too strong. Everything whites out and once again, I am back to throwing biscuits into some endless void inside me. They are out of date and the biscuit is soft and yielding rather than crisp to the bite. The filling is perilously sweet. I don't care. I am back where nothing happens but food.

I eat ten and something happens. I feel sick. Not just physically, although I do feel biliously full, I feel tired and sick of myself. I am sick of the unthinking behaviour that I have allowed myself to fall into at the first chance. If I crumble immediately then what has this last few months been about? Has there been no progress? I look at myself in the mirror and see how my body has changed. I am half the man I was. I only have one leg. My skin droops like an empty sail lost without the fat that once filled it. My beard is braided with rubber bands and my hair is hoiked into bunches, because why not? I go from feeling elated and promising myself I will change and get fit - then it all collapses at the sound of a packet of biscuits.

My mum once said to me that I am special and that I am destined to do something great. It's the sort of bollocks all mums say, but for some reason, the love and the trust implicit in her comment hits me for the first time, and I see the gulf between what my mum felt for me and what I feel for myself. I think of when Father Donnell told me that if I could see myself the way Jesus sees me and compare it to how I see myself, then I wouldn't think it was the same person. For the first time, I see the hatred and the loathing that I allow to sit inside my chest. I see a fat black slug resting on my heart which I feed and care for. Why do I do it?

I don't want to go back. I understand now what Helen meant when she said that she wanted to try leaving. I think she meant that she wanted to give herself the chance to change and that sometimes that can only happen somewhere else. I understand her sadness for me. My mum believed in me. I look at Brown asleep on the bed. She relies on me. Despite my behaviour and how I feel about myself, I see so clearly now that I am and have always been surrounded by love. This world is broken, but it doesn't mean that I must be broken too. I have a chance to be better. In a moment of rage, I take the biscuits out onto the balcony and begin to rant at them. Wraths uncoil from their dormant positions across the estate and I hear Karl shout that he is going to kick my fat arsehole inside out. I tell him to shut up, or I'll cut him down and see how big and hard he is when his legs are poking through his shoulders.

I start to throw the biscuits out of the flat.

Fuck that slug!

Fuck Karl!

Fuck this fucked up world!

Fuck biscuits!

And then a thought appears in my mind. I am sitting in my bedroom, speaking to customers selling Disney trips while wrapped in a stupid foil sauna suit. I'd worn it for two days and nearly lost consciousness several times, but I'd also lost nearly 5 pounds, so despite the lunacy I declared the experiment a success and celebrated with pizza and biscuits. Within a few days, I gained 9 pounds. I see very clearly now the futility of rushing from famine to feast and back again. It is dizzying and I see how that behaviour was part of my problem. I sprint in one direction and sprint back. I get exhausted and depressed that despite all of this sprinting, I only ever seem to stay still. I ward off that depression with food. I sprint again. I sprint back again. I stop throwing the biscuits off the balcony and hop back into the flat, leaving Karl and the wraths to rage on outside. I carry the packet of biscuits to the food cupboard and place them carefully next to my giant bottle of multivitamins. I will allow myself half a biscuit every other day and I will be in control. Not the food. Not the urges. The black slug shifts slightly.

The biscuits I've eaten are lodged in my stomach and I can't stop burping so I decide to see if exercising helps. I get my weight diary and look at the lines of figures charting how many reps I was able to do yesterday. With the exercises, I have no strategy, other than wanting to create a general improvement. For once I'm not creating ridiculous targets for myself or setting deadlines. I just aim to get better. It doesn't matter if yesterday I'd done 15 press-ups consecutively and today I can only do 12. If the overall trend is going up and I am celebrating each new personal best, then that is all I want.

I sit on the floor to do my crunches and leg lifts. My gut is still a massive hindrance that I have to work around, but the difference in my range of movement from when I was over 600 pounds is incredible. I still find myself surprised by how I can reach and bend so much more freely. At my heaviest getting down onto the floor was a legitimate risk. I lived in fear that if I somehow managed to get down, then there was a chance that like a stranded beetle, I might not be able to get back up again. Eventually, the Housing Association would find my skeleton lying supine on the floor. Now though, even with one leg, I don't think about it, I just do it. Nike would have been proud.

When I first started to exercise, I used one of the two-litre bottles of water and simply pulled it in my right hand and brought it up to my chin. I could do 30 of those before my tiny, feeble bicep burned and I was blowing hard. Then I moved the bottle to my left hand and did 30 on that side. Then I tried holding the bottle by my hip and lifting it to the horizontal as if I was flapping my arm. I did 15 of those on both sides. Then my forearms. Then I did 50 squashes on one of Brown's tennis balls until my fingers and wrist ached. Then I did the other side. I made a meticulous note of these numbers and enjoyed seeing them getting higher each week. At the end of ten days, I swapped the bottle for the sand-filled doorstop that we used to keep the lounge door open on windy days. My scale told me that was 9 kilogrammes. That brought my numbers way down, but I didn't panic and every day I chipped away and focused on trying to do one more than the day before.

Outside the window, Karl is still awake and screaming about the bumps and the groans emanating from the flat window as I exercise.

"What are you doing to yourself you fat fucking pervert? I bet you're diddling yourself, aren't you? If you can find it!"

I pull the curtain across the opening to give myself some privacy and shut him out. I prefer to look out over the city while I exercise and let some breeze in, but I don't want Karl to have something else to belittle me for. For a moment, I stand by the food cupboard door and physically will my hand not to rise to the handle. I focus my entire mind on it.

"I choose who I am" I declare loudly to the room. "Ben Stone chooses who he is. Wow! What a great guy that Ben Stone is! He's the sort of person that I want to be! Why do I like him so much? Why has he been voted Earth's greatest man six years in a row now? I'll tell you! It's because *he* chooses who *he* is. He chooses not to hide. Don't hide Ben. *Please*."

My breathing calms. My hand stays by my side. I drink some foul warm water and go back to my work out. I hum songs to myself to drown out Karl's foul commentary. My brain responds to my body's movements and my soul lifts. I set several personal bests and make sure to thank Karl afterwards; he doesn't like that and I watch him wriggle and gasp on the end of his line like a fish.

Every time I finish a workout, my body burns with the acid in my muscles. I drink litres of water to replenish the liquid that I have sweated out. I feel the warmth that I have generated in my body, and I twitch the growing muscles under the skin. They are a beginner's muscles, but it feels like seeing a green shoot poking through the soil – there is that awe-inspiring sense of growth and the creation of new life. As I had when I'd first been contemplating my thigh muscle, it feels as though I am emerging beneath my skin. Like inside me, there is a different person who is outlined by these muscles and I am luring him to the surface, through the layers of fat.

Of course, as well as Karl, there is an obvious impediment to me getting serious about working out. Namely, that I now only have one leg. My stump is completely healed over now. By jamming the mirror in between the mattress and frame at the bottom of the bed, I can study the stub of my leg. The skin is a lighter pink colour with purple scar lines mottled across the surface. Although the tip of the stump has a numbness to it, the patella moves uncomfortably close to the surface of this scarred skin. If I poke it I can feel it nudging some unknown bundle of nerves, which makes me feel queasy. Despite its brutality, it seems to have healed clean and the rot of diabetes hasn't yet taken hold any further up the leg. Your operation is a complete success Mr Stone, you were lucky to be in the hands of Dr Stone, he's one of our foremost have-a-go amateur surgeons.

Even the patches of dry and scaly skin on my left leg that had bloomed in my heaviest days are mostly faded and look like normal skin now. This is almost certainly to do with the extreme drop in weight and my improving fitness. I know that diabetes is closely connected to weight, as a constant stream of experts advised me to lose weight if I wanted to avoid having my leg amputated, but I am not sure if it is possible to simply stop being diabetic? Definitely not for Type 1, but Type 2? It seems implausible, but then the only conclusions I can draw are from my continued existence. Aside from some truly sickening headaches in the early days after I stopped taking the Metformin – the fact that I am not dead is all the encouragement I really need.

I eventually become adept at moving around the flat using the broom crutch. I have to recalibrate my sense of balance though, which takes a lot of falls and a lot of holding onto walls as I move about. There are patches on the walls where my finger and palm prints are visible from across the room. So far, I've not experienced any of the pains that some people get when they lose a limb, but I certainly get an uncomfortable sense of *ghosting* sometimes. It feels like a danger that is present in my mind and compounded by my ongoing weight loss, that I might simply stop being. If my leg can go and my weight can nearly halve, then where does it end? I remember watching Back To The Future with mum, and seeing Michael J Fox fade into non-existence and I sympathise with his predicament. I fantasise about creating a prosthetic leg, which would give me back some sense of permanence and convince me I am not disappearing. Fortunately, I have plenty of time to experiment with building one.

What I have discovered is that it's not easy to build a prosthetic leg. This is especially true when the only things that you can build it out of are items you have access to in your flat. I pull up the floorboards in the back of mum's bedroom, which gives me enough material to create a wooden leg, after the classic pirate model. I abandon this after a few modifications, simply because the point where the peg leg connects to the stump is too painful. Even with significant padding on the top, it puts too much pressure directly on the patella, which makes me cry out with pain when I take even a tentative step on it. It needs a design with a circular aperture that I can place my leg *inside*. That way it will cushion the kneecap within the joint, but it will mean that the prosthetic can hug the stump and help it to stay on.

My next thought is to try cutting up a pair of jeans, which I then pack with material and gaffer tape to my thigh and onto the wooden leg. This time though the issue is that it doesn't provide enough stability and the filling of the jeans wobbles whenever any weight is put on top of it, which means that I still need to put all my weight on the crutch - in which case there isn't really any point in creating a prosthetic. I need something that I can mould around the remnant of my leg, which will also be strong enough to support my weight without collapsing underneath me. The answer presents itself in the small storage space we have above the cupboard that holds the flat's gas meter. Alongside a box of mum's photo albums and records, which might be worth a fortune if there are any record collectors left alive, there are some items that mum has put in a box marked for Bric-a-Brac. In the box is some of my comic collection (which I promptly return to the lounge for reading) and some old toys – including an unopened magic set that teaches you how to do the connected rings trick and the 3,428 pieces of the Lego Eiffel Tower set.

In my mind, I think I hear Father Donnell commenting that there is something supernaturally appropriate about making a prosthetic leg from Lego, so I bring the large box through to the lounge and start to experiment. Lego is an ideal building material because I can tailor the pieces perfectly to my stump. It also has a tensile strength, which means that it can support my weight. From the smaller pieces, I make a circular collar which I fit around my stump and then create a central cavity which I pad to avoid putting undue pressure on my kneecap. Then it is simply a case of experimenting with building the shaft of a Lego shin section which can add strength.

My initial design for a foot quickly evolves from a flat Lego pad, which repeatedly snaps off. The lesson is that Lego might make a good limb, but it does not make a good ankle. Eventually, I pull up all of the metal threshold strips that sit between the rooms of the flat. They are individually easy to bend into a Z shape, similar to the blades that competitors use in the Paralympics. The problem is that individually they don't hold my weight. However, when I combine five of them together, the lamination means they are strong enough to act as my new foot. After hundreds of different iterations, I have a prosthetic leg design that I am happy to commit to glueing together. I then wrap the whole thing with an entire roll of Sellotape. Not only is it strong enough to support my weight, but after much practice and stumbling, it allows me to stand with equal weight on the two bathroom scales for the first time. To my amazement these now show that I weigh 347 pounds. I am back to two legs and one scale.

I put Brown on the scales as well, to see how her recent trip to the walking field has impacted her weight. She has gained 1 kilogramme on the trip. Good girl! At this rate, I'll have to check the drone's manual to see what the weight capacity is. The model of drone I have is primarily used to carry industrial film cameras for dramatic tracking shots in glorious 4K, so a small dog shouldn't be too much of a problem. The other evidence that Brown is definitely feeding herself on these trips is the stench that her digestive system produces. When her rat farts fill the flat, I've taken to dabbing Vaseline under my nose. It reminds me of a time when I had to slather my belly in the stuff to avoid the friction that everything once seemed to place on me. As horrible as it is, even that is preferable to the smells that emit from Brown. She doesn't even have the good grace to look embarrassed.

There have been a total of three sorties now and I feel more confident with each flight. The problem we face is that the batteries on the VR headset have gone now and I'm streaming the connection from the drone to my laptop, which is draining the battery faster than I'd like. I think I can do one more flight using the laptop, before needing to switch to the phone. I'm reluctant to run down the battery on my phone, simply because it seems the most likely to provide some connection with the rest of the world. I've not had any notifications from any of the apps, but my hopes still rise every time the phone boots up. Perhaps this time, there will be the ping of a notification and I'll click it and open a photo from Helen showing a glorious sunset over the Disney castle. What a beautiful thought.

CHAPTER 16

18ᵗʰ July 2011

9 years, 17 days before

340 lbs (154 kg)

Ben had thought a lot about the last time he had been outside. On one level, he romanticised the very notion of outside, so that in his recollections of that day there was a nostalgic wash of rich summer light and a sharpness to the colours he saw, there were laughing children playing in the street and the sounds of an ice-cream van's chimes ringing loud. But Ben knew that no amount of the sepia-tinted propaganda his brain could generate should dislodge the fact that beyond his front door lay real horror. Every time he relived the moment it was partly with a misremembered fondness for the world, but he always returned to an emphatic understanding that he had made the right choice to stay inside for the rest of his life.

The day it happened started off so normally. He was going through a phase of wanting space from his mum, so he told her that he was going out to study. On his way out, he would call at the supermarket and stock up on crisps, drinks and Skittles, all bought with the new-found wealth from his experiments in eBay selling. He would throw these items in his scuffed rucksack alongside the packed lunch that his mum made him. He would then search the streets and countryside for places where he could be alone. Often, this ended up being the local library where he had learned long ago that the librarians were experts in leaving people alone. The other place Ben liked on dry days was a small thicket out in the hills that he'd seen one day while riding the bus. He knew it was private land, but he had never seen another living soul within the wooded area, and he could sit on the mossy grass and look up at the trees and the sky beyond. He had started to make a rudimentary shelter there, too. Occasionally, he would read, but often he would simply pass the time and eat.

On this particular Monday, it had been raining when he left the house, so he'd made his way to the library and to his usual table near the fire exit. He liked this spot because it was on the top floor and at the end row of shelves among the archive of local planning issues, so he was very rarely disturbed. He often pulled several books from the shelves and stood them on their hard spines to create a defensive barrier, so even if he was spotted, someone would have to actively search out who was hidden behind Planning Decisions 1990-2000 Volumes 1 to 8. Ben had passed the day reading. He mostly denied himself the pleasures of fiction, but he liked to browse atlases and maps. There wasn't any particular effort made towards learning things about the world. Ben just liked to identify places that seemed like they might be quiet. He particularly liked maps of forests. He could focus on places that seemed so calm that mentally he would inhabit those spaces for hours at a time. Often, he would come to and find that such was the concentration of conjuring those spaces, he had drooled a bit.

It was nearly home time and Ben felt his phone vibrating.

"Hi Ben – it's your mum."

"I know – it says that on the phone when you ring remember?"

"Don't be smart – are you on your way to rugby practice?"

"No, training was cancelled," said Ben, lying reflexively. To assuage her demands for physical education he'd never told his mum that he'd stopped playing rugby since the day of the tournament. Mostly, he just muddied his legs outside the flat to keep up the pretence. Ben was pretty sure she knew, but so far she'd not directly challenged him on it.

"Please, would you do me a favour? I wouldn't ask, but Janet had a cancellation and can fit me in today, so I could do with you picking some things up from Tesco." His mum's pleading tone infuriated Ben, but also made him relent.

"OK, what do you need?"

"*We* need something for tea and a few other bits. I'll text you a list, thank you!" his mum said and hung up.

Janet coming round meant that the flat would smell of bleach for a few days and there would be little snippets of hair on the floor of the kitchen no matter how much he swept. Ben sighed and carefully deconstructed his barrier to put the books back on the shelves. He shouldered his bag and nodded at the librarian on his way out.

The rain from before had given way to a muggy heat and Ben instantly began to sweat. He was wearing black trousers and a large black T-shirt which a few months ago had been big on him but now stretched over his gut. He automatically tugged at the fabric to create some space for his stomach and instinctively pulled the shirt down at the back so that the shirt was hanging down over his arse. He hated it when he saw bigger people and the crack of their arse was visible. It made him shudder, and whenever he was out, he would pull at the front of his shirt and tug it down at the back so much that it actually wore the fabric at the pinch points.

He put his head down, turned up the music on his headphones and headed up the long, moving walkway into the supermarket, sighing with relief as the heat was beaten back by the powerful air conditioning of the store. Instantly, he wished that he had a jumper to pull around his shoulders. He checked the list his mum had texted and realised that it was enough to need one of the small trollies, which were corralled at the bottom of the walkway. He suddenly felt paranoid in case anyone saw him doubling back down and thought he was weird, and he decided that he could probably cram all of the items into two baskets, so he picked two large baskets up from the top of the walkway and started to work his way through the list.

On top of the items his mum had asked him to pick up, he added Bourbon biscuits, cornflakes, ready meals, six bags of Skittles, two bottles of fizzy drink, wraps, vegan butter and crisps. He doubled back to the fruit aisle to pick up some strawberries from the list. As he reached for a punnet at the back to make sure he got the latest use-by date, he realised that someone was right next to him and reaching for something on the shelf below. He backed off so they could reach and smiled bashfully at them through his drooping fringe. It was an older woman – she was about 70, Ben guessed. She was dressed in a shapeless beige blouse that he somehow understood was expensive. She was talking to him, so Ben reluctantly pulled one of his headphones out of his ear and listened.

"- you should be eating more of, if you want to lose weight," the lady said and nodded at the strawberries.

"Sorry?" Ben said. "I had my headphones on."

She seemed annoyed and tucked her short brown hair behind her ear in exasperation. Ben couldn't figure out what he had done, although a horrible suspicion had started to form.

"I *said*, that the strawberries are about the only thing in your baskets that are going to help you lose weight. Just look at the labels on these," she said and reached into one of the baskets that were cutting into his wrists. She picked up one of the tubes of Pringles he'd chosen and turned it slightly so that she could read, but also so that Ben could see the little grid of information on the side as well.

"Look at this – 9 grams of fat, which is 15 per cent of your daily total. But what you have to ask yourself when you're looking at these is, what serving size you're talking about because the information they put on there isn't for the entire tube, it's for a serving. Now you look on there and see what the serving size is, I can't see, the writing is too small – what does it say?"

"Per 28 grams, approximately 16 crisps," Ben said. He felt his voice ringing hollow inside his chest. Something was wrong. It felt like a rash of heat was creeping up his back, and at the top this warmth translated into a pounding in his ears. The sound that filtered into his ears changed and it seemed he was hearing through two empty Pringles tubes.

"Now you look at the strawberries," the lady was saying but Ben couldn't engage and her words fluttered away.

Something was badly wrong. He took a breath and the air wouldn't go in properly. He blew out as if he was inflating a balloon and took a sip of air. It wasn't enough, so he sipped again and again until his lungs were full. He puffed out the air again. The sound of his breathing tunnelled into his head. He then realised his breath was only filling his mouth, not his lungs – he had to breathe deeper! A dark border appeared around his view of the fruit on the shelves. He turned slightly and looked at a pack of white mushrooms bulging against the cellophane roof of their container. It appalled him somehow. He looked at the grooves of the celery. His breath was still only in his mouth. He rested his baskets on top of packets of beetroot and felt the stiffness of his wrists.

"Uh, you…" he started but his voice was minuscule. He was being weird. She knew it. He smiled at the lady to try and reassure her but he knew that his grin was crazy. He suddenly had to get out. He abandoned his baskets and focused on the doorway and quick-stepped towards it. He held his hands up to the security guard, scanning shoppers as they came in and mumbled something about his wallet. He barrelled past him and onto the walkways. Still, his breath wouldn't come and as he left the shop, the jets of the blue super-cooled air gave way to the cat-breath heat of the day. Ben felt his breathing get even more ineffective. He lifted his face to create more space in his chest and found that he could still sip his breath into his mouth, just.

As he made his way onto the street, he felt his heart begin to hammer. Not in its regular pattern, but in an erratic, syncopated rhythm. Should he go to the hospital? And tell them what? That he had a jazz heart? Get a grip. This couldn't be right, could it? By swimming his shoulders forwards, he found he could bring in enough air to keep him alive. Then he felt the roll of his shoulders was making it obvious that something was wrong. People would see and point at him. No, not the hospital, he should head home. That was where it was safe. Waiting for the bus. Paying for his ticket. Turning himself around to reverse into the bus seats, as he couldn't fit his legs or stomach into the seats otherwise. Knowing that people were watching him and knowing that people hated him. The cold, smudged glass against the back of his head, chilling his neck. The surreal feeling of watching his thumping heartbeat pound through his eyelids. The terror of what he would do if anyone spoke to him. The stink of the flop sweat rolling off him, as he pushed his way through the rutted path that cut across the green outside Ellis Tower.

Finally, reaching the electronic front door and presenting his key fob which flicked the door to a saviour green and allowed him into the familiar entrance hall which smelled of dust. Waiting in agony for the lift to fetch him and deposit him on the fourth floor. The familiar creaking of the lift cables. Looking at his face in the polished surface at the back of the lift and realising that he was not well, he was dying. Feeling his life fading away and fumbling with his keys in the corridor and then shutting the door behind him.

The welcome feel of the door behind him.

The relief of its thick weight. Its green gloss paint. The spyhole that shrunk the world down to a fisheye view of a corridor and reduced it to something he could manage. His fingertips held onto the tacky gloss and he smelled the flat. The bleach of Janet's hair products, under that, the floral patterns of his mum's perfume and the comfort of the carpets and his home. The sound of a hairdryer and his mum's booming laugh. Ben was home and his heart responded. He felt it climb down from behind his teeth. The oxygen in the air found the pipe into his lungs and it tasted better than the finest wines ever created. He was home. He would be fine.

CHAPTER 17

1ˢᵗ January 2021

4 months, 28 days after

281 lbs (127 kg)

When your birthday is on New Year's Eve, people often feel sorry for you and think it must be horrible to be overshadowed - but what they never see is that if you were born on the 31ˢᵗ December like me, then every year the entire world celebrates with you on your birthday! Imagine never having to twist arms to ensure that people will go out on your birthday! Imagine how great it is when everyone is happy on your special day! Full disclosure, I haven't been out on my birthday since I was 12 and in actual fact, I've never had a conversation where someone expressed regret for my birthday falling on New Year's Eve, but I always imagine that is what my rebuttal will be.

This year, I have planned my birthday celebration in detail and it is a humdinger of depravity. First, there is a grand feast planned – one entire bourbon biscuit. This is to be accompanied by a small bottle of a melon liqueur called Midori, which is incredibly sweet and cloying, but it's pretty strong and I think it will be an appropriate tipple to celebrate another trip around the sun. There's a recipe on the back of the bottle for something called a Japanese Slipper which is Midori, Cointreau, crushed ice, lemon juice and a honeydew melon slice. I haven't got Cointreau, crushed ice, lemon juice or a honeydew melon, so I decide to just neck a few shots of Midori neat to get the party started. That makes me feel like throwing up, so I mix it with some water and drink it long from a highball glass.

At midnight to bring in the New Year, I am going to have a real treat – I am going to power up my phone and play a song. In a post-electric world, wasting battery power is the cardinal sin but my rationalisation has been that a world without music – especially on your birthday - isn't one that is worth living in. Sadly, Spotify is the same as all the other apps that rely on the internet and nothing actually happens if you try to open it. This is a shame as it means I have had to choose from the MP3s that I've actually downloaded to my phone's storage, but who does that any more? My own phone contains two folders of music - a collection of Halloween Sound Effects MP3s, which I'd bought to create a YouTube video. Fortunately, I also have something far better: *PUP,* the eponymous debut album of Canadian punk rock band, PUP. I choose the track *Dark Days,* because it's a great song which sticks in your head for days, giving me value for battery usage, and the more I think about it, the lyrics might be about the secret to survival. It's certainly eerily fitting for me: "We celebrate life at the end of the earth/When everything is gone/there'll be nothing left to lose." Ok, so I still have quite a lot to lose with regard to weight, but it certainly speaks to me.

As I savour the chewable grotesqueness of the Midori, I get everything ready for the party. As the alcohol kicks in, it convinces me to follow through on a bad idea I had earlier. I decide to raise the cherry-picker platform so that Karl is nearly level with the balcony. I have nothing much planned for the day and I think it might be interesting to experiment with Karl and see if I can make any useful observations about what triggers the wraths. Given that I have a captive wrath at my disposal, it seems to make sense to me. Or at least it makes sense to the Midori. Tragically, I suppose it is also because I want some form of human contact. Even if that human contact is spewing murderous rage at me, would it really be massively different from when my dad's cousin Arthur turned up one New Year's Eve with a gift of three McEwans Lagers and proceeded to bray about how he felt immigrants were ruining the country. Mum kicked him out before he had his first sip of lager.

"Get me the fuck down, you turd! Fuck you, I'm going to stick a fucking screwdriver in your face, I bet you bleed gravy you hipster shite. Tell your weird fucking dog to fuck off as well. Come on then!"

Karl isn't happy about going up in the world. When he starts bellowing, Brown speeds out to the balcony with such conviction that I briefly worry that she is going to launch herself at him. However, she just takes up a position at the very edge of the balcony and barks silently but furiously at Karl when he cuts loose with the invective. The "hipster shite" thing is fair comment. To dress up for the occasion, I've parted my long hair and looped it into two pigtails that are then looped into my parted beard. With my face in the middle it makes a nice pattern of 'O' shapes. Karl is right, it is pure hipster shite, but in my defence, experimental grooming passes the time.

"I've actually lost a lot of weight recently Karl."

"You're disgusting. You make me sick. People like you should be culled. What's with the leg? I bet you're just after a better parking space. You're a fat, one-legged turd who's going to sputter out with a heart attack and I can't fucking wait."

"Don't be like that Karl – it's my birthday. I'm 26."

"26 tons, you fat pie. Keep eating and hopefully it'll be your last."

I am already regretting the idea to invite Karl to the party. Lesson learned: don't listen to Midori.

I draw the curtains in the living room and go into mum's room where I've positioned the curtains so that there is a tiny gap through which I can watch Karl. Deprived of a stimulus to attack, he just hangs in his harness looking angry and gravity swings him until finally, he comes to a halt. I watch him over about 30 minutes with Brown sleeping on my lap. Gradually, his eyes become fixed and he doesn't move as much. His hands fold themselves into fists and pull into his sides. Finally, his eyes glaze over. For the first time, I notice that he isn't sleeping as I'd always assumed, it is more like he is paused, or as if he's been put into standby mode. Karl and the rest of the wraths don't eat or drink, so clearly they are being kept alive by some other process. If I were a scientist, I would have taken samples of Karl's blood and muscle tissue and figured it all out. As it is, I just watch him and wonder.

I go back into the lounge and pull out my food diary and turn to the workout page. I leave the curtains shut and start on the rounds of stretches, squats and lifts. I have recently added running on the spot – well, I say "running", but it's more like high-tempo wobbling as my limp is still fairly pronounced. But even though it is difficult, it helps me to work on my balance, so I feel it is worthwhile. I am really pleased at the progress and have just cracked a one-minute sprint barrier where I lift my knees fully up to my chest when Karl pipes up.

"What are you doing in there? Shut up! It sounds like a herd of elephants fucking."

So that proves that it isn't just a visual stimulus that wakes the wraths – they are definitely sensitive to sound as well. I pull back the curtains.

"Hi again, Karl."

"You sweaty fat fuck, kill yourself. Do everyone a favour and stick your head in a noose. Or just take a few steps and give the pavement a big fat kiss."

"Thanks for the suggestion Karl, but I'm exercising. I'll leave the curtains open and let's see if there's a limit to how long you can bang on for."

There isn't.

Throughout a 50 minute workout, Karl exhausts his repertoire of fat insults and euphemisms and at times simply falls back on the old standard of screaming "FAT FUCK!" at me until his face turns magenta. It is weirdly encouraging, like one of those drill sergeants you see in films. I set more personal bests and finish my workout. As the sun goes down, I wash in the bathroom, lifting the various flaps of my loose skin to carefully wipe around with a wet cloth. I still haven't got over the novelty that I can now hold the skin of my stomach back and wash my penis. Truly, this is a day of celebration.

I dry off and make my way into my old bedroom. It is reaching the point where I am small enough that I could move back into my old bed. I decide it would feel like a weirdly regressive step, like being transported back in time. In my wardrobe, I find the suit that mum bought me for her cousin's wedding when I was 16. It is a black suit, naturally, and I remember I spent the wedding feeling out of place and anxious – it was the last social event I'd been to before becoming a shut-in, so the suit is still nearly new. I pull on the trousers and laugh as they fall about three inches short, I'll put on some white socks to make up for that. The trousers button easily. When I'd worn it before, I'd felt swollen and uncomfortable, now I am on the opposite trajectory the lines of the suit make me feel human and smart. It is maybe even a bit baggy. I button up a white school shirt, which falls short at the wrists and shrug my way into the jacket, which buttons up without complaint. I decide that is formal enough and leave the tie in the wardrobe.

I fix my hair into a simple ponytail and smooth my beard out into a point. I make my way back into the lounge and find Brown pacing back and forth. The curtains are drawn, so Karl is going glassy-eyed again. On a whim, I find a piece of red ribbon and curl the ends with the open blade of the scissors and attach it to Brown's collar. It looks festive, but it only lasts two minutes before she chews it up. She never likes to dress up and I should respect that. Feeling fancy, I pick her up and spin uncertainly around on the floor with her, imagining orchestral music swelling as we dance. She doesn't like the spinning and jumps down. I give up trying to make my dog celebrate with me and pour another Midori out and sit on the bed thinking about the unprecedented year that has passed. It naturally begs the question of what is going to be in the future.

The hours pass and midnight comes. I open the curtains and lower Karl back to his normal position against the wall – I've had enough persecution for one evening. I get Brown and sit on a folding chair on the balcony. Before, this was where me and mum would have front row seats for all of the firework shows in the area. She used to squeeze my hand and say that these were the VIP views that no one else could ever have. Now there are no fireworks, but it is enough that for once the air is cool and the earth feels good. Brown burrows under my arm to ward off the cold and I power up the phone. No notifications, no surprise there. I open the phone's music player, plug in my headphones and select *Dark Days*. It's been so long since I heard music that I jump when the skittering guitars play out and my pulse surges with the thunder of the drums and the song begins. *This endless night, this funeral dirge, we celebrate life at the end of the earth. When everything is gone, there'll be nothing left to lose.* I have to scream along.

Karl's voice cuts through the music.

"Stop screeching you bloated shite!"

In the pure darkness, the wraths at the base of the building stir at the sound of my singing and Karl's protests. I drown out their noises with the phone's volume at the maximum and let the song play on and scream all the louder, allowing the music to wash my head and soul clean. It ends and I power the phone off and sit and enjoy the ringing in my ears. The sounds of the wraths' fury and fighting fill the air. I sip my Midori and hug Brown's head to me, and together we pray that the world has a happier new year than the one that has passed.

CHAPTER 18

12th March 2006

14 years, 4 months, 23 days before

142 lbs (64 kg)

Ben pushed the button that heated the leather seats of the Astra. He looked out of the window as he felt the heat start to emanate from the seat. He imagined that he could sense the outline of the element that created the heat. Ben powered the window down and enjoyed the breeze blasting his hair into a wild shape. He looked puzzled as the window closed itself, he turned and saw his dad doing the window up on the master control on his side. He then locked the windows with a little button on the control panel. A tiny red light illuminated on his armrest.

"What are you doing putting the seat warmer on at the same time as having the window down?" Charlie asked.

"I just wanted some fresh air," Ben explained.

"You're either hot or you're cold, pick one. What have I told you about pressing all the buttons anyway?"

"Not to," Ben replied, trying to keep his tone light. They'd had lots of chats over the half term about his tone. Ben had learned the word "surly". He'd also learned that it was amazing how long a week can last.

They drifted into silence as the car drove on, through an

industrial section on the outskirts of a town Ben had already forgotten the name of. All he knew was that they were about two hours from his home and his mum. Ben shifted position in his seat and looked out of the window, but he was really studying the reflection of his dad in the glass. Charlie wore a plain white T-shirt which had ridden up under the opposing pressures of the friction against the seat and the overhang of his belly. The skin of his dad's belly was pure white, like a large scoop of mashed potato. It rested on the top of his thighs which were clad in a pair of the black jogging bottoms he favoured.

Ben looked at his own reflection and sighed. He was becoming portly, which was the term his mum had used. She had assured him that this was just puppy fat and he'd soon grow out of it. He felt a wave of low-lying anger towards his dad and Ben vowed that he would never get that fat. He remembered an activity that they'd done in Sunday School, where they'd talked about the sins of the father being visited on the children and then they'd coloured in a picture of God's benevolent bearded face beaming down from the clouds – which seemed to be how every Sunday School session concluded, regardless of what they discussed in the class. As he considered his dad's reflection again, Ben realised that he was more worried about being visited by the chins of his father, and he laughed to himself.

"What's funny?"

"I just saw a sign for Butt Lane," Ben lied and Charlie laughed too.

Charlie and Anne had divorced when Ben was three and consequently, he had very little recollection of a time when his dad was ever a presence in the flat. The thought of his dad and his mum together seemed absurd to Ben now, not just from a compatibility point of view, but Ben felt they were mismatched on a deeper basis – as if they occupied separate realities. The only way he could explain it was the sense of wrongness he felt when he watched a Bugs Bunny cartoon and Bugs fought with the animator and was exiled onto a blank page.

Charlie had moved out of the flat when his mum had discovered he'd been having an affair with his secretary; Charlie's life was littered with clichés like that. There was no counselling or trial separations. Charlie admitted the affair and within the hour, his belongings were neatly packaged in bin bags that flew from the balcony of the flat and split apart at the foot of Ellis Tower. Charlie didn't rant or plead; instead, he sheepishly gathered his life into the boot of his car and sheepishly, he fled.

For years, the only contact Ben had with his dad was that in early December, a parcel would arrive in the post containing a Christmas card and a series of presents which every year served to convince Ben that either Charlie had precisely no idea who he was, or he chose presents by throwing darts at an Argos catalogue. Gallingly, Charlie never included a receipt. Every January, Anne made Ben write a letter thanking Charlie, which Ben would reluctantly concede to, but he would also subtly misspell Charlie's name every year. As well as the random gifts, there would also be the new season's Liverpool FC top. Even if he could have squeezed himself into it, Ben would never have worn it out of deference to his mum's devotion to Man United. Ben found he lacked the passion to truly care about football, and as he grew he realised this sentiment also applied to his dad. There was no rancour, or open animosity, just a void where his feelings should have been.

Ben would have happily lived out his life with a Secret Santa for a father if Charlie hadn't married for the third time after his second wife left him. Charlotte was 23 and adamant that she wanted it all and she wanted it now. House, car, children, pets, two holidays per year – at least one abroad. Ben's dad was in his late forties at this point and seemingly content to fritter the rest of his days away at the local pub, supping lager and helping the regulars to turn the once-white walls of the pub a true tobacco yellow. Charlotte was resourceful though, and through judicious administration of lager and lingerie, she got Charlie to seal their relationship with a child.

Their daughter Kim was born in 2005 and Charlotte became convinced that what she really needed was an older sibling to care for her. Fortunately, the only thing Charlie had to do to provide this was to repair the estranged relationship and bring Ben into their family. Her secondary motivation was that if Charlie was successful in bringing Ben to live with them, then the Citizens Advice Bureau had assured Charlotte that not only would Charlie's hefty alimony payments to Anne stop, but the money would be required to flow in the other direction. Consequently, Charlotte began to needle Charlie to reach out to Ben and Charlie, ever in search of a quiet life, allowed himself to be convinced that out there was a son and heir who was potty trained and ready to learn from his old man.

Letters started to arrive at Ellis Tower, which begged for a second chance at "being the father he'd never had the chance to be." This led to phone conversations where father and son "ummed" and "so'd" their way through awkward exchanges. Then visits were agreed. Charlie arrived for a weekend and took Ben to the football. Half terms were assigned, and Charlie's Astra dutifully arrived to transport Ben the four hours and forty-two minutes to Portsmouth. Ever magnanimous, Anne gently persuaded Ben to give Charlie a chance, fearing that he'd regret it if he cut his dad off without at least getting to know him. Ben went along, but he kept waiting to be told that there had been an implausible, highly comical mix up at the hospital and that this wasn't his dad at all. If only there wasn't such a strong physical resemblance.

Charlie lit another cigarette and Ben instinctively reached for the window control, which did nothing when he pressed it. He looked over and saw the tiniest smirk play across Charlie's lips. Ben inhaled the wisps of secondary smoke. He always liked the first ten seconds of the cigarette smoke that clouded the car when his dad smoked. Ben found that it made something in his head buzz in an appealing way. The rest of the time was a choking horror, as the fog thickened. Ben threw caution to the wind, adjusted a button on the dashboard to put the air conditioning on and felt the purity of clean air breaking through the fog.

Ben's dad indicated and pulled off the road at a roundabout. He swung into a familiar-looking car park and followed the arrows under the golden arches. Ben's dad loved McDonald's. He felt that the drive-through was the zenith of human achievement – imagine a dining experience where you don't even have to get out of your car to have high carb, high-fat foods delivered to your window. It felt Roman in its decadence, a point he'd often made out loud because he liked the way it sounded.

"Welcome to McDonald's, how can I take your order?"

"Big Mac meal, chocolate milkshake."

"Regular or large?"

"Let's go large, as the actress said to the bishop." Charlie smiled at Ben, who suffered a fractional death.

"Is that everything?"

"No, what do you want Ben?"

"Um, what do you have that's vegan?" Ben asked, shouting across his dad.

"Sorry, did you say vegan?" the cashier said through the loudspeaker.

"Yes, do you have anything vegan?"

"We have a veggie burger."

"Is that vegan?"

"No, I don't think so."

"Come on, we've done the nut roast thing all week, you don't need to be vegan at McDonald's. I won't tell anyone. Have a burger." Charlie implored.

"I don't want a burger, I'm a vegan."

"You could just eat the bun and the lettuce."

"It's all covered in mayonnaise, which is made from eggs."

"So, you can't even eat eggs? They don't kill chickens to make eggs you know – they just fall out of their arses!"

"Look, Dad, it's fine. I'm not hungry anyway."

"My manager says that the apple pies are vegan."

"Great, I'll have an apple pie, thank you."

"You need more than that to keep you going, we're not going to get back until late."

"Can you just do me a plain bun?"

"I don't know. I'll check."

They waited for the voice to return. Three cars had pulled into the drive-through lane behind them by this point. The car at the back beeped his horn.

"Why don't you just have a burger?"

"Because I'm a vegan," Ben explained.

"Listen – what have I told you about being surly? Just because your mother has decided to save the world and live off mung-beans, doesn't mean that you have to follow suit. It can't be good for you. You're a growing lad."

"I'm not following her, I just happen to agree with her. She wouldn't even let me be a vegan until I started at high school. I wanted to do it from when I was seven. Animals don't have to die for me to live."

"Well, you can't get enough calories just eating grass. It's not right, you'll be weaving your own shoes soon."

"Ok Dad," Ben said with just enough emotion to make it clear that he actually said something else.

The drive-through voice returned.

"We can't just do a bun I'm afraid because we wouldn't be able to charge it on the tills."

"Get a fucking move on!" someone in the queue shouted out of their car window.

"Don't worry about it, he'll have a cheeseburger and an apple pie."

"Is that everything?"

"Yes, that's everything."

"Drive round to the next window, please."

Charlie burned rubber and overshot the window by several feet. He burned more rubber as he threw the car into reverse. It was a pretty impressive manoeuvre in an Astra.

They collected their food and Charlie drove away from the McDonald's car park, fearing the retribution of the other customers who had been forced to wait an extra minute. He pulled up in a lay-by in the industrial estate.

He took the bag from Ben and disgorged its contents across the Astra's central column, balancing fries against the gear stick and jamming little pots of ketchup and BBQ sauce by the handbrake and instrument panel. Ben pointedly ate the sesame seeds off the top of his cheeseburger one by one, creating a pock-marked bun. His father noticed but decided not to engage and instead ate his meal with vehemence. Ben finished the seeds and took a bite of the apple pie. It was molten inside and he seared his lips and the tip of his tongue with his first bite.

"Ow! Shit," Ben shouted and took up his dad's chocolate milkshake and pressed his lip and tongue against the side.

"You can have a sip you know," Charlie said in a softer voice.

"No. I don't want to. I do not want to."

"OK! OK!"

Charlie finished and burp-sighed with contentment. He peeled the strip of red plastic from a new packet of cigarettes and lit up. He unlocked the windows and dropped Ben's by a couple of inches as a way to clear the air between them.

"Listen Ben, I wanted to have a bit of a chat with you on the way back."

Ben felt his scrotum tighten. This wouldn't be good. His dad's conversations over the half term had mostly just been extended lectures, which Ben felt had been working towards a point. Ben felt too tired and he was suddenly hungry. He contemplated eating the burger, but only for a fraction of a second.

"You're a big lad now and you're at high school and I think that means that you're old enough maybe for us to have a conversation about some things that maybe your mum might have missed out when she's talked about me and Charlie."

Ben could never quite believe that he called Charlotte "Charlie", but seemingly he loved the confusions that it caused.

"Dad, I don't know. I don't really want to get involved."

"But that's the thing Ben, love, you are involved whether you want to be or not."

"But I don't want to be."

"But you are. You can't just wish it away."

Ben felt hot and checked to see if the seat warmer was still on.

"So, listen Ben. I think a lot of this whole situation would be much clearer if you read something."

Charlie reached into the door pocket on his side and pulled out a few pages that had been folded into thirds. Charlie held them out to Ben and slowly, with evident reluctance, he took them from his dad as if he was being passed cooling rods straight from a reactor core.

Ben unfolded the paper and saw that it was a form for an adoption agency. He felt as though someone was piping cold water into his stomach as he recognised his mum's small, looping handwriting. He noted that it was photocopied, which confused him.

"What's this?" he asked.

"Have a little read, Ben, I think it will help you understand," Charlie tapped the cigarette into the Astra's much-abused ashtray.

"It looks like an adoption form."

"It's perhaps not easy to read but it's all there. Charlie thought you deserved to know and I agreed."

Ben scanned the form, somehow fearing that if he actually read the words then it would make the whole thing real. It wasn't hard to understand though – it was a form that was starting the process of putting him up for adoption. He checked the date on the form.

"But I wasn't even born."

"No, your mum wanted to give you up as soon as you were born. She felt that it would be fairer on you and the parents."

"But she's my parents."

"The parents who would have taken you I mean."

"Why are you showing this to me?"

"I know that you think I'm just some deadbeat dad, who has never been there for you and I've made mistakes, but I'd like to be there for you. Charlie and Kim would as well."

"I get that, but why are you showing me *this*?"

"I think it's important you know what your mother is really like. If it wasn't for me, you'd be who knows where. I think you'd be better off living with someone who always wanted you."

***

It was late when Ben walked down the corridor and stopped outside the door to number four. He was conscious of how strongly he smelled of smoke. He felt as though he could see a beige miasma of smoke around him like an aura. He knocked on the front door and his mum opened it and looked surprised.

"Ben! Oooh, I missed you!" She wrapped him in a hug that forced the air from his lungs. "Why didn't you use your key?"

"Mum, did you put me up for adoption?"

She looked at him with an expression of confusion.

"Adoption?"

Ben passed her the forms that his dad had left him with. She took them and looked at them quickly and then tucked them in the back pocket of her jeans. She stood back from the door. The gap let the smell of baking creep out. The warm scent mingled with the stale cigarette smoke.

"Come inside," she said.

"I don't want to, I want to know what this is all about."

"I suppose your dad gave you the forms? I'm shocked he kept them, he was always losing everything, but this he keeps."

"So, it's true?"

"Come in, we shouldn't talk about this on the doorstep."

"Dad wants me to go and live with him."

Anne's face registered anguish and Ben felt his resolve plummet. He was so determined to be angry with her. He picked up his bag and turned away from his front door. He started walking towards the lift. His dad had said he'd wait for him in the car park. Ben didn't want to go with his dad, but he didn't know if he could stay here either.

"Yes, it's true! I wanted to put you up for adoption. I felt too young. Your dad was working all hours and I didn't trust myself to care for you. I got the forms from the agency one day and I filled them in. Your dad found them and went mad. He said I'd be fine. We never discussed it again."

Ben stopped ten paces away from his front door.

"Why didn't you want me?"

"I did want you! I *did* want you! I wanted you so much that it made me scared. I worried that I'd smother you, or throw you off the balcony. When you're pregnant so many stupid thoughts go through your head. Will you be enough? Will you be a good mum? In the end, I thought someone who wasn't off their nut would do a better job for you."

Ben turned and Anne saw the tears running down his face and ran to him, the door shutting behind her. She gathered him up and hugged him fiercely.

"Ben, I don't mind if you really, really want to live with your dad. I'd miss you more than anything. But what I won't let you do is leave thinking that I don't love you, or that I want anything other than the life that I've got. You make me so happy and so proud. Every day."

Ben cried and hugged his mum.

"I don't want to live with Dad. He's a twat," he mumbled between sobs.

"I know he is love, but you had to find that out for yourself."

"I want to stay here."

"And you can, for as long as you want."

"I want to stay forever."

"And you can. I wouldn't have let you go anyway, you're too important."

"Thanks mum."

"Plus, my keys are in the flat."

CHAPTER 19

9th February 2021

6 months, 5 days after

240 lbs (109 kg)

If you want to know what your BMI is, then you take your weight in kilograms and divide it by the square of your height in metres. To give a working example, today when I step onto the scales I weigh 240 pounds. 240 divided by 2.2 gives you a metric weight of 109 kilograms. I am six foot four inches tall, which is 1.93 metres. 1.93 squared equals 3.72. If you divide 109 by 3.72 you get 29.3. My BMI is 29.3. A BMI of anything over 29.9 counts as obese.

I am not obese.

I am overweight.

I'm overweight!

It may sound like a stupid thing to be overjoyed about, but it's *actually happened*. I am no longer obese! I walk into the lounge like John Cena taking to the ring and I'm singing that cheesy '80s song from *The Karate Kid*. I'm shadow boxing and climbing the steps like Rocky. I'm flexing to the inert audience of murderous wraths outside my window and curling my forearms and posing like The World's Strongest Man. I am brawn. I am buff. I am sex. Gaze ye on my naked form world and witness the fitness.

The world is silent, but I can tell that it's checking me out.

I power through my workout and even if I don't quite hit 50 press-ups in one set - I start shuddering at 45 and switch to knee down press-ups for the last five – it's fair to say that I've come a long way. I tried getting my entire body into one leg of my biggest pair of trousers the other week, and it wasn't even that hard. It was hard to get out again, but that's a lesson learned. I've even become slightly obsessed with standing in front of the mirror – I'm not going to be gracing the front pages of Men's Health any time soon, but then who knows, given the competition I might be the healthiest man alive.

One thing that's massively helped my mobility is that I don't have boils on the underside of my belly now. Instead, I have four patches of darker skin where they used to be, with a little circle of dried skin in the middle like the remnant of a puddle. The boils have simply dried up, taking all that rank pus with them. In fact, I don't really have a belly in the same sense as before. I just have this drooping sheet of flesh that swoops from the top of my chest down to my thighs. If I want to I can use it as a table cloth. I also find it useful for hiding Brown's tennis ball underneath and enjoying her canine confusion about whether it would be appropriate to go digging for it. She cocks her head and sub-woofs until I take pity on her and get it out. I think she thinks I've eaten it.

Because of my exercise regime, the growth of the muscled sub-human underneath the skin has continued and in various places around my body, my loose flesh gathers tightly around bands of muscle. My abs look like satsumas pressing against the side of a carrier bag. In mum's room, I find some of her hair clips and realise that with the bulldog grips I can pin all of my excess flesh behind my back and look semi-normal – even healthy from the front. Alternatively, I can use one of her scrunchies to bunch up enough of the skin in the centre of my chest, so that it looks like a really fucked-up ponytail. It may be gross but it means the skin doesn't impede me as I move around the flat. For ease, I often just tuck the various flaps of skin into my pants.

I have had to alter a few choice items of clothes because all of my clothes are comically baggy on me. I'm no tailor, but the end result is functional and screams end of the world chic. In truth, even though she was so much shorter than me, it would probably be easier to let out some of the clothes that still hang in my mum's wardrobe, but I have no idea how to do that and it all seems very Bates Motel, so I'll make do with baggy skin under baggy clothes.

It's been more than two months since I built my Lego leg and apart from re-doing the gaffer tape "skin" it functions about as perfectly as I could hope for. I even find time to break out the Sharpies to decorate the leg with some old school graffiti, which starts to make it feel more like it belongs to me. It's been strange to get used to the solidity of the leg. I'm aware it creaks slightly as I walk and the way it impacts my balance if I attach it slightly differently. The hardest thing has been to accommodate the pressure it puts on my right hip, which gets sore through the slightly wonky version of walking I do. There's a series of "yoga flows for hip opening" in one of mum's magazines and I've been doing those morning and night to relieve the worst of the pain. I've also been doing the breathing exercises they recommend and that really helps too. There's one called "bee breath" where you stick your fingers in your ears, breathe through your nose and make a buzzing noise as you exhale. It's really wonderful, but Karl doesn't like it.

The only other problem with the leg is that after I've spent a few hours on my feet working out or doing laps of the flat to get my 10,000 steps in, I get red marks around the skin on the stump and above the knee. These initially formed painful blisters that put me back on the crutch until they had burst and the new pink skin underneath had stopped being so painfully fresh. I don't get blisters now, but the leg still rubs. It's a constant trade-off between finding a tight enough bind so that the leg stays on and stopping it from cutting off the circulation or chafing. The best adaptation I've made has been to roll an old rugby sock all the way outside of the leg and stick that into place at the top of the prosthetic. This means that I can roll the sock onto my stump and all the way up the leg. This mostly holds it in place, to the point that I'm confident enough to walk and jog around without feeling like I'm a high kick away from flinging my leg out of the window. When I was eight, I got a rubber arrowhead stuck to my forehead, which left me with a perfect round blemish as a reminder of my stupidity for a fortnight. Inspired by this memory, I think there will be a vacuum solution to keeping the leg on, but I need to find something like a large toilet plunger, preferably a new one, to experiment with.

Getting 10,000 steps every day has been tricky, but a useful way of perfecting my balance and learning how to move confidently again. The problem is that the flat is less than 50 paces from one end to the other. The spyhole shows both Mr Ethiss and the lady from the lift still entwined together just outside my front door, so I can't even use the corridor to pace in. Consequently, it means a fair amount of turning and marching on the spot, but it passes the time and burns more calories. As I look in the mirror and see my body changing, I'm more aware than ever that by exercising, I am simply speeding up my journey towards the point where I will need to find a source of food for myself. But I feel like I am doing the right thing. There will always be problems, all I can do is to focus on what I can solve now.

My plan for the day is to wash the water bottles, then finish reading The Book of Revelation and my favourite issue of Closer. I'll then wait until nightfall and take Brown on her fifth flight to the walking field. She tolerates the end of the world pretty well, but aside from a break in her usual eating patterns, nothing much has changed for her. And as smart as she is, it's not like she can get crushed by the concept of the breakdown of society. It's nice to hang out with someone who only gets sad when her tennis ball is lodged down the side of the fridge, or she can't quite position herself under her favourite blanket. If anything, she seems to have enjoyed the peace and quiet that Armageddon has brought with it – she's not big on other people generally, so I don't think she would be overly concerned to know that mankind has finished.

We doze the afternoon and evening away. The sun sets and I take a few minutes to stand at the back of the balcony and watch the sun turn the sky into an orange mess. Brown's mood picks up as I do a pre-flight check on the drone – she knows what it means when I take the tarpaulin off the drone and ritually remove the lens caps and clean the cameras. Mechanically, the drone is looking as good as new, the blades are all flawless, the rotors are turning easily, although I spray it with WD40 anyway, but that's more because WD40 is up there with cut grass as one the greatest ever smells - possibly even the best. The hydrogen tank has about a third left in, but I grab a full one from mum's room and secure it in place on top of the drone. I think about how shifting the canisters used to seem like such an effort and leave me out of breath, but now I use two of them as part of my weight routine and can fly-lift them for 50 reps. What have I become? Brown circles my feet and pulls at the pet carrier to signal that she's ready and excited for another flight.

I think my over-caution regarding the hydrogen is partly to offset the concern that I'm reaching the end of the road when it comes to display options. The laptop now only has 5% power, which isn't enough to trust it for an entire flight and my phone is down to 11%, which in battery-saver mode might be enough for two or maybe three more flights. There's no question that when the phone battery goes, I'll have to consider my options carefully. A long-considered, but frequently put-off plan is to brave the horrors in the corridor and see what resources Mr Ethiss' flat may reveal. For now though, I'll stream the video footage direct from the drone to my mobile, which can be mounted on top of the transmitter.

There is a mottled cloud cover tonight, which is a surprise, and I wonder if it's going to get colder. I make a mental note to try and figure out how I could collect the dew as a source of drinking water. Maybe tomorrow I'll restore order to the world, get the power back on, revive Google and look it up. Brown breaks my train of thought by jumping fully to my waist and trying to bite my hand. I open her pet carrier and she obediently jumps in and settles. As always, I kiss her head and pray that God guides her flight and gives her happy hunting. She tries to nip my face as I kiss her head again and I reluctantly close the lid and triple check the timers and settings.

I power up the drone and I get the familiar sensation of the sound of the eight motors powering up and a blast of wind. As usual Karl somewhere below starts to chunter about how he's going to skullfuck everything. It's surprising how you can get inured to someone screaming top-shelf profanity at you. Sticks and stones may break my bones, but words will never hurt me. I check the phone's battery, which shows at 10% and take the drone up a little too quickly. The rope uncoils beneath the drone until it goes taut and the pitch of the motors jumps as it pulls more energy to drive the motors harder still. The carrier jerks off the ground and I gasp and hold my breath as I worry that Brown might be bumped out and fall. Nothing happens and I exhale with a whooshing noise like the article about yoga breathing suggested for calmness. Everything is fine. I experience a horrible lurch in my stomach as the drone moves out into the night and I pray harder still for my beautiful dog who just wants to eat.

I thumb the display and pull up the thermal view from the camera. I pan the camera to sweep the streets below and as the noise of the drone filters down to the creatures, they come around and start to follow the source of this new irritation. They seem almost purple with fury as they chase the noise of the drone. As it heads further away from town, the numbers following the drone on the streets drop. Soon, Brown is alone over the woodlands and I switch thermal imaging off to try and save the battery.

I fly fast and direct to the walking field and bring Brown gently down to the ground. Even in the dark, it's a simple landing and as the rope coils to the ground, I move the drone away to the North so that I don't accidentally land it on top of Brown. I scan the camera around and see that the pet carrier is safely sitting on the ground about 15 feet away from the drone. This patch of the land is towards the top end of the walking ground, close to some weeds and shrubs that I'd spotted on the fourth trip. I thought they might be a fertile hunting area, or provide other sustenance such as grasses or plants, maybe even a rabbit, which might not make the flat so toxic on Brown's return.

The timer goes off and the lid of the pet carrier springs open. As usual, Brown exits the carrier immediately and sniffs around to find a good spot to have a wee. She cocks her leg against the side of a bush right at the edge of the camera's line of vision. I see a murky image of Brown turn quickly as a pair of large muddy wellington boots stride across the view of the camera and kick Brown hard in the side. I shout "No!" as I see her tiny body fly out of shot.

In a panic, I flick the camera back to thermal imaging and see a large wrath stomping across the land. My land. Towards my dog. She's three miles away from me. I panic and wonder what I can do as I pan the camera again to watch the wrath advancing towards Brown. She has rallied from the assault and is gamely barking, not knowing that this creature isn't able to care or feel fear even if she could make a noise. I do the only thing I can think of and power the drone up. The drone responds instantly and the blades of the machine come alive and something about the waft of the air and the noise does just enough to catch the attention of the wrath. It abandons its search for Brown and comes back towards the drone instead. I flick the drone into the air and the rope uncoils beneath. As I'm gaining altitude, I dip the camera and see the wrath standing staring at the drone shouting into the night. I notice that the wrath has a wide, kind face and seems to be dressed for a day's shooting, complete with a gun bag over its shoulder. It's furious about the source of irritation slipping beyond its grasp, but belatedly I also notice that it is standing on the rope that connects the drone to the pet carrier. The drone pays out the rope behind it and it goes taut and the controls strain in my hands.

The wrath looks confused as it feels a tugging at its boot and it very, very slowly realises that the rope is attached to the drone. It reaches out a huge hand and takes hold of the rope in front of its face. It holds on and pulls the drone down. I gun the motors to maximum power and the meters all red-line, but it's no use. As the wrath pulls one hand down and places the other onto the rope, my drone is gradually dragged towards the ground. The wrath looks up and realises that the hated, noisy drone is being brought closer and so it keeps pulling, hand over hand. I switch to thermal and spot Brown in the background, cowering from the wrath. I take in the wider scene shown on my phone screen and feel as certain as I can be with such a quick scan that there are no other heat signatures on the field. Yet. I then hammer both control sticks with my thumbs and power the drone blade first into the face of the wrath. There is a flurry of a liquid spray that shows like a shower of white sparks on the thermal image display and some grinding that I can register through the controller all these miles away. The drone crashes to the ground and a liquid slowly oozes over the view from the camera. I can't see Brown. I can't help her. My dog is stuck out in this murderous world and I have no way to bring her home.

CHAPTER 20

Dr Shaw moved to the kitchen and washed his hands. He rolled the sleeves of his shirt down and came back into the lounge. Ben was struggling, reaching over his stomach, trying to pull his right trouser leg down with his grabber arm. There was an awkward moment of intimacy, as Dr Shaw noticed and reached across and did it for him. Ben mumbled a thanks.

"How's the diet going? We'll get a more accurate idea when we bring the scales in next week, but how do you feel it's going?"

"I'm making progress," said Ben. "I'm finding it hard to eat much of anything at the moment. I'm not sure if it's nerves or the fact that I'm eating so many vegetables, but I find that I'm full after about two bites. Doesn't seem to matter what it is – why do you think that is?"

"Well, as you say, it would be understandable if you're feeling a bit nervous. Even leaving the flat is going to feel pretty terrifying I imagine." Ben coughed and tried to suppress the feeling of falling into blackness he got whenever he contemplated leaving the flat. Dr Shaw continued. "You also have to remember that you've got diabetes and that has a number of symptoms that *could* lead to a diminished appetite."

"I've still got a big appetite though, I want food all the time. But when I start eating, I feel like I've been eating for hours. I did want to ask if it could be this thing I did called the hypnotic gastric band? It was on a website I saw and I thought I'd give it a go. It was one of those relaxation talks where you have to lie down and climb down some mossy steps into a peaceful clearing, that sort of thing. Then it talked about your appetite waning and you suddenly being aware of every mouthful. I didn't think it worked at first but that was about a week ago – could it have been that?"

"Well, it *could* be, but I think it's more likely connected to the diabetes. There's a condition called gastroparesis which relatively common in diabetics and that often leads to an uncomfortable feeling of fullness. We'll be able to see where we are with that when we bring you in and do a colonoscopy. Do you have any questions about the amputation?"

"Yeah, how do you actually do it?"

"Well, it's not that complicated really – there are three main stages. The first is to cut the skin and muscle and open up the leg – it's a bit like the skin of an orange being pulled back. We then deal with the bone, which in your case will be relatively easy as we're losing the whole of the lower leg beneath the knee. We then sever the ligaments which hold that on and remove the leg. We then pull the folds back over everything to create a stump and, hopefully, bring everything together neatly."

"What do you do with all the arteries and things?"

"Well, we seal those off, the idea is that it will improve your circulation and leave us with a nice stump that we can get a prosthetic on, but we'll go into that more when you're in hospital. Have you had any more thoughts about the move and what you'll do afterwards?"

"I don't want to leave, but they're going to refuse to put me back in here. I got a quote from a haulage company about how much it would cost to put me back in if I paid privately, they reckon fifteen grand once you have all the insurance in place."

"Wow."

"Yeah, the council weren't even happy that I'd asked. They want me to just move into the ground floor flat and shut up and die."

"I'm sure that's not the case Ben, you have to try and see it from their side – there's a lot of complexity and cost involved in having someone like you in a flat like this. They'll be worrying about health and safety and accessibility."

"I'm worried about my home, though. This isn't just where I live – it's been everything to me for my entire life. I've not left in nearly a decade. I know every floorboard of the place. It feels like it is me."

"But another place could feel like that in time."

"But the flat does now."

"Well, I'll leave that one to you. Do you have any other questions about the operation?"

"What's the chance that I'll die?"

Dr Shaw finished buttoning the cuff of his sleeve. Ben thought briefly that he was going to ignore the question.

"I can't give you an exact number on it, but we have to accept that there are risks. We'll do everything we can to protect you from those risks but the ones that I would say are significant are firstly the chance of dying during the operation. Because of your size we have to be really careful that we give you the right levels of anaesthetic to keep you sedated during the operation. We also have to make sure that your blood pressure is stable during the operation and, again, because of your weight, that's not going to be easy. The more weight you can get off before the operation, the easier that becomes."

He paused to give Ben time to absorb what he'd been told.

"The second risk is more for after the operation. We are taking the leg off below the knee, but depending on how your body responds, we will need to see if another amputation is necessary. If it is, then it might be mid-thigh, or even to hip level. Finally, it's a risk that because of your isolation here we need to be very careful about infection. Normally, when people are out and about they're exposed to a number of different bacteria just through getting on the bus or being in work. With you because you've been here for so long on your own you will have a much narrower library of bacteria that your body knows how to fight off. So we have to be aware of that. Does all of that make sense? Have you got any questions?"

"I'm OK. I just want to make sure Brown is looked after."

"Well, if you want to give yourself the best chance, then keep losing weight. Can I ask you a question?"

"Anything, as long as it's not the one about how do I go to the toilet."

"Ha! No. I was wondering what you're most looking forward to seeing outside."

Ben pursed his lips in thought. For some reason, the image of Helen standing in his kitchen asking him to go to America with him jumped into his mind. The only thing outside of the flat that he wanted to see was her. But where was she? He searched for a less complicated answer to give the doctor.

"Hmm, I've not really thought about it. I guess I'd like to see the flat."

"This flat?"

"Yeah. I've spent so long looking out of the window that it would be interesting to see the window and the balcony from a different angle."

"Interesting. Is there anything else you want to know about?"

"I don't think so."

"Ok then – so we're all set for Tuesday 4th August. We're already liaising with the team from the council and from the emergency services. They're going to be in touch soon to arrange a meeting so we can all understand what the others are doing. We're confident that we can move you safely and comfortably, that's the main thing. You're going to have to get used to people coming in and out as they prepare, but ultimately it's all going to be worth it if we can get you back to full health and maybe even get you settled in an environment that's going to be healthier for you long-term."

Disneyland thought Ben. That's the only place I'll swap this flat for. Settle me in Disneyland.

CHAPTER 21

I think through what I saw at the walking field again. I'm almost sure that the wrath was killed by the drone, but my mind won't rest at the thought of Brown alone out there. I spend a few minutes confirming that the drone is completely destroyed. It doesn't respond to any attempts to power it up and the cameras have gone dark. On the positive side, I definitely saw Brown moving, which suggests that she survived the attack, but who knows what injuries she has sustained? It also stands to reason that if one wrath can get into the field, then others can too. It might also mean that Brown can get out. Even as I sit here thinking, she could be disappearing from my life forever. On my quick swivel of the cameras, it didn't seem that there were other heat signatures on the land, but I'd only had a glimpse and that isn't enough to be sure that right now, my dog isn't injured and trying to defend herself against wraths who will kill her without thinking.

I swear at the top of my lungs and hate myself again for putting Brown in a position where she could be harmed. I have to go to her. I have to. I push down the rising bile in my throat and force myself to think and plan. I need to find a way to get to the walking fields and that means leaving the flat. The simplest thing is to go out of my front door, but there are two problems. First is that Mr Ethiss and the lady from the lift are in the corridor and they will attack me as soon as I open the door. Quite simply, I have to attack and kill them first, I have no choice. The second issue is how am I supposed to get to Brown? I can walk, but it will take an hour at least. I've never even sat in the driver's seat of a car before - just another experience I have cheated myself of, by choosing the life of a shut-in. Also, unless I am insanely lucky and manage to find a modified car which has fuel and the keys waiting in the ignition, I'm not sure that I can even drive a car with my prosthesis. Fuck it, if I need to, I'll run there. I just have to get going.

I run around the flat and load a backpack with a bottle of water, the binoculars, my phone, two of the kitchen knives, the long hob lighter from the kitchen and a towel. I pick up a length of wood which started life as a chair leg and stick another knife onto my prosthetic leg with gaffer tape. I go into the hall and begin to unblock the various barriers I've erected in front of the door. I get a hammer and thump away the wedges I've hammered into place to keep the wraths at bay. I bang the flat of my palm against the door and look out of the letterbox, so I can see the wraths. They are still entwined on the floor, but at the noise of me smacking the door, their red eyes open and they stare at the door with a renewed ferocity.

"Sh'up! SH'UP!" the lady from the lift screams through her broken jaw.

"This used to be a good place to live until you food bank ponces moved in with your noise and your dogs!" Mr Ethiss adds.

I bang on the door a few more times and make sure they make their way over to me. They start to pound on the other side and I can feel the door rattling in its frame. I don't have long before they break through. I go into mum's room and roll out one of the half-full canisters of hydrogen and throw it onto the bed. I have spare lengths of tube that are used to attach the canister to my now-deceased drone and I quickly thread the tubing onto the valve at the top.

"Come out here, Fat Boy!" Mr Ethiss wails as he pounds on the door.

The lady from the lift screams something incomprehensible.

I pull the canister into the hall next to the door and gently lift the flap of the letterbox again. All I can see are the midriffs of the wraths as they punch and kick at the door. The plaster from around the doorframe starts to crack and dust falls in little puffs. As quick as I can I feed the tubing through the letterbox and slowly turn the red nozzle at the top, letting the hydrogen billow out into the hallway. Fortunately, pure hydrogen has no smell. As it is released, it chills the air, but the wraths are too occupied with getting in to attack me to notice. I am able to let the gas run into the hallway for thirty seconds before I guess that it will probably be enough. I tentatively hold the nozzle and reach into my bag for the oven lighter. With one finger, I hold up the letterbox, as I kneel by the door.

"Hey Mr Ethiss! Lady! Down here!" I shout to get their attention. The wraths bend over to see how they can reach me through the narrow slot. Their red eyes come level with the slot and in that instant, I see that the humanity in them has been snuffed out. Their hands push through the slot, scraping the skin from their fingers.

"Sorry," I say and click the lighter at the opening of the tubing.

A huge *whoomp* blasts out in the corridor and a red cloud ignites and quickly disappears. Even through the small slot, the force and heat of the blast and the impact pushes me back and the door rattles in its frame. At the same time, a roaring whistling flame emerges from the tube as the hydrogen ignites and directs a five-foot gout of flame into the corridor, immolating Mr Ethiss and the lady from the lift.

I quickly turn the nozzle on the canister and pinch out the remnants of flame that are dribbling from the melted tip of the tubing. For a first attempt at making a flamethrower, I would say it is a success. I pull my sleeve over my fingers and gingerly lift the letterbox flap. In the hall, a charred section of the corridor outlines precisely where the hydrogen has ignited. I can see two forms on the floor, writhing in their burning garments. The roof and parts of the hard-wearing floor tiles are on fire.

I stand and pull open the door. A smell of crisping skin and singed hair mingles with the smoke and I step over the two wraths and walk down towards the lift, where I retrieve the fire extinguisher from its mounting on the wall. I pull the pin from the mouth of the extinguisher and aim the black tube. As I walk back up the corridor, I fire a narrow jet of white powder from the extinguisher into the hall and coat everything with a fine dust, which quickly extinguishes the small blazes that have started. Reaching my front door I steel myself, loft the fire extinguisher and bring the base down on the lady from the lift's head. She pushes out an exhalation and then nothing more sounds from her. Mr Ethiss has wriggled onto his back and with one charred eye, he watches me, as I repeat the process with him. There is nothing I could have done. It is now a choice of them or us.

I grab my backpack from the floor where I've dropped it, shoulder it and push down the corridor towards the stairs. I remove the knife from my leg holster and hold the length of wood in my right hand, prepared for any other wraths who might be lurking. The stairwell is quiet though, and I scurry down the four flights in the early dawn light, trying to overcome the strangeness of going downstairs and to keep my balance. I descend into the entrance hall and look around in surprise as I notice that it is a completely different colour to how I remember and that the noticeboard is now at the bottom of the stairs, rather than by the door. It looks like they've upgraded the doors as well. I feel like an imposter. I remember that there used to be a bike storage cupboard at the back of the entrance hall and hope that it is still there. Sure enough, the cupboard is there and sitting at the back is a large woman's bike with a basket on the front. It would be a virtually silent form of travel and it's certainly quicker than running all the way, even if I can only pedal with one leg. I dump my backpack into the basket and pull the bike out, only to notice that it has a thick metal chain securing the wheel to the stand, which is concreted into the ground. Fuck. I'll have to look for a bike on the street.

I grab my rucksack and make my way to the front door. I turn the thumb lock and push the door open. As I step across the threshold, the coolness of the blue air strikes me. I hold the door behind me open with one hand, as I notice the long, brown stalks of dry grass that have grown up through the paving slabs on the path, which are being pushed around by a breeze. At ground level, I am struck anew by the scale of the destruction around me. Everywhere, smashed cars, dead people and carnage. There has obviously been a fight near the front door; two bodies are jumbled together in a mess of decomposition. I try not to look too closely.

Looming over the flats is the crane, still poised ready to whisk me to the hospital. I can see Karl dangling immobile under the cherry picker. I feel so small. I feel like a 16-year-old obese lad running from a mean woman in a supermarket again. I can't go back into the world. With my hand still holding the door to the building open, I experience a surge of panic so urgent that I audibly whimper. My breathing is thick and once again the belief that none of the air is making its way into my lungs lodges in my brain. Spikes of adrenaline poke through my body. I reach up and artificially push my chest in and out with my hands in a parody of breathing. My head dips towards my chest and I feel tears stinging my eyes.

My dog needs me! Come on! Move! Why won't I move?

I stand trapped between the building and the street, panic building in my mind and my heart hammering through my ribs. A drop of moisture hits my nose and I brush the sweat off my brow. I have to move. Another drop of moisture hits me and I look up into a sky that for the first time in months is sunless. It has been so long since it rained that I have almost forgotten that it can. It is such a bizarre thought that this precious resource that I have spent so long guarding and worrying about could just fall from the sky. More raindrops fall and I notice that the clouds I saw last night have thickened into a deep, grey sky. I hold my hands cupped and watch, fascinated, as the drops gather. I lick my palms. Away in the distance, the clouds are massing with real intent.

"Fucking rain!" someone nearby shouts and I spin around to see a man who I assumed was dead, as he was tucked under the bumper of a car. He rises awkwardly to a standing position.

"Why does it always have to rain?"

Someone near him chimes in. "This fucking country is ridiculous, may as well go and live in the fucking sea."

Another voice. More shouts.

"The forecast said it would be fine," screeches a girl.

The scene in front of me starts to rearrange itself. As the rain wakes them, the wraths stand and move. Some start to fight with each other, and gradually the street comes alive.

I hear a gentle click and look behind me, just in time to see the door to Ellis House close.

I inhale hard through my nose and try to be as inconspicuous as possible. I tug at the door and confirm that it has shut firmly. I am so unpractised at going outside that I haven't even contemplated absolute basics like the need for keys. I'm not even sure I have the keys anymore – I haven't needed them in so long.

"What's your fucking problem, Sunshine?" a wrath about thirty yards away shouts and starts to make his way over to me, with the unfamiliar walk that the wraths have.

I turn and tug at the door again. The glass is woven with little wire squares, suggesting that I wouldn't be able to kick it in and push through it in time.

I wait until the wrath is nearly on me, then I turn and bring the knife from my side across his throat in a horizontal slash. Thick, dark blood gushes from his neck, and he holds his hands to his throat and falls backwards. I feel sickened, but a voice in my head says loudly that I have to choose: them or us.

Another four wraths notice the man fall and start towards me.

I run.

I bound as fast as I can around the side of the building, mentally noting how my loose skin bounces and wriggles and how, at speed, my prosthetic feels looser. I will have to find a way to anchor both in place if I survive. I shin over a wall at waist level and find myself at the rear entrance to Ellis House. There is a large porch on the building and I try the door. Locked. In desperation, I cast around and notice more figures in the car park looking at me. They start to walk over to me. I attempt to jump up on top of the roof of the porch. I manage to get my fingers over the edge, but it isn't enough. I try again just as the first wrath reaches the wall behind me. I take a moment and remember the thousands of star jumps

I've been doing. I crouch down and jump - this time I get a better purchase with my whole hand on the roof. I scrabble my left leg up against the building as the wraths in the car park break into a run. I manage to hook my left foot over the side of the roof and pull myself up. Pull-ups save my life. I resolve to stop hating them so much.

By this time, the rest of the wraths have rounded the building and are joining with the ones from the car park. More of them, woken by the now-heavy rain, have noticed their shouts and come lumbering over to investigate. Soon, a crowd of forty or so wraths have the porch surrounded and are screaming about pulling me to pieces and the misery of a British summer.

I look around the roof. There is nothing. No way to make a miraculous leap onto the nearest balcony, and no handy lanterns to swing from. I brace myself and stamp my left foot onto the roof. It seems solid. I frantically follow the roof lining, to where it meets the side of the wall and I pull at the lead flashing, which comes up easily. Underneath is the start of the rubberised roof material, which is sealed to the wall. I take my knife and slit the rubber roof, scattering the grit and peeling a long strip of the roof material back. I turn just in time to see hands coming over the side of the roof, and I stretch out my metal foot and kick the fingers off the side, leading to a cry of "I'll gut you, bastard!"

Underneath the roof is mottled chipboard that looks like lots of small pieces of wood glued together. I try to see if I can get my fingers in between the side of the board and the wall, but it is too closely positioned. Even if I could, I wouldn't be able to move it while I am standing on it. If you can't go round it, you'll have to go through it, I think. I cut a space about a foot wide in the rubber covering and peel it back. Once exposed, I lift the knife above my head and drive it into the roof. The blade doesn't hit true and it bends the tip and breaks off near the handle. I scrabble in my bag for the other knife and nearly cut my fingers. This time, I try a smaller digging motion and quickly work out a fleck of the board. I dig again and another fleck comes out. I pause to swipe the knife over more fingers that have come over the edge of the roof and watch with satisfaction as three wraths plunge back to the ground. Back to the tiny hole I've created and with another stab, my knife hits another section of the roof.

By now, a hundred wraths are pushing at the walls of the porch and trying to work out how to climb up to the roof. I work a finger into the hole I've created and frantically pull at the board until it starts to come loose, not caring about the splinters it drives into my hand. Soon, a hole is exposed revealing a white board underneath. I continue to pull frantically at the chipboard until enough comes away to reveal a hole just big enough to fit me through. I stand up and jump with my full weight onto the white board. My feet plunge through and an entire section of the plasterboard from inside the porch comes loose and crashes to the floor. I lose my balance as more of the roof gives way and I fall in a shower of dust and plaster crumbs onto the floor of the porch, bending my prosthetic foot back slightly and scraping deep gouges in my sides. I notice for the first time that there is an internal door between the porch and the building. I pray that it is not locked and pull. It swings open. With a gasp of relief, I quickly speed through the hall and back up the stairs and return to the fourth floor.

I risk a look out of the window at the top of the stairwell and see three wraths standing uncertainly on the porch roof examining the hole, with more pulling themselves onto the roof. I run down my corridor, noting the charred remains at my door. I run into the flat and slam the door shut and start hammering the wedges into place again when I notice that it doesn't shut properly any more. I then see that the bottom hinge has been blown apart in the explosion. I push the door back into the frame as well as I can, but it won't hold anyone for long, not least a wrath intent on destruction. I slot the security chain into position and acknowledge that it is a futile gesture, but it seems that futile gestures are all I have right now.

CHAPTER 22

20ᵗʰ July 2020

15 days before

605 lbs (274 kg)

"I just want you to know that having communion now isn't just because of the operation. This isn't a Bart Simpson approach to faith," Ben explained, trying to fill the silence as the priest swept the bed of the ephemera of Ben's daily life: lotions, a selection of Brown's toys and biscuit crumbs. He sat down and pulled a heavy, black leather bag onto his lap.

"And what would a Bart Simpson approach to faith be, my son?" Father Donnell said indulgently.

"There's an episode of The Simpsons and Bart says something like "I'll go for a life of sin, followed by a prest-o-change-o deathbed repentance." I just didn't want you to think that I asked for you to do communion because I was scared I was going to die. I've thought it through. There are things about Christianity I don't understand and some more I don't like, but I believe in God and I want to learn more."

"I think it's the belief part that God cares about, we all try and figure out the rest as we go, some days I think I have it cracked and then others, I'm as clueless as you. Well, maybe not quite that bad," Father Donnell said, taking a small brown gauze bag out of his leather carry-all, which he placed by his feet. From the cloth bag, he removed a circular bronze box that looked like a small make-up compact. He uttered a few words heard only by himself and God and kissed the box.

"What's that?"

"It's a pyx, it's a box designed to carry the host."

"Would the prest-o-change-o strategy not get past the Almighty then?"

"Well, given that He weighs our hearts and our actions, I suspect He's used to a little human subterfuge by now, but nothing would surprise me. I'm sorry to say that I suspect Bartholomew Simpson will be asking Satan to eat his shorts when he dies, but this opens up a theologically complex discussion around the souls of animated characters, so let's move on."

"What about-" Ben began.

"Ben, I hope you'll take this in a spirit of friendship when I say, shut up and let me concentrate."

Ben fell silent and stroked Brown's neck and smoothed out her ears.

"What happens if you do fake it then?"

"As ever, our brother Paul has this covered. There's a line in 1 Corinthians 11, where he says, "For anyone who eats and drinks without recognising the body of the Lord eats and drinks judgment on himself". I was told when I was training that to take communion without due sincerity was to invite death."

"How do you remember all that? The 1 Corinthians stuff. The Bible's massive."

"Well, I've had practice." The priest stood up and took some of the items off the movable table that stood next to Ben's bed. "So do you feel you can continue with suitable sincerity or shall I pack up for the day because, frankly, I'm knackered?"

Ben looked chastised and nodded.

"Sorry."

"Don't be soft," the priest said, smiling. "Taking communion for the first time isn't going to kill you any more than that operation will. Communion is about meeting with God and acknowledging that Jesus died to save us. It's also one of the few magic tricks I can do, so you should enjoy it. You're supposed to be kneeling at this point, but I think we can skip that for now. Can you kneel when you've had your leg amputated?"

"I'll tell you in a fortnight."

"Ok – let's get this show on the road. By the way, as it's just me and you, if you have any questions, just let me know. I know you will. Just read your bits on the card – the ones in bold."

The priest had by now poured out a small glass of red wine into a crystal cut glass that he had taken from his bag, laid a silver platter on the table and added a thin white disk about the size of a beer mat, which Ben eyed warily. Father Donnell put a laminated square of text on Ben's lap and Ben picked it up to read ahead.

The priest picked up the communion wafer and held it in both hands and intoned in a deep voice.

"Behold the Lamb of God, behold him who takes away the sins of the world. Blessed are those called to the supper of the Lamb."

"Have you done the magic then?"

"Yes."

"So that's the body of Jesus?"

"According to the miracle of transubstantiation, yes."

"I didn't see it move."

"It didn't move."

"So, it starts as a wafer and then turns into the body of our saviour?"

"*Yes*. It's a miracle."

"Are there the same calories in it when it's a wafer and when it's the body of Christ?"

"Read your bit."

"Lord, I am not worthy that you should enter under my roof, but only say the word and my soul shall be healed. It's funny that it says enter under my roof isn't it when you've actually entered under my roof."

"It's just the text of the communion."

"OK."

Father Donnell raised the wafer above his head and brought it down to eye level and showed it to Ben.

"The body of Christ."

Brown came instantly to life from her prone position next to Ben and within a fraction of a second had nipped the wafer away from the priest and sat on the bed, crunching it up.

"Ben!" The priest cried dumbfounded and Brown sensed something was amiss and leapt off the bed. The priest gave chase and swung his leg threateningly to try and clip Brown's backside but missed. "Your dog has eaten Jesus! Spit it out Brown, this isn't funny! That's Our Lord and Saviour!"

Ben was screaming with laughter. Tears streamed down his face as he laughed so loudly that the sound was stolen from his lungs. The priest continued to rage, "She's like a ninja that one, she didn't even make a sound, the ratbag!"

Ben continued to laugh until his massive frame ceased shaking and he realised that the priest was actually annoyed. This just made him laugh more.

"Roy, I'm so sorry. If it's any consolation it was only me who saw and it's not like I've got anyone to tell, is it?"

Ben used the grabbing arm to reach one of the shelves to the right of the bed and pulled down a brown plastic pack of biscuits.

"How powerful is the miracle of transubstantiation, Father? Could you do it with a bourbon?"

The priest seethed, but reluctantly took a bourbon from the pack and ate it. He took another and placed it on the silver platter. Brown looked on hopefully from the doorway, unsure if this was a test or a game. Her ears raised in query. Ben shook his head at her as the priest closed his eyes and began a lengthy prayer, asking forgiveness for the spoiling of the sacrament and for God to marshal more than his usual reserves of patience and love to bless the activity in this flat. He also prayed in explicit detail for Brown to get heinous diarrhoea. Eventually, he retraced his way through the Eucharist and held out the platter to Ben, complete with the bourbon biscuit, and said, "The body of Christ." Ben waited and took a piece of the biscuit and said "Amen". The priest repeated the prayer with the small glass of wine and Ben took it and drank.

Later in the afternoon, Father Donnell packed his leather bag and Ben thanked him. Father Donnell shook Ben's hand.

"It's funny, apart from doctors I think priests see more dead and dying men than anyone else. It's a tremendous privilege to be able to be there for someone as they die. You learn a lot about people in those moments. There are two things I can tell about you – you don't want to die in that operation and you do want to live after it. I pray that both of those things are given to you."

"Thank you Father. It's been a difficult week. I feel better for the communion and sorry again about Brown."

"Anything you need prayer for?"

"I'm just trying to understand what's going on. I think I need prayer for understanding. I can't quite get my head around something that's happened."

"To do with the operation?"

"No. I just want to know what God's plan is for me. At the

moment it's like he's lined up all of these barriers. You're right, I don't want to die and I do want to live, but I wonder if that's what God has planned for me."

"Ben, you'll have heard the one about God moving in mysterious ways, but I think it's just that we're unable to see things from His perspective. All of these things down on the ground that seem not to make sense, but if we just looked at it from above then they would. I'll pray for you to get some perspective. In the meantime, think of Jeremiah, chapter 29: verse 11, *For I know the plans I have for you, plans to prosper you and not to harm you, plans to give you hope and a future.*"

"I saw the doctor this week and he said -" Ben stopped and looked pained. He bit his lip and pulled a biscuit from the pack and put it in his mouth.

"He said?"

"Nothing. I'll be fine. Thanks for everything."

The priest reluctantly stood and gathered his things.

"I'll see you Ben. God bless you."

CHAPTER 23

10th February 2021

6 months, 6 days after

238 lbs (108 kg)

The drizzling rain falls as I peek out on the street and wonder what to do. Down below, every wrath in the area seems to be hellbent on getting into Ellis Tower. As I watch, I see some stragglers sprinting towards the back of the flats, desperate not to miss out. I listen at the front door and I can hear the sounds of destruction and ranting as more of the wraths follow each other through the hole I created in the porch. There's no chance I can fight them all. I think of Brown and try to shut out the image in my mind of the boot connecting with her ribs, flinging her across the walking field. I run into the lounge and wonder if I could push the bed against the door and if so, how much time that will buy me. And the thought quickly follows - what is the point of buying time? I don't want more time in here. I want to be outside and I want to live. And I want to get my fucking dog back.

A thought flashes in my mind and I latch onto it. It's a risky plan, but I can't think of anything else. Lord Jesus, please bless this insanity. With purpose, I quickly move to mum's room, grab two of the hydrogen cylinders and drag them into the lounge and lie them on the bed. I return and drag the others through. There are three half-full cylinders, one empty one and one full one. I search quickly through the remnants of the drinks cupboard, but as I suspected, the Midori was the last of the alcohol. There's just a bendy straw and a measuring cup left in there now. I rush back to mum's room and go through a box of cosmetics on her small dressing table. I turn each bottle around looking for a symbol that shows the item is flammable. There are three bottles of nail polish, which is odd because I never remembered mum having painted nails, but there on the back is a small fire icon. I open the top of one of the bottles and sniff it and recoil at the heady chemical smell that filters out. Perfect. I un-wad some cotton wool from a bag in the box and using a cotton bud, I poke the cotton wool into the necks of the nail varnish bottles and jam them in my pocket. In the corridor, I hear smashing and a voice crying out something about rain and blood.

I rush back to the kitchen to find a lighter from the kitchen drawer and shake it to make sure it has fuel. I run back into the hallway, stopping only to open the valves on all the canisters of hydrogen. I then brace myself against the front door and shriek at the top of my voice, "Come and get me, you bastards!" I kick my side of the door and shout "Hey! Hey! Hey!" over and over. It only takes seconds before the pounding starts against the other side and the hinge groans under the assault. I set my feet against the opposite wall and lock them out. I strain with every new muscle in my body as the pushing and smacking against the door grows. The chorus of voices doubles and trebles and soars, creating an unholy choir of profanity. Murderous threats and the generic complaints of arseholes mix together to form a wall of sound. My feet slip and I can see my metal foot is biting into the plaster of the wall.

I take a breath and then stand and run.

I make it into the lounge before the door crumples inwards.

Fortunately, the hinge on the top fails and the door falls against the wall, leaning like a ladder. The wraths at the front of the frenzy are smashed against the door and I watch as those behind them try and push past until the ones caught in the front shriek and their eyes bulge in their heads. I whip aside the curtain in the lounge and step out onto the balcony. As I hoped the street below looks quiet, as most of the nearby wraths have been tempted into the riot in Ellis House. I lean out over the balcony, holding on to the slippery railing with my right hand. I panic as my foot slips on the metal floor but recover my balance before I fall. My left hand stretches over the cherry picker's control panel. I nudge the boom control joystick and far below the engine fires up with a cough. The platform starts to judder and I quickly guide it closer to the balcony.

I step onto the wet metal platform of the cherry picker just as the first of the wraths makes it into the lounge. He's a large man with piercing red eyes and a newly broken arm that dangles obscenely from his shoulder. He looks around and spots me. He turns towards the window. I move the cherry picker two metres from the balcony and quickly study the panel and flick a switch which allows the top platform to drive the base unit. I hit the joystick and below, the large wheels turn and the cherry picker pushes ahead, agonisingly slowly. I see that the unit is snagged on a body. The wrath takes his chance and leaps from the lounge across the balcony and grabs onto the guard rail of the platform with his good arm. His broken arm flaps in a circle and slaps the rail, snapping the wrist. I continue to drive us as I see a wave of wraths entering the lounge now.

We are six metres out from the flat now and another wrath, an elderly woman who still has her handbag, jumps from the balcony trying to get to us. She falls well short and plummets to the damp ground, looking thwarted. The wrath on the rail throws a leg over the side and frantically kicks at the controls and at me. I can feel our combined weight and his movements starting to tip the cherry picker and for a second it teeters as if the whole machine will spill forwards and dash us all on the floor. I pull it back by stopping the wheels and moving the boom closer to the platform.

More wraths fly from the balcony, trying to grab onto us. I pull my fist back and punch the man as hard as I can in the face. I feel his nose collapse, but his grip still doesn't give on the railing. I rummage in my pocket for the lighter and set it burning under his nose. I see the hair in his nostrils fizzle away in flame and he grasps at the lighter with his hand. Gravity asserts itself and he falls to the ground face down. Far below, a halo of blood appears above his head.

I steer the cherry picker further back from the flat. The wheels of the base unit dislodge the body and suddenly we're moving and we're fifteen metres away. I light the cotton wool in the three bottles of nail varnish and throw first one and then the other two towards the building. The first is swatted at by a wrath who topples off the balcony to reach it. The second hits the wall above the door to the flat and the third falls into the mass of wraths in the lounge. The one that hits the wall smashes and an eerie blue-pink flame takes hold on the brickwork. Within a fraction of a second, that flame connects with the cloud of hydrogen that has been leaking out of the flat for the last three minutes, and a fireball erupts that illuminates up to 30 feet above the building.

The entire roof of Ellis Tower jumps up in the explosion, and the impact and raw heat hits me after a second and pushes me against the side of the cage. I see ten or eleven wraths blasted clear out of the window and when I look back, there's more of them writhing in the flames of the flat. Somewhere in the innards of the building, the flames connect with another source of gas and another, bigger explosion rings out with such heat that I can feel my face glowing. I instantly feel a sense of loss, but I can't think what for. My one regret is that photos of mum are burning and I should have thought to save my weight and exercise diary. In the frantic rush, I realise that my rucksack was still on the balcony. I focus on the joystick and push the cherry picker down off the pavement and onto the road as my home burns.

Karl screams that he's being abducted as we go but as I hoped, blowing up the flat has taken care of enough of the wraths from the estate to give us a clear passage, at least initially. I ignore Karl's shouts and steer the cherry picker through the abandoned traffic on the roads and try and plot a route to the walking field. Having only ever flown it before, I have to rely on a series of landmarks that I recognise from flying around the area. Navigating through the roads is difficult and several times I have to steer the cherry picker across to the other side of the road to get around an abandoned bus or a smashed up lorry that clogs up the road. The cherry picker is just quick enough to outrun any wraths who do give chase, but our progress still feels agonisingly slow. Twice, I need to drop the height of the platform to get underneath telephone wires that loop across the street. By the time I've lowered the platform enough, Karl is dangling about two feet above the ground.

Throughout the journey, Karl keeps up a constant stream of abuse directed towards me, the harness he's attached to and anything and everything that he sees. While I'm leaning on the joystick on a long, straight stretch of road that seems relatively free of impediments, I find where his harness attaches to the platform. A clip on the end of his tether is fed through a safety point and the loop needs to be unscrewed to create a gap in the side of the clip. This then needs to be unhooked from the safety point. I manage to unscrew the clip and try to push the clip loose, but with Karl's full weight dangling from the harness, I can't lift the loop the inch or so it needs to move to force it out. I stop driving altogether, to see if I can lift the tether with two hands, but it's no use and Karl starts screaming even louder. I kick myself for not keeping hold of a knife or any weapon. Curtains in a nearby terrace twitch and a wrath bangs on the inside of the glass, so I'm forced to give up, power the cherry picker back up and continue, while Karl narrates the journey with his complaints.

On Brown's flights we cross the motorway, so I follow the blue traffic signs and power the vehicle down the southbound slip road. The motorway is frozen in time from the moment when the wraths began, and sporadically I see cars, trucks and buses abandoned or crashed along the road with bodies and crumbs of glass spilt across all three lanes. The hard shoulder is mostly clear though, so I only occasionally need to weave in and out of the vehicles and crashes. Soon, I notice a large white farmhouse in the fields on the left of the road. I recognise the two large round slurry tanks on the land behind from flying over them so many times, and I mentally plot that the walking field must be about half a mile behind them.

When I'm level with the farmhouse, I bring the cherry picker to a halt and quickly lower the platform towards the ground. I'm too focused on Brown to wait, so I jump from the side of the cage onto the floor. Just as I hit the ground, I suddenly realise that I didn't re-do the clip on Karl's tether and turn, just in time to see Karl's restraint come loose from the safety point and clank to the floor of the platform. I sprint for the side of the road, never more grateful for the hours of walking and sprints I did in my now-destroyed flat. As I reach the side of the road, I turn to see Karl trailing the tail of his safety harness and disappearing behind an overturned lorry.

I think of Brown and climb over the metal crash barrier and scramble down the embankment, my metal foot sinking into the soil. I quickly realise it's not designed to be an all-terrain foot and I try to stick to solid ground. I find myself on a rutted farm track with deep potholes that are newly full of rainwater. I keep to the side, ready to go off into the fields if needed and work my way up to the house. It seems empty, but at every step I expect a wrath to launch at me from around the corners. I creep around the slurry tanks and find myself in a field of wheat that has long since grown long and toppled over. The remnant of the wet crop pulls at my feet and an urgent smell of petrichor rises from the field as I stomp my way through the field and beyond into the rising tree line. Sweat is pouring off me and I feel weak, but I'm not sure if that's from dread at what I might find in the walking field or from the first exercise I've had outside for nearly ten years. I come across the twin ruts of a service road and realise that this must be the access route that feeds the field, so I turn back and follow it.

In less than a mile, I am confronted with the familiar palisade fencing and the layers of chicken wire that secure Brown's walking field. It's a surreal experience to be face-to-face with something that you've only ever seen rendered through the lens of a camera. It feels like that momentary disorientation of remembering a dream. I follow the perimeter around and have only inspected two hundred metres before I see how the wrath has managed to gain access. Four of the slats that make up the fence have been pulled outwards, which has pulled some of the other posts down, creating a low point in the fence that would be easy to climb over. How could I be so fucking stupid? I created this fate for my dog. I could have just chosen to sort my weight out and take her for long walks myself. Maybe then I would have been able to go with Helen. Maybe then I could have lived a life, rather than just hiding.

With a desperate heart, I pull the fence panels further down and step over them, slipping slightly as I make my way onto the field. As loudly as I dare, I call out, "Brown? C'mere girl." Nothing. I try again a little louder. At the far end of the field I see a body lying on the ground and walk over to see the wrath with the drone's blades embedded in his face. There's a five metre perimeter around him spattered with blood and flecks of bone, which looks slick in the rain. He trapped his shooting bag underneath himself as he was forced backwards by the drone. The rope attached to the drone is still under his foot, and with a rising sense of horrid certainty, I follow it across the concrete and find the small blue pet carrier. I see Brown's body before I reach it, and I start to shout as I run towards the carrier.

"Brown!"

I reach out a hand and touch her wet and cold flank.

She twitches and lifts her head up in shock, as she rouses from a deep slumber.

"Brown! You're alive! You're here!" I scream as she gets to her feet in the carrier and stretches her back. I pick my beautiful dog up and nuzzle her close to me as she licks my face with joyful recognition. I hold her face to mine and tell her again and again that she's a good girl. I register the look of surprise in her face and realise a second too late that she is looking over my shoulder. It's a second that gives Karl just enough time to swing a giant fist at the side of my head and then there is nothing.

CHAPTER 24

28th July 2020

7 days before

602 lbs (273 kg)

Despite its name, super-obesity doesn't actually confer any special abilities, it's just the technical term for someone whose BMI is over 50. It might not be a superpower, but it does bestow an extremely sensitive radar for the supposedly subtle signals that people think they're smart enough for you not to notice; whether it's a mother's warning look to her child not to say anything out loud as they stare at a fat person they pass on the street, or the suppressed giggle passed between groups of women as they see someone obese. Women were more likely to comment, Ben had found, but they rarely did it overtly. Men were more likely to address you directly. There was probably a lesson in there somewhere, but if so, Ben wasn't interested in learning it.

Ben was more interested in the micro-look that had passed between his consultant and the nurse who had come on the home visit to take blood. The look clearly said that this was the point they had previously discussed when she would give them some room. It worried Ben more that the nurse did exactly that; excusing herself to take the samples out to the courier, leaving Ben alone with Dr Shaw.

Ben liked Dr Shaw. He had a pleasant face and was immaculately coiffured, Ben felt sure someone who took that much precision with his parting was probably a safe bet to rummage around your insides. Currently, Dr Shaw's face didn't look entirely at ease.

"Ben, when we met before, you mentioned a feeling of being full very soon after eating. How has that been?"

"Still the same. As we get closer, I definitely feel like it's more to do with nervousness though. I'm not sleeping well and I've been getting the trots a lot, which only ever happens to me when I'm nervous about something."

"Have you noticed anything about your stools in general – you say that they're looser?"

"Um, no, not that I can think of. Just that I've been back and forth to the commode – I think that's helped me lose some weight as well – I must be doing five hundred steps a day just to the bathroom and back."

"Ben, you have cancer."

Ben laughed dutifully and waited.

"Sorry, I thought you hadn't finished. I've not got cancer, I've got diabetes. You're chopping my leg off next Friday."

"Ben, I'm sorry but you have diabetes *and* cancer."

Ben pulled at his shirt which was tight around his neck. He felt sweat break out on the back of his neck. Why couldn't he get his breath? His mind flashed back to that moment all those years ago, when he had struggled to get home from the supermarket and had closed the door behind him for the last time.

"Would you like a glass of water?"

The consultant's question derailed Ben's blooming panic and he stared at this insultingly neat man as if he was seeing him for the first time.

"How can I have cancer?"

"I'm sorry Ben, but having diabetes doesn't preclude you from getting another illness. You are very young to get cancer, but you're obviously more likely to get it because of your size."

"Because of my size? This is because of my size? Why can't you just say fat? What's stopping you from saying that this is all because I'm a big, fat failure?"

Dr Shaw let Ben's comment dissipate in the air.

"Ben, I need you to understand that this is not a normal, clinical situation. Ordinarily, we would do a colonoscopy and further tests to see precisely what we were dealing with before we even discussed a diagnosis with you. But that would mean you would be in the hospital for longer, and I know you're already concerned about Brown and organising care for her. I know it's also going to have an impact on your ability to come back to the flat, so I wanted to tell you as soon as I was sure."

"And you are sure?"

"We know for sure that you have cancer, yes. We don't know what cancer it is, or what stage it's at, we will only be able to determine that when you come in for the operation and we'll do a colonoscopy and more tests at the same time, so you don't have to have the risk of the anaesthetic again."

"So how do you know I've got cancer? You could be wrong?"

"There's a new blood test which allows us to detect very specific proteins which are only created by cancers, so we can say with certainty that you do have cancer."

"What type do you think it is?"

"I'm uncomfortable being put on the spot in that way Ben, I-"

"Listen, in this room, there's only one person who's allowed to be uncomfortable and that's me. What sort of cancer is it? You mentioned a colonoscopy which is the pipe up your arse, isn't it? You think it's stomach? Guess if you have to!"

"My guess is that it's colorectal cancer; the feeling of fullness and the diarrhoea are fairly common symptoms. I am sorry, Ben."

"If it's that one, can you treat it?"

"Yes, it's not easy and your weight would complicate the treatment, but we would try."

"How long have I got?"

"That's not a fair question."

"I'm just going to Google it when you're gone."

"*If* I'm right, then Stage 1A would be the best-case scenario and there's a 71% chance you'll survive for five years or more at that point. At worst, you'd be looking at about a 5% chance. Obviously, with appropriate treatment, you could be completely cured."

Ben cried then, a short shout of anguish that took him by surprise and his face crumpled. Brown came snuffling in from the balcony and leapt onto the bed, her whip tail flashing from side to side. She looked murderously at the stranger and Dr Shaw stood to get some tissues from his bag and also to put distance between himself and the dog. He held one out to Ben, radiating benevolence. Brown watched his every move.

"Ben you need to realise that this situation is unusual – we don't yet know what cancer it is, or what stage it's at. That's why we need to focus on getting you through the op and understanding what is going on."

Ben pulled himself up. He grabbed the tissue and swiped at his eyes. He blew his nose and stroked Brown's muzzle, the soft velvet of her ears. She relaxed slightly but retained her wary surveillance of the consultant.

"I'll give you one thing," he said.

"What's that?" Dr Shaw asked.

"I'm not worried about the amputation any more."

Dr Shaw laughed.

"And who knows," Ben continued. "Maybe it's cancer of the right shin and we can kill two birds with one stone."

CHAPTER 25

I think my stupid hair saved me. As I was rushing around the flat earlier, I rolled my hair into two Princess Leia buns, because ponytails and pigtails had a habit of flicking me in the eyes and I didn't have time to braid it. So, I'd massed bunches of hair into two rough ponytails and then scrolled them round and tucked them in a sort of thick knot that sat on either side of my head. I'm not saying it is a good look, but as far as shock absorbers go, it is the best hairstyle you could hope for. When Karl smacked me in the head, the hair had soaked up enough of the blow to simply render me momentarily senseless rather than knock me out cold.

I wake up to a burning agony in my lip and nose as I come around and realise that I am being dragged face down across the concrete, my hands raised above my head. I lift my head from the floor and use my hands to swipe blood and gravel from my face. As I look over my shoulder, there is Karl, smiling maniacally at me.

"I'm going to hold your chubby fucking head under the water and watch the last bubble of air come out of your fat-stained lungs."

Karl has hold of my foot and my prosthetic blade and he is leaning backwards to use his body weight to yank me across the ground. I belatedly realise that he is pulling me towards the dip in the centre of the walking grounds where the rain has created a filthy pool of water.

Brown comes from just out of his eyeline and latches her teeth onto his left arm. Her ears are swept back and the muscles in her jaw ripple. I see a look in her eyes that I've never seen before – not even when she attacked the lady in the lift. This is her war face. She bites down with force and her teeth bore into Karl's arm. Karl looks annoyed and takes his right hand off my leg to grab Brown's collar. As he lifts the collar pulls tightly across her throat. Brown holds on valiantly, but eventually, she has to let go. Karl holds her up by her collar and her legs cycle in the air as she tries to find a purchase.

Still holding Brown in his right hand, Karl tries to tug me across the ground with just his left arm, only to register surprise when he finds that he is falling backwards, holding not my entire body but just my prosthetic leg. As he falls, he drops Brown and she takes the chance to dive on him and savage his face.

I ignore the burning heat across my face and scream at myself to get up and move. I push the stump of my left leg into the ground and straighten my arms to crouch on my left leg with my palms on the ground. I lift myself up and start to hop away from Karl, who has now managed to push Brown off. He sees me retreating and screams after me.

"You pussy! You chicken! You scum! You would never have survived in the trenches! Hop off, I'll track you down, but I'm going to drown your shit-hound first."

I turn and stumble as I see him holding Brown aloft by the collar again, new gashes in his face as he turns towards the pool. I recover my balance and start to hop as fast as I can away from Karl. I don't have long, I know that, but it isn't far. I just have to keep going. I fall to my knees but the thought of Karl holding Brown under the water makes me push myself to my feet again, and when I fall for a second time I roll over and over on the floor, towards the wrath and his shotgun.

I reach the body and roll over his blood and gore on the ground. He is lying on his back with the gun sling underneath him. I grab frantically at his coat and push him over just enough so that I can access the zip of the case. I fumble with it and finally slide the long shotgun out. It looks like an antique model and has two barrels side-by-side and is just over four feet in length. I push the stock of the gun under my right shoulder, crouch down to accommodate its length and crutch faster than I've ever done before, back towards the pool.

Even from ten metres away, I can see Karl kneeling in the middle of the pool, with his back to me, intent on keeping the object in his hands under the water. I splash through the shallows of the pool and feel myself start to trip. I raise the gun in a panic as I fall. I aim roughly towards Karl and pull the gun's double triggers. Nothing happens. I sprawl forward into the water and drop the gun as I break my fall with both arms. Almost instantly, I push myself back up, first onto one leg and then up out of the murky water. I grab the gun and pull at the triggers again and for the second time there is no crack of noise or fire. I try fiddling with a metal switch on the top and shoot a third time. Nothing.

Karl turns to me with his arms still held under the water.

"Can your dog breathe out of its tail?" he says and he smiles.

I lurch forward and, holding the gun by the barrel, I whip it round in a circle. The butt of the stock smashes against Karl's forehead with a thick, slapping noise. His head snaps back and he falls back into the water. Brown's motionless body bobs to the surface and I grab her. She is lifeless and limp and I struggle to push myself up out of the water as I fall off balance again. Kneeling on one knee and supporting myself with my stump, I can hold her up above the water by her back legs. I tip her upside down and shake for all I am worth. A small gush of water falls from her mouth and into the pool. I tip her back around and clamp her jaw shut. I place my mouth over her nose and blow hard. I wait a few seconds and blow again. I do it again and, finally, a froth of liquid spurts out of her nose.

"Brown!" I shout, as I hold her upside down again and unclamp her mouth and watch intently as her eyes roll in her head, but slowly and magically they come back into focus.

Karl launches himself into us from behind and clasps his arms around my shoulders, clamping his hands over each other. We tip forwards into the shallow water and I feel Brown trapped underneath me, frantically scrabbling to get free. I push back and stretch out my arms wide to try and break his grip, but Karl is too strong. I lean my head forwards, deeper into the water then whip it back and connect with his nose, hard enough to make him give an inch. I push back again and create just enough space for Brown to escape. I shove her and force her towards the shallows. I break the surface and gasp in air. I am above water just long enough to see her struggle groggily out of the water as if she is sedated. I urge her to keep running. Run away. Escape!

Karl finds his grip again and squeezes his arms around my chest, forcing me back under the water. He dunks his head in after mine and clamps his teeth around my ear and tears his head backwards, ripping the top half of my ear off with remarkable ease. The heat explodes across the whole side of my face and I scream in pain under the water and buck and writhe, moving his grip slightly lower on my body.

His hold relies on my body being a solid mass but I now have loose flesh that doesn't stay fixed in place and this allows me to rotate until I am at ninety degrees to him. I kick my leg straight and force my head above the water and snatch a breath. It is then that I realise Karl is still wearing his safety harness and has the long tether still attached, like a tail. I catch him off guard by pushing my arms further down and I manage to reach between his legs and snag the tether with the tips of my fingers. As he squashes the breath from my lungs under the water, I pull the end of the tether up and through my fingers. With a yank, I snap it up between his legs. He grunts and I do it again. He breaks his grip on me, to try and stop me doing it again. In that instant, I pull my left arm free and reach up and feed the tether back around his neck. As soon as I manage to get a loop around his throat, his hands go to the tether to guard his neck, but it is too late. I whip the tether around again, trapping one hand. The strap is now fully around his throat twice and I lean back and pull the end of the tether high until I choke the very last breath out of the monster. His face goes red, then purple and I keep pulling and pulling until it is frozen in a dark scream.

Brown approaches me from the shallows of the pool as I continue to pull and she skips from side-to-side to get my attention. I come to and see that Karl is dead. I drop the tether and call Brown towards me and she braves the waters to jump into my arms. I sit in the water and hold her close to me, next to the body of our enemy. She opens her mouth in a soundless bark.

"Who's a good girl?" I ask. She knows the answer.

I hold my lovely dog in the grim waters, as the grey drizzle blows around us until Brown starts to shiver and I somehow push us to the edge of the pool, where I find my abandoned leg. I sit and look at Karl as he lies motionless in the cold waters, looking at the rainfall with unseeing eyes. Our fight is over. I sit up and pull my leg back on.

"Time to go," I say to Brown.

***

We don't make it far.

We hobble away from the walking field and down the access road, but by the time we reach the farmhouse, Brown is shivering hard. I feel sick from the pain in my ear and face. I am disorientated by the sensations of wind and rain on my face. The smells of the farm are strong and make me feel nauseous. My stump throbs and I am cold and need to rest. Brown doesn't seem to know how to behave – she roams and sniffs at something in the hedge and then scampers back and weaves so close to my legs that I keep tripping over her. I realise that we have never been outside together before. I take a moment to stroke her head and try and calm her. We both have a lot to learn about being out in the world.

I smash a window at the back door of the farmhouse, using the butt of the shotgun. Inside, the house is dim and chilled. We go cautiously from room to room, looking for wraths. The only occupant is the decomposed body of a woman in the main bedroom. I only know it is a woman because of the clothes she is wearing – a long, black dress with matching black shoes that she has kicked off next to the bed. She lies serenely on the covers of the neatly made-up bed. Her skin is still on her skeleton in patches but it looks more like tanned hide now. Surrounding her like an aura is a dark stain on the duvet. On the bedside table is a bottle of Baileys and an empty bottle of pills. I conclude that she was like me and had survived the arrival of the wraths, but maybe she simply lost hope of rescue or recovery and decided to end it all. I pray that God gathers her to him, and leave her in peace.

There is wood stacked in the outbuilding closest to the house and despite the risk, I light a fire for the comfort that it gives us, as much for the heat. We warm ourselves by the flames and Brown suspiciously inches herself ever closer to the source of heat, never having seen a log-burner before. The mains water is off here, too, but the rain is lashing down and quickly fills several containers that I set outside. Incredibly, the large pantry off the kitchen is still mostly full, and after such a long time of deprivation, it feels odd to see a glut of cans, jars and packets lining the shelves. Brown demolishes three tins of corned beef in quick succession and although there are fewer vegan options, I warm a pan of water on the fire and make rice, sweetcorn and chopped tomatoes. Even this pathetically basic meal is overwhelming, so full of flavour and simply remembering the experience of eating again – getting food stuck in my teeth! I manage to eat half the pan before I feel bloated and nauseous. I'm not sure if this is the cancer, or simply because I haven't eaten in such a long time. I realise that I will have to ease myself slowly back into the process of consuming food again. I want to learn from my experience with the bourbons and to ensure that there will be no going back to my old ways.

Nearly two weeks pass at the farmhouse as we recover. We sleep in a spare room upstairs, feeling comforted by the house's remote location, Brown's excellent hearing and the large cache of shotgun shells I discover in one of the sheds. We rest by the fire and I read from the selection of books in the study. I find an old, but mostly unused ladies' bike in another shed, and repair the punctured tyre. I lash a crate to the handlebars and Brown and I slowly master the art of riding a bike with one leg. I decide that a change of looks is needed and so one evening, I take a pack of safety razors, heat some water and shave my hair and beard to the roots. Brown is upset by this new look, and it takes her a few hours before she stops curling her lip whenever she catches sight of the new-look me. I feed her Spam and she soon decides to get over any wariness.

Over the fortnight, as we eat and sleep, I feel my strength returning and realise how low my energy has been. Now I am fuelled properly, I feel an urgency returning to my muscles, and as I continue to do my daily exercises, I find that I can push my body harder. I can sense the cancer is there, but it is lurking just out of sight for now. I watch with joy as a glossy sheen returns to Brown's coat and she too seems to pulse with energy and excitement. We carefully explore the local area and Brown supplements her pantry diet with rabbits and rats, which she seems to have developed a taste for. I raid the farmer's wardrobe and go from being garbed in billowing black to a country gent. I even upgrade my prosthetic by widening the blade of my foot so that it no longer sinks into the mud. I discover a pair of lycra leggings in the wardrobes which also gave a much greater hold between the stump and prosthetic.

The day we leave, I pack up a rucksack with enough food and water for a couple of days, and an array of weapons. I sling the loaded shotgun, which I have modified with a kitchen knife bayonet, over my shoulder. I have another, smaller, wickedly sharp chef's knife holstered on my prosthetic leg. Brown settles into the milk crate which I have padded with a blanket. I run my hand over the stubble of my head and take in the farmhouse. Is it too soon to go? The farmhouse has been a place of sanctuary. I am sad to leave, but having spent so long enmeshed in the flat, I know the danger of getting too comfortable. One day would I look out of the farmhouse's window and see with surprise that another decade had passed? There are things we need to do.

The world has allowed us a pause. I believe there are others like me out there who survived, and there are the wraths too. Both need help. I'm not sure how I am equipped to help, or even if the wraths can be helped, but I believe that I am meant to try. I am as sure as the lady who reached out to touch Jesus' cloak. I know that I am supposed to stand up, to go out into the world and that what needs to happen next will find me. Brown wants to go and find more corned beef.

I push the bike down the farm path to the motorway and take it up onto the road. I kick my leg over the crossbar and pedal silently past the cherry picker, which now seems to belong to a different lifetime. I ride further South on the hard shoulder down to the next junction and circle back around to the cemetery on the outskirts of town. I'd only been once before when I was a child, but I somehow remember the sweeping road up to the small, squat crematorium and the memorial fields beyond, which are now overrun with long grass and wildflowers. I scan the graveyard and see that no one is around, I carefully venture along the rows, with Brown keeping close to my heel. I don't know where mum is buried, and there doesn't seem to be any logic to the order that the graves are arranged in. Some who had died recently were placed alongside graves that were so old that they had started to lose the definition of the text, abandoning whoever lay beneath to final obscurity.

It is nearly dark before I find mum's grave. I push back the grass and see she has a simple memorial. A rectangle of white marble chips and a single headstone rising from the centre. There are no flowers and only a simple inscription:

Anne Mary Stone

Born November 11th 1961. Died November 14th 2017.

"I knew you would make it."

At first, I think the text is a bleak joke about her health, but then I remember that in one of our last conversations before she died when she was in the hospital, we discussed how if the worst happened then I probably wouldn't be able to go to her funeral. She wanted me to know it was OK and that she wasn't scared of dying. She had arranged for a friend to read a eulogy if I wanted to write one for her, which I did.

"You might not make it to the funeral Ben, but that's OK, I know you'll make it one day," she said.

And here she is, still being right. Still loving me. Still encouraging me, three years after she died. I kneel next to the grave and speak to her.

"You're right mum, we made it. Brown is here too. You would be proud to see her, she's beautiful. She's the best dog in the world."

Brown opens her mouth and pants at me, her long pink tongue lolling from her mouth. Good girl.

"I made it, too. I don't know why I made it. I prayed for God to save me, and he did. Me and Brown are going to see if we can return the favour and maybe save the world. But first, we're going to Disneyland."

THE END

MY SINCERE THANKS....

Jane Almond-Deville
Laura Bellamy
Kerry Comb
Flic Everett
Iven Gilmore
Ann Harrison
Chris Harrison
Sophie, Ash and Teal Harrison
Wayne Hughes
Emma Jones
Craig Morris
John Ossoway
James Pierpoint
PUP
Catherine Quinn
Emma Shanahan
Frank Shanahan
Harry Shanahan
Matilda Shanahan
William Sheard
Graham Waugh
Yolander Yeo

My abject apology to the people I have forgotten.

Printed in Great Britain
by Amazon